LAST

LIGHT

a BEACON FALLS novel   featuring LUCY GUARDINO

CJ LYONS

LAST LIGHT

a BEACON FALLS novel · featuring LUCY GUARDINO

CJ LYONS

EDGY READS

PROLOGUE

LILY MARTIN HATED how quickly night fell after the clocks turned back in November. Peter said the whole thing was a Wall Street conspiracy, but he tended to blame everything on New York City bankers who didn't understand the scrabble of working the land, trying to feed the nation as well as your family. Peter liked to think of himself as a hardworking, upright, honest man and loving husband. Even if he wasn't.

Maybe with the nights growing longer and cooler, the rain would finally come. It'd been a long, dry summer and autumn, making for a poor harvest. She turned off the main road from town, dust billowing behind her as the Subaru wagon bounced over the washboard ruts of the hard-packed lane leading past fields of cotton and sorghum, trying to outrace the setting sun.

Motion in the rearview mirror caught her eye. Sweet Glory was still asleep, despite the bump and grind of the lane, drool slipping into the bib tucked into her onesie. Such a good baby, no trouble at all.

Unlike her big brother. "Turn around and stop your squirming," she told Alan, who was halfway over the rear seat, foraging through the grocery bags in the way back. He twisted to face front, chocolate smearing his mouth, hands, and Cub Scout uniform.

She hit the accelerator. That chocolate was going to stain for sure if she didn't set it soaking. She'd bought the uniform at the thrift store in San Angelo. She'd had to mend rips in the shoulder seams, but it was the best she could do and she wouldn't have those other mothers thinking she couldn't manage keeping her son in decent clothes. "What did I tell you about eating before dinner?"

"Sorry," he said.

Lily hated the whine in his voice. Sure, he was only six, but she was afraid he'd grow up to be one of those spineless boys who took what they wanted without thinking of others, always taking shortcuts and lying their way out of honest work. Just like his father, God help her.

"Sorry doesn't pay for groceries, young man. Those cookies were bought special for tomorrow when Caleb comes to visit and you know it."

"Yes, ma'am." He hung his head, contrite, but his gaze angled up under the fringe of dusty brown bangs, assessing her expression in the rearview.

She sighed and glanced at the baby sleeping beside him. Sweet Glory was her last chance out of this place, her chance for a new life. They could run away. Tomorrow. Tonight. Be together, forever.

"Well, they're coming out of your allowance, that's for sure." She yanked the wheel, pulling into their drive. No sign of Peter's truck. Good. Cub Scouts had run late and so had juggling the kids with the grocery shopping, and now all she'd have time to cook before Peter got home would be Hamburger Helper. If Peter bothered coming home. Friday night, payday. There was a good chance he'd end up over in San Angelo at the gaming tables.

"Help me in with the groceries."

She got out of the car, the setting sun angled at the top of the house's corrugated tin roof blinding her. When she looked up, squinting, Blackwell Manor, the next property over, seemed to float above the rays of sunlight and clouds. As if the mansion and the rich people privileged to live inside resided on a heavenly plane compared to folks like Lily. She blinked away foolish fantasies, but couldn't resist hiding a sliver of hope in her heart. Someday, maybe, she'd be living in a house like that with a good man, a man who loved her.

Alan banged the car door as he hopped out.

"Hush, don't wake the baby."

Together they carried the first load of groceries inside, leaving Sweet Glory sleeping in the car with the doors open to the mild November breeze.

"Can I watch TV?" he asked, not waiting for her answer as he dumped his bag on the kitchen table and ran to plop himself on the sofa in front of the TV.

"Only until your father gets home. But first wash your hands and face." If he got chocolate over her sofa...Alan leapt back to his feet and raced past her down the hall, holding his hands out so he didn't touch anything.

"Wait, give me your shirt. I'll start it soaking."

He barely slowed enough for her to tug the shirt, still buttoned, over his head and up-stretched arms. Then he was gone.

The boy was perpetual motion. She'd hoped he'd calm down now that he was in first grade and school was all day, but no. Seemed like he saved up all his energy for when he came home and she was too tired to wrangle him.

She put the frozen food away then took the shirt out to the sink in the laundry room behind the kitchen. After she'd picked off the chocolate and graham cracker chunks and immersed it in soapy water to hopefully soak away the rest, she went back out to the car, leaving the front door open, and hefted two more bags from the rear of the station wagon.

Peter's parents and his sister's family were coming for Thanksgiving, so she'd been trying to stock up on nonperishables whenever they went on sale. Today she'd found a whole stack of canned beans and corn, all half-price just for little dents that didn't harm what was on the inside.

She turned, shifting the heavy bags in her arms, hugging them tight to keep them from slipping free, and headed back to the house. Something stopped her as she passed the station wagon's rear door. She dipped her head down, certain the sun reflecting off the window had created some kind of optical illusion.

But no. Glory's car seat was empty. Only the drool-stained bib remained.

Shock froze Lily, as cold as the setting sun was bright. "Glory!" she shouted as if the seven-month-old could answer her.

Much less climb free of the car seat. What in Lord's name? Panic tightened her throat and she lost her grip on the bags. They dropped to the ground, cans clanking and rolling and bouncing under the car.

Lily yanked open the car door, certain Glory had somehow slipped below the car seat's restraints. She lay across the back seat, hands flailing as she checked the space below the front seat, behind the car seat, over the seat in the way back, then shimmied into the narrow space between the two front seats. No sign of Glory.

Frantic, she scrambled back out of the car, not caring about the way her dress rode up. She tripped on one of the damn cans of green beans and caught herself against the open car door, her breath coming in gasps.

"Glory!" she screamed.

She shielded her eyes from the setting sun, whirling around, scouring the horizon, searching for an answer.

"Alan," she called, surprised her shrieking hadn't brought him running already. Movement came from the shadows gathered around the open front door. The sun was now directly behind the house, the roof a blaze of gold, blinding her as she stumbled toward the door.

"Alan, where's Glory?" she shouted, angry now, certain this was some kind of silly, childish prank.

The figure who appeared at her door wasn't her son.

"What are you doing here?" she stuttered, shocked, confused. "Where's Glory?"

"Glory's here." The figure turned so she could see the baby.

And the knife held to Sweet Glory's throat.

CHAPTER 1

ABILENE, TEXAS, PRESENT DAY

DAVID RUIZ HATED hospitals. Had vowed when he returned from his final assignment in Afghanistan—the one that left him half dead and the soldiers he was embedded with all dead—that he'd avoid hospitals at all cost.

It wasn't the smells or sights or memories of white-coated ghosts tending to young men who were suddenly mangled apparitions of their former glory-selves. Wasn't even the blood—hell, he'd worked the crime beat in Baltimore while finishing J-school. Blood was an old friend, meant a better story.

He pulled his dusty Ford Escape into Abilene's Mercy Medical Center's parking lot. Hunched over the steering wheel, he stared through the bug-splattered windshield up at the five-story glass and concrete building. It sat at an angle, two wings stretching out from a central hub. He guessed some architect had sold them on the design, probably thought it looked like angel wings opened wide to offer comfort and solace.

Only problem was the weathered concrete and glass tinted against the Texas sun created more of a feeling of oppression and despair. *Abandon hope, all ye who enter*, he thought as he climbed out of the SUV.

This was why he hated hospitals. They stole your free will; relegated you to a number housed in a database; told you what to do, when to do it, worse than any Army drill instructor; all in the name of providing a chance to live. Offering hope that your life wasn't fucked up beyond repair.

But it was all just a crapshoot. A game of existential roulette. And behind their masks and arrogance, the doctors knew that. Otherwise, why the hell would he be walking across this asphalt parking lot made sticky by the Texas sun, alive when he shouldn't be?

He pushed through the glass doors, air conditioning rushing at him like a slap in the face from a woman who'd held an icy drink in her hand. Stood for a moment to get his bearings, taking in the scents that all the antiseptic in the world couldn't hide, noting the large cross hanging above the receptionist desk, the quiet hush of the empty foyer.

And fought to shake off the feeling that there was someone at his back, ready to ambush him. He stepped forward, surprised at how much the simple act wrung him out. If he couldn't find the courage to face the baby-cheeked old lady at the desk, how the hell was he going to make it to his destination?

His steps were a stumbling shuffle, hardly the confident stride of a twenty-nine-year-old investigative reporter who'd seen the worst the world had to offer.

At least he thought he had. Damn, he hated hospitals.

Almost as much as he hated Texas. Yet, here he was.

"David Ruiz," he announced himself to the clerk. He was too tired to modulate his tone and it emerged sounding more like a chainsaw grating on metal than human.

The old lady glanced up, startled by his abnormal voice—he still wasn't used to that, wished he hadn't forgotten his electrolarynx in the truck. As a prop, it came in handy times like this. "You're a patient of?"

"I'm here to see my mother, Maria Ruiz."

"Alrighty then." Her fake smile shone bright as she searched her computer. Then her smile dimmed. "Oh."

"She's in the end-of-life unit." He said the words so she wouldn't have to. His tone was blunt, devoid of emotion, making her wince and look away. He sighed. Too tired to explain to a total stranger. Not that explaining ever truly changed anyone's first impression.

A helpful therapist, hoping to get him to commit more fully to his speech rehab, had shared the research with him: people cemented their impressions of strangers not by their appearance but rather by how trustworthy their speech, cadence, and tone were judged. Cadence he could control, but tone and trustworthiness? Even with the help of his vocal coach, those were beyond his capabilities. "Hospice."

"Room three-twelve," came her equally flat reply. No eye contact, no acknowledgment of his humanity—or his mother's. Simply a dismissal as she looked away and pretended to be totally absorbed in her computer. But her eyes didn't track with the words on the screen and a thin film of sweat beaded on the back of her neck. His fright-night axe-murderer's voice scared her. She wanted him gone.

So he left. Funny thing was, it wasn't all that long ago that he would have been able to charm someone like her. With a sly wink and subtle hint, he'd quickly have them gushing about how they'd seen his televised reports from the war and how handsome he looked and how brave he was, returning to a war that everyone else was leaving, and could they have his autograph?

He still looked the same. Well, almost—no one noticed his prosthetic eye; it was a perfect match to his real one. There were no visible scars now that his hair had grown back. The only external clue to his brain injury was his voice: flat, cold, devoid of emotion or humanity.

Kiss of death for his TV career, but in many ways, maybe the best thing that had ever happened to him.

Funny how everything you thought was Truth turned out to be a bunch of lies.

David stood outside the door to his mother's room, waiting while a nurse finished adjusting the infusion pump that provided Maria's pain medication. Typical Maria, she had ignored her symptoms, denied that anything could come between her and her son and the life she dreamed for her family until it was too late.

When he was a kid—after he was old enough to stop believing in Santa Claus, his father's innocence, and other fairy tales—he'd accuse her of being delusional, living in a fantasy world where she could make dreams come true. Now that he was an adult and had seen more than his fair share of dreams shattered, he wondered if it was more a case of Maria fighting to protect her tiny family from harsh reality.

"Hi, Mom," he said as he entered and leaned over the bed

to plant a gentle kiss on her forehead. The cancer had infiltrated her bones, creating constant pain at the slightest touch.

"David, my David," she murmured, her eyes glazed. He thought she might drift off—she was spending more and more of her time in the netherland between sleep and wakefulness—but she gave herself a shake and pushed the button to bring the head of her bed up so she could face him. "Have you gone yet? Have you seen your father? He needs you, David. And you need the truth."

The gush of words left her breathless, gasping. He adjusted her oxygen cannula, noting the bruises left by the tape holding it to her cheeks. The mask would be more comfortable the nurses said, but Maria refused it. She hated anything that might impede her last chances to communicate. Maria had always been a talker, just as her son had always been the one to ask questions.

He smoothed out her orange and green crocheted afghan before taking the chair beside her, making sure he was at her eye level so she wouldn't have to strain to see him. She was the one person who didn't seem to mind his new speech patterns; she understood the emotion behind his words without needing to hear it.

"You must go to him, David. Before it is too late."

The one person alive on this planet who knew him better than he knew himself and she was dying. Yet, she didn't want him here with her; all she wanted was for him to reconcile with his father. How could he say no to her final request?

But he was merely going through the motions for her. Lying and trying his best to hide it from her. He'd never reconcile with his father, never forgive.

"No, I haven't been to see him yet. The Justice Project attorney is working to get me permission for a special visit this week." He was glad his voice hid his emotion—it had been eight years since he'd seen his father and he'd be happy to never visit him again.

As if she read his mind, she stretched a bone-thin hand to cover his on the bed rail. "You need to go. You need the truth. And so does your father."

He shook his head. "What truth? He confessed. He took the plea. The prints on the gun were his. We might get him out on a technicality, but that doesn't make him innocent."

Her sigh emerged as a rattling noise that made him wince and look away. He'd heard that noise before in soldiers about to die.

"When did you lose faith, David? You used to believe."

"How can you still?" he argued. "Twenty-nine years you've followed him from one prison to the next, dragging me along, fighting a battle even he never asked you to fight. The man's in prison. Where he belongs. Why can't you see that?"

To his surprise, she smiled. Not at him, at some hidden memory. "He's innocent. I know it. Just as I know you are the one to save him." She turned her head, stared at him straight on. "Promise me, David. Promise me you won't give up on him."

He already had, years ago. Given up on the idea that his father could be innocent, that he wasn't the son of a vicious, cold-blooded killer, that justice hadn't already been served. Michael Manning was exactly where he should be: behind bars.

But David had never been able to deny his mother anything. "I promise," he whispered. Her fingers tightened on his hand with surprising strength. "I promise I'll keep fighting to get him released."

Not the same as believing in Michael's innocence. And not promising any future relationship with the man who'd given David half his DNA.

Maria nodded. It was enough. "Thank you, David. I know you always keep your promises." She sucked in the oxygen. Her gaze drifted toward the window with its view of the endless Texas sky. "I'd hoped to see him. One last time. But..."

David choked back a sob, wishing he could promise her that, anything to bring comfort to the woman who had sacrificed so much for her son and the worthless man who'd fathered him.

"I know, Mom." He patted the air above her hand, not wanting to cause her any pain with his touch, his words as empty as the gesture. "It'll be all right."

She closed her eyes, eased into her drug-induced twilight sleep, her features at peace, accepting her son's lie.

Chapter 2

LUCY GUARDINO LOVED everything about being a woman. In fact, her favorite photo of herself was taken when she'd been requalifying on the FBI weapons range, firing a Remington 870 pump-action shotgun while eight months pregnant, grinning like a madwoman.

As she slid her new Beretta M9A1 into the paddle holster on her waist and glanced in the mirror to check that it wasn't too obvious beneath her blazer, her gaze went to the rumpled bed where her husband, Nick, had just this morning reminded her of the many, many pleasurable advantages her gender provided. Oh yes, Lucy loved everything about her life, about being a wife, a mother, a woman...except...

Shoes. She pulled her dark curls back from her face and glanced down at her sock-clad feet peeking out from beneath the hems of her slacks, the white plastic ankle-foot-orthotic brace glaring against the hardwood floor. It'd been four months since she'd almost lost her leg after being mauled by a vicious dog. The surgeons said it was a miracle she could walk again, much less mostly without need of a cane. But the nerve damage—there was no easy cure for that. She'd always need the brace, would always be in pain.

Always have to find damn shoes. During her medical leave, she'd worn sneakers while rehabbing, but today was the first day of her new job, leaving the FBI for a consulting firm that worked cold cases. An office job—she refused to think of it as desk duty—with a team to manage, people to meet and greet, an image to project.

Sneakers were not going to cut it. Neither were her almost-as-comfortable hiking boots.

She'd dressed in her best testify-in-court suit but had forgotten she usually wore low-heeled pumps with it—shoes she couldn't fit her AFO brace into.

Lucy opened the closet door and was greeted by a host of Nick's button-down shirts, slacks, and his handful of suits— seldom worn now that he'd set up his own practice as a trauma counselor and wore jeans most days. Even so, his side was much more colorful than hers—and more crowded. All she had were four conservatively cut pantsuits like the one she wore, a dozen blouses in various shades of white and off-white, and a few lonely date-night dresses she hadn't worn in she couldn't remember how long.

She pushed the suits aside and found what she was searching for: her black tactical boots. Perfect. Comfortable, the AFO would fit, no problem, and while they'd be a bit clunky—

"Mom, no," Megan said from the door behind her. Her tone held all the outrage of a fourteen-year-old fashionista witnessing a crime against style. "Drop the boots and back away from the closet."

"I need to wear something—" Lucy protested, holding on to the boots. Last time she'd worn them, she'd been with the Pittsburgh FBI SWAT team, roping out of a helicopter during an urban combat training exercise. Such fun.

The stab of fire from her left foot reminded her that those days were gone forever.

"So, is this Beacon Group an accounting firm?" Megan asked, scrutinizing Lucy's black pantsuit. "Or is this new job of yours as an undertaker?"

"It's my first day. I'm not sure what the dress code is." And she wanted to make a good impression.

Until now the Beacon Group had functioned as an information clearing house, coordinating efforts of law enforcement agencies, nonprofits like the National Center for Missing and Exploited Children, and a myriad of volunteer-run groups. After being inundated with requests for investigatory assistance—not uncommon in these days of budget cuts and refocusing of priorities on domestic terrorism and violent crimes—Valencia Frazier, the owner, decided to establish a field investigation team as a pilot program.

Led by Lucy. No badge, no arrest authority, no resources. Yet, she was supposed to build a team that could crack cases years—decades even—gone cold, often without access to the original evidence or witnesses, with only case reports and photographic documentation. Sometimes not even that.

Putting together puzzles with no idea what the picture on the box was, with missing pieces as well as pieces from other puzzles jumbled into the mix.

Almost as much fun as roping out of a helo in Lucy's mind.

"What's their sense of style like?" Megan asked, taking the tactical boots from Lucy.

Lucy had run a background check on Valencia Frazier and her organization, knew their annual budget and closure rates, but the report hadn't mentioned anything about a "sense of style."

"How are their offices decorated?" Megan translated. "What did the people you met there wear?"

"The offices are in a Queen Anne house that's over a hundred years old. Valencia's family—the Fraziers—were among the original settlers at Beacon Falls."

"So old and stuffy, uptight?" Megan grimaced. "Maybe undertaker does fit."

"No. Valencia's not like that. She's—" Lucy hesitated. "Elegant. Understated. Audrey Hepburn—but in her fifties."

"Audrey Hepburn would never be caught dead in a pantsuit. Let's start with losing the blazer." Before Lucy could protest, Megan slid it off her shoulders.

"I'm not leaving my weapon behind." As a former federal agent, Lucy was able to continue to carry her guns—usually she had at least two on her person and one in her bag. She'd given up her ankle holster and switched her body gun to the sleeker Beretta instead of the .40 caliber Glock the FBI had issued, but no way in hell was she walking around naked.

Megan stepped back. "No. Keep the gun. That's your style—badass, kick-butt detective. Like those black-and-white movies you and Dad love so much. In fact, a shoulder holster would be sexy."

"And totally impractical."

"Just saying. Wait, I have an idea." She disappeared, heading down the hall to her room.

Lucy glanced in the mirror. She was thirty-nine, would be forty in a few months, and her teenaged daughter was dressing her. But, she had to admit, the blouse and slacks without the jacket did kind of work. She wore no jewelry except her wedding ring and a paracord survival bracelet Megan had given her to replace the one that had saved Lucy's life back in January. This new one was black threaded through with silver wire that would make for a perfect garrote or lock pick, depending on your needs.

A jewelry box sat on the dresser, its lid dusty. Lucy never wore earrings or necklaces on the job—too easy for an assailant to grasp and use against you—but she had a few nice pieces Nick had given her over the years. She rummaged through them until she found the ones she wanted: filigree silver shaped in the form of calla lilies with freshwater pearls dangling from their centers.

"What about these?" she asked as Megan bustled back into the room, her arms brimming over with colorful scarves, beads, and a pair of dark purple cowboy boots.

"Now you're getting the idea." As Lucy slid the earrings on, Megan draped scarves across her shoulders, assessing the various combinations.

"I always end up dunking them in my food," Lucy protested.

"Yeah, too frou-frou anyway." She swept the scarves aside and switched to the necklaces, most of them Mardi Gras beads that Lucy wouldn't wear even to a costume party. No way in hell was she going to spoil Megan's fun, though. She could always change in the car before she got to Beacon Falls.

Megan shook her head, discarding each set of beads until she had one strand remaining. It was smaller than the others, the beads elongated and curved, in shades of eggplant purple, silver, and teal. Megan pulled up Lucy's dark curls, doubling the strand over and around Lucy's neck until it sat at her collarbone. "Perfect."

It did look good. "We still haven't solved the—"

"Oh yes, we have." Megan held up her cowboy boots. They were ankle high with flat heels Lucy could probably manage without her cane. She was really hoping, despite the doctors' prognostications, to wean herself off the damn cane.

"They're purple. And turquoise and pink—"

"Magenta," Megan corrected. "The purple matches the necklace, gives a little contrast to your suit, and you'll never see the teal-and-magenta embroidery at the top under your slacks. Plus, I'm a half size larger than you, so the brace should fit and you can double up on socks for the other foot. Just try it."

Lucy sat on the bed and allowed Megan to slide her foot with the brace into the boot. As promised, it fit. What was even more surprising was the way her daughter had assessed the situation and found a solution. Pride washed over her. Her baby girl was growing up.

"How's that feel?" Megan asked as Lucy stood up. She took a few steps. The boots were surprisingly comfortable, giving her injured foot enough support without rubbing against the damaged nerves.

A wolf whistle interrupted her. Nick stood in the doorway, grinning. "Wow, you clean up nice." He joined them, kissing Lucy and rumpling her hair. "Megan, grab your stuff, I'll drop you at school."

Megan ran back to her room. Lucy turned to Nick, the weight of the day hitting her. She didn't need to say a word. He stepped to her, circling his arms around her from behind, resting his chin on top of her dark curls.

"What was I thinking?" she asked. "Joining a group of amateurs?"

"Amateurs with a damn good track record." He was right. Valencia's organization had a better clearance rate than most police departments' cold case squads. But still...

"They're all so young. Tommy Worth, the pediatric ER doc, is the oldest, and he's only thirty-four. Their tech guy doesn't even have a degree. Instead, he has a juvie record." So unlike the High Tech Computer Crime squad she'd partnered with at the FBI. Those guys had more initials after their names than a can of alphabet soup—not to mention their genius level IQs.

"It will be all right," Nick whispered. "You'll make it work. You always do."

"I wish I was as certain as you are." She didn't even bother to mention the final member of the team Valencia had put together for Lucy: a twenty-six-year-old former Marine MP who'd somehow managed to win a Bronze Star yet hadn't been able to hold a steady job in the seventeen months since she'd left the Corps.

Lucy had a feeling there was a lot more to TK O'Connor's story than what showed up in Valencia's terse summary. She'd done a basic background check on TK, just like she had the others, but it had been a cipher, as if the woman had been living off the grid since her return stateside. On paper, TK barely existed. Lucy could not help but wonder what the former Marine would be like in real life.

"You don't have to do this," Nick reminded her. "We can make it with your FBI medical pension and my work. You can stay at home, do whatever you want. Learn Italian, write your memoirs, teach, anything."

Retire. How Lucy hated the word. In her mind, it was the equivalent of *surrender.*

"Hang on. I thought of one more thing." Megan breezed back into the room, vanished into the closet, and emerged with a black leather jacket that Lucy hadn't worn since her undercover days. It was fitted, waist length, too short to conceal her weapon, which was why she never wore it, with bright silver zippers at the front, cuffs, and diagonally situated pockets.

"You're going to knock 'em dead," Nick whispered as he helped her on with the jacket.

Lucy wasn't so sure. The jacket still smelled of perfume and cigarettes. And maybe was too young for her? She twisted, scrutinizing her image in the mirror. One good thing about months of unrelenting rehab—other than her leg, she was in the best damn shape of her life. Maybe she could pull it off.

She wrapped her arms around her family, tugging them to her, ignoring the spike of pain when she shifted too much weight to her left foot. "What would I do without you guys?"

"Start your new job naked?" Megan suggested, ducking Lucy's fake punch and heading to the door. "C'mon, Dad. We'll be late."

"Got your karate gear?"

"It's jujitsu, not karate."

"Judo?"

"Jujitsu."

"*Gesundheit,*" Nick finished what surely was his three hundred and forty-first rendition of the joke. Both Megan and Lucy laughed even as they rolled their eyes and shook their heads at each other.

Megan herded Nick down the stairs, waving over her shoulder. "Good luck, Mom!"

Chapter 3

"THE BEAUTIFUL THING about gravity," TK O'Connor called back over her shoulder as she planted one foot on the railing above the abandoned hospital's narrow staircase and then launched herself to the wall on the opposite side, "is that she has no favorites. Sinner, saint, we all fall."

She zigzagged over the railings, three feet above the steps, her feet never hitting the ground. At the top of the stairs, she pushed off the wall, flying into a front flip before landing.

Wilson grunted behind her. He had at least six inches on TK's five-seven, with a longer reach, but his greater bulk put him at a disadvantage with some parkour moves. She'd designed this particular urban free-racing course with those in mind. Today, she was going to finally beat him. "You want to worship gravity? Like as a god?"

"Goddess," she corrected, leaping into the hospital's empty dumbwaiter shaft. "Gravity is a she. Mother of the universe. Even Einstein worshiped her."

She liked how her voice thundered back to her as it echoed against the brick walls of the narrow shaft. Originally designed to open on both sides to carry equipment where it was needed, the doors and hardware were long gone, leaving openings up and down all seven stories, like a boxer with half his teeth knocked out.

TK used her momentum, bringing one foot up to plant firmly against a solid wall, then vaulted through the opposite opening on the floor below. Most of the outside wall was gone on this side of the building, leaving the foundation littered with small mountains of crumbled cement and bricks. Pittsburgh was filled with buildings like this, especially here on the Southside, where gentrification was only now catching up with decades of urban decay. Making it a parkour runner's dream landscape.

She raced through the maze of debris and turned the corner, the sky opening up in a golden-blue umbrella above her. Now came the challenge move: up and over a twelve-foot cement foundation wall. The approach was short, making it difficult to build up momentum. TK sprinted forward, slammed both palms high up on the wall as she pushed her shoulders back, giving her legs room to run up the wall. When they caught up with her body, she flew up into a handstand, then flipped upright.

"You don't defy gravity," she said as Wilson began his approach on the wall, tackling it head-on as if he'd rather plow through it instead of going over it. "She embraces you, anchors you, then finally sets you free."

Wilson scrambled for a handhold on the ledge, missed it, and tumbled back. He landed with a thud on the concrete floor.

"I think your goddess is a bitch." He groaned, stood, and

backed up a few steps to try again.

TK crouched on top of the wall, nodding. "Yep. But an equal opportunity bitch. That's my point. None of this favoritism bullshit. No matter how high we fly, in the end, gravity always wins."

Wilson slammed into the wall again. This time his trajectory was off by miles, leaving him unable to get past his first foot plant. He lay on the floor looking up at her, chest heaving.

When TK planned their runs, she always left the toughest obstacle for last. It was selfish, giving her a slight edge since her slimmer, more flexible build made parkour's urban-obstacle free racing easier. Not that Wilson ever gave her any slack when they sparred in the ring, even though he had the longer reach and greater strength.

"It's all about momentum," she told him.

He grunted and rolled to his feet, recalculating his approach, and this time he was able to scramble up the wall, using his muscles to haul himself up and over. It wasn't pretty or elegant in the least, but it got the job done. Too late. TK had already leapt past the mounds of broken concrete littering the former reception area, raced down the graffiti-covered hall, through the side exit, and was waiting for him when he finally chugged his way to the tree she'd designated as their finish line.

She grinned at him, looking for some acknowledgment of her victory, but he simply reached for his water bottle from his pack.

As he drank, he glanced back at the former hospital, a gloomy hulking shadow marring the golden light. Beyond it Pittsburgh's Southside was waking up to greet the day.

"You'll need an alternative to that last wall for the group

run. Make it a cooperative exercise," he finally said. "And we should do the dumbwaiter as a chimney with spotters." Today's run was to prep the course for the class they taught on Thursday. "You keep forgetting parkour is about community, working together. It's not a competition. It's not about winning." He eyed her; she looked away, pretended her shoe needed tying. "Or about escaping."

"Learning to trust your body and your instincts as well as your partners," she droned, repeating the instructor manual. TK had taken up parkour only a few months ago after she'd stumbled across one of Wilson's groups running a course, but he'd quickly taken her on as a co-instructor.

"Even a Marine understands leave no man behind," he said bluntly. Wilson had been an Army Ranger and had seen his share of combat.

She grunted, conceding the point. It wasn't the first time they'd had this conversation. They jogged side by side, cooling down as they headed back to Greene's Gym down by the waterfront.

The gym was in an old two-story warehouse that once serviced barge traffic on the Mon. It was prime real estate now that Homestead was being gentrified, but Sal Greene refused to sell. Instead, the warehouse owner was finally committing to some much-needed renovations, trying to placate both the old gym rats who liked working out in a place that had no machines as well as his new clientele who loved the "authenticity." And felt like they were getting a better workout if an old man who looked like he could have been an extra cast from *Rocky* yelled at them during it.

"Construction starts next week," Wilson said as they

rounded the corner to the gym. "Where you going to move?"

TK sighed. Her arrangement with Sal was teaching parkour, mixed martial arts, and self-defense classes in exchange for free room and board at the gym. It was the only way to keep a roof over her head since she'd separated from the Corps and returned stateside, when, after eight years of Uncle Sam seeing to her care and feeding, homelessness had become her new reality.

"Not sure."

"I thought now that you got that gig with Beacon you might move into a real place."

"I'm still work-for-hire, which doesn't work out to so many hours a week. But there's some hotshot retired FBI agent coming on board. They'll decide if I get to stay on full-time." And if she got a chance to do what she really wanted to do: get into the field and out of the damn office.

"That must suck. Getting all spit and polish for a new CO."

"Tell me about it." Resentment bled into her voice, but Wilson was right: it did suck. Having to prove herself over and over again. And she'd read up on this FBI chick, Lucy Guardino. The woman had been with the Bureau for fifteen years, would no doubt expect her new team to genuflect and worship at the altar of rules and regs. TK had had quite enough of that, thank you very much. Fellow grunts, she'd die for her team. But that respect was earned, not commanded.

In the past six months, she'd done good work for the Beacon Group, including identifying a decades-old John Doe body and finding a missing person who had been living under an assumed name. It was what the Group was all about: solving cold cases and bringing justice—and some sense of closure—to the families left behind. TK had surprised herself by enjoying the work, but she wanted more. She wanted to tackle the real cases, the unsolved murders, the stuff nightmares were made of. At least for normal people.

For TK, after what she'd been through in Iraq and Afghanistan, murders that took place years ago didn't hold a candle to her own night terrors. But studying them, along with working out and devouring language tapes, helped to keep her mind occupied with anything but the all-too-real horrors that were her memories.

Wilson held the door open for her—the closest thing to conceding her victory today that he'd ever give her. "Worse comes to worse," he said as he followed her into the cavernous space that stank of machine oil, sweat, and testosterone, "you can always bunk with me."

"In your dreams, Army." She laughed to soften the blow, but living with someone, anyone, especially a man, was out of the question. She'd rather go back to the streets. Alone.

Maybe there was a reason why TK couldn't run a parkour course any way except to flat-out win...because the last time she'd trusted someone, she'd lost. Lost everything.

CHAPTER 4

BEACON FALLS, THE hamlet where the Beacon Group had their headquarters, was an easy drive from Lucy's home on Pittsburgh's Southside, especially since she could take back roads winding over the hills of West Mifflin.

Twelve minutes after leaving her house, she was heading up the drive that led to the large Queen Anne on a bluff overlooking the gorge above the Monongahela River. For centuries the people who lived here—first Iroquois, then the French, and eventually British colonists—had outposts here, lighting bonfires each night to warn others of the treacherous waterfalls that waited, invisible, around the sharp bend of the river.

Lucy parked her Subaru between a BMW motorcycle and a Volvo in the small paved lot on the near side of the house. The bluff was high enough that she could see across the river to the east for miles, and from the other side of the house, she'd have an unobstructed view up the Monongahela River to the Pittsburgh skyline. Excellent tactical advantages. No wonder armies had fought over this tiny piece of mountaintop.

At the far edge of the bluff stood a tall iron tripod topped by a large bowl cradling a flame. Beside it, gazing out above the morning mist that obscured the river below, was a slim woman with black hair streaked through with gray, wearing a dress so simple in its lines that it had to be from a designer, topped by an intricately knotted length of silk. Valencia Frazier. Lucy bet she never dunked her scarf in her food. The woman was the epitome of grace and elegance.

"I love starting my day out here," Valencia said, beckoning Lucy to join her at the eternal flame. "When the mist is thick or the clouds hang low, you can almost imagine that it's three hundred years ago...or three hundred years from now. As if anything is possible."

She inhaled deeply, locked her arm with Lucy's, and turned away from the stunning view to face the house. "I'm glad you're here with us, Lucy. I think together we're going to help a lot of people."

"Glad to be here," Lucy said as they strolled along a brick-lined path back to the house.

The Queen Anne was a dusty shade of lavender that looked blue in some light and pink in others. The trim was a darker shade of purple, almost matching Megan's boots. It was a solid house, comforting in the way it perched on the mountaintop with the confidence of having withstood a thousand storms and the certainty it could face a thousand more.

"When I began the Beacon Group, almost two decades ago now, I never dreamed it would grow to play such a vital role for so many victims and their families." Valencia stopped to glance back at the beacon with its flame once more. The plaque at its base memorialized Valencia's late husband, Charles.

Lucy had read about his murder case and the battle Valencia had waged over nine years to find his killer. "You should be very proud of what you've accomplished."

Valencia's smile was a wistful glimmer and Lucy knew she would trade it all to have her husband back with her.

They crossed the gingerbread-adorned porch and entered through the main doors, intricately carved mahogany, handcrafted with loving hands. Inside, the walls of the foyer were adorned with paintings from artists even Lucy had heard of, names like Remington and Catlin, depicting the history of Beacon Falls. The Fraziers had arrived here in 1752, traders and fur trappers who were among the first whites to call Beacon Falls home. The British had displaced them for a while, sending them north to join the Iroquois nation, but eventually, they'd fought their way back south again and regained their land.

Valencia led Lucy past the reception area in what used to be the front parlor and up a gracefully curving staircase to the second floor, where Lucy's new office was situated in the Queen Anne's rounded turret. Windows on three sides offered a view corporate honchos in the city would kill for.

"I'm afraid there's no time for you to get settled," Valencia said as Lucy dropped her bag and jacket on the settee beside her new desk. "We've had an emergency request." She led Lucy down the hall past former bedroom suites that had been converted into work areas.

"A missing person?" In addition to cold cases, the Beacon Group assisted law enforcement with critical missing person cases. Given Lucy's experience with the FBI's Child Abduction Response Team, missing persons would also fall under her new team's purview.

"No. A homicide. Three of them to be precise." Valencia paused outside the closed door of a conference room. "An entire family annihilated."

Lucy stopped short. She'd been listening to her music on the way here, kick-ass rock 'n' roll to psych her up for her first day trapped at a desk. Had she missed something? "I didn't hear of any—"

"I'm not surprised." Valencia opened the door. "It happened twenty-nine years ago in a small town in Texas that doesn't exist any more."

They stepped inside. Lucy kept her unanswered questions to herself, letting Valencia set the pace. The woman knew how to bait a hook that was for certain.

The conference room had a dining table with eight chairs around it along with an old-fashioned porcelain brick fireplace and elegant tapestry drapes edging the large picture windows that lined the back wall. But the rest of the room was decorated in the latest technology: a state-of-the-art projection monitor that took up the entire side wall, several laptop computers, and speaker phones spread out along the length of the table like trays of canopies at a dinner party.

At the far end of the table was a black man in his twenties manning a computer. He was the first to notice their entrance, glancing up at them with a welcoming smile beneath the dreadlocks that framed his features. Behind him stood a blonde, also in her twenties, wearing cargo pants and a Pucifer T-shirt. The man she was in a heated discussion with was older, mid-thirties, dressed in a conservative button-down and khakis.

"You can analyze the old evidence all you want, Tommy," the blonde was saying, "but the only way to dig up anything new is to go boots on the ground. We need to re-interview everyone, see what they're hiding."

"Um, guys?" the man at the computer put in as he spotted Valencia and Lucy at the door.

"Maybe it's not as easy—" the man started, then broke off when Valencia cleared her throat. Everyone fell silent and turned to face Lucy and Valencia.

"Thanks a lot, Wash." The blonde slapped the back of the first man's chair. Lucy realized he didn't sit in one of the regular chairs aligned around the table, but rather a wheelchair. It had a low back, was sleekly designed, and painted racecar red.

"You must be the Fed," the woman continued. Despite the fact she appeared to be younger than either man, she was obviously the leader. "I'm TK, TK O'Connor." Instead of approaching Lucy to take her hand, she dropped into a seat, crossing her arms over her chest as if waiting for Lucy to dazzle and amaze her.

"Nice to meet you, TK," Lucy said before Valencia could intervene. "I'm Lucy Guardino."

The older man had better manners, rushing forward to shake Lucy's hand. "Don't mind TK. She's always grumpy until she gets her coffee. I'm Tommy Worth. Pediatric ER doc, so I usually handle any medical or pathology records. And this," he turned to indicate the man in the wheelchair, "is George Washington Gamble, our resident tech guru."

"They call me Boxcar," George said.

TK frowned. "What? No one calls you Boxcar—"

"Well, they *could*. Why are you the only one who gets to use a nickname, *Tiffany?*"

"Ignore him," TK said in a voice of dismissal.

Lucy chose instead to ignore TK's order. This was her chance to take charge. She walked to the end of the table to take George's hand. "Boxcar, like in dice, right? Because G-G could look like two sixes."

He grinned, nodding his head. "Hey, you're the first one to get it. But seriously, call me Wash—after my middle name. Most everyone does."

"Good idea. Boxcar might not give the professional impression we're aiming for."

"Yeah, right." He nodded like it was his idea to deep-six his nickname. Lucy turned back to Valencia, raising an eyebrow as if to say, *See, this is why I wanted to hire professionals.*

Valencia seemed unperturbed by the antics of her civilian staff. She poured herself coffee, using a delicate porcelain cup instead of the larger mugs the others had, and slid gracefully into a seat at the far end of the table. "I was just telling Lucy about the Martin case."

"Why the rush on a case twenty-nine years old?" Lucy asked.

"It's a case the Justice Project brought to us," Valencia answered. "One of their key witnesses is in hospice and if they can't find evidence to support their appeal before she dies, their case dies with her. TK, you can fill Lucy in on the details on your way to Texas."

TK beamed at Tommy and Wash. "Told you, boots on the ground is the only way to go."

"May I have a word?" Lucy pulled Valencia out into the

hall and closed the thick oak door behind her. "None of them has any investigatory experience. I can't send them into the field."

"This isn't the FBI. There aren't going to be armed felons chasing them. It's a simple matter of sitting down, drinking a few cups of coffee, teasing memories from people who may not have told the police everything they knew at the time of the original crime."

"Until you ask the wrong question of the wrong person and things turn ugly."

"Lucy." She settled her hand on Lucy's arm in an almost maternal gesture. "We've been doing this for years. So have the Doe Network, NamUs, the Southern Law Poverty Center, and all those other unsung heroes who volunteer their time to help victims get the justice they deserve. Most of the time, we don't need to leave the building. It's a simple matter of picking up the phone or going online."

"I'll go," Lucy decided, knowing Nick and Megan would be angry. This job was supposed to give her more time with them, not send her off to Texas with no notice on what was almost certainly a wild-goose chase.

"We didn't hire you as a field investigator. We hired you to lead. To build a team we can send out into the field when necessary. Like now."

Lucy was a lead-from-in-front type. Even when working with fully trained FBI agents who she trusted with her life, she would still take point, especially if it was dangerous.

"A team of highly qualified investigators," she argued. "Not a trio of amateurs."

"They're the best we have, and the Justice Project doesn't have time for us to waste."

Her tone had an edge; Lucy had insulted not only Valencia's people but also the work to which she'd pledged her life. Lucy took the hint and backed down. "Well, Wash obviously isn't going. What about the others? Do either of them have any training or experience in investigations?"

"Tommy has fellowship training in forensics, specializing in abuse and sexual assault."

Lucy frowned. She couldn't see the pediatrician being much help—maybe if they had live victims to interview or to do a forensic evaluation on, but not a case like this. Which left only TK, the former Marine MP whose military record had been almost totally redacted, even from Lucy's Top-Secret clearance. All Lucy knew was that she'd served for eight years, including deployments to both Iraq and Afghanistan.

No wonder the woman tried to take charge. But TK didn't radiate the command authority most of Lucy's Marine friends did. Instead, an edgy energy sparked from the younger woman.

"Why'd TK leave the Marines?" From Nick's work, she knew all too well that many returning veterans had issues the military left untreated.

"You'll have to ask her. But it was an honorable discharge and she received several commendations. Including a Bronze Star." Valencia stood even straighter than her usual perfect posture, ready to defend her team. Lucy liked that about her even if she didn't appreciate the sudden change of plans.

"I'll take TK with me." Former Marine MP, at least TK would know how to handle herself if things got rough. "That way I can evaluate her in the field."

Valencia's smile told Lucy that the older woman had

gotten exactly what she wanted. She'd have to watch this one—beneath all that elegance beat a heart of steel. "Sounds perfect. My assistant has the tickets booked. You leave in three hours."

"If I don't like what I see," Lucy countered, "then I get to build my own team. Of qualified professionals. And your amateurs can go back to working the phones and surfing online archives. Deal?"

"I wish it was that simple. I'm afraid that with our limited funding, we're only able to hire three fulltime staff for your team. If they don't work out—"

"They lose their jobs?" Shit. At least at the FBI, if you were dismissed from one assignment, they would quickly find you another. Here at the Beacon Group, she was responsible for not just her team's lives but also their livelihood.

Valencia gave her a nod. "I sincerely doubt it will come to that. I think you'll see that civilians can have unique insights you might not get from indoctrinated law enforcement officers. After all, with most of these cases, the police have had trained investigators working them for years and have gotten nowhere. Our closure rate is seventy-four percent, much higher than most police department's cold case squads."

"But that's not with field investigations," Lucy countered. "Out there, it's a whole different ball game."

"That's why we hired you. To build a team that can handle what local authorities don't have the resources to deal with. I look forward to seeing what you can accomplish."

"Okay then," Lucy said, accepting Valencia's challenge and not-so-subtle reminder that it wasn't only Lucy's team on probationary status, but also Lucy. Who said retirement would be easy? Especially when she still had to face Nick and Megan with the news that her first day on the job was taking her to Texas for God knew how long.

She opened the door to the conference room. Wash was rattling away on his keyboard while Tommy leafed through a stack of case reports. Only TK sat doing nothing, leaning back in her chair, balancing it on two legs, a smug smirk aimed at the door.

"TK, go home, get packed. I'll pick you up for the airport in an hour. The rest of you, build me a coherent summary of the forensic findings and any evidence we have. I want facts, not interpretations. Oh, and transcripts of all the interviews. Line item them, compare them to each other and their previous statements. Highlight anything contradictory or inconsistent. I need to know where the holes in the case are so we can focus our investigation."

TK popped her chair forward, landing with a soft thud.

"Ma'am, yes, ma'am," Wash said with a mock salute and a grin, while TK stood, looking none too happy.

"I can go alone," TK said. "I'm sure you're needed here. To supervise." Her tone was cordial, but there was no mistaking her meaning, especially when she punctuated it with a glance at Lucy's cane.

"I'll pick you up in an hour." Sometimes there was a lot to be said about having the last word. Lucy spun on her heel, glad the others couldn't see the wince of pain the movement brought, and stalked out the door.

Hell of a first day, that was for sure. And if TK's attitude didn't improve, it was going to only get worse.

CHAPTER 5

WHILE SHE PACKED, TK plugged her ear buds into her latest language tape. Conversational Portuguese.

She'd begun using the language tapes back in Iraq when she'd first been drafted to go out into the field and serve as unofficial liaison for all things associated with their host nation's women, from searches of their persons and living quarters to questioning them and their children, often learning valuable intel no man would have gleaned. One of the unexpected benefits, aside from being able to function without an interpreter, was that the tapes soothed her anxieties and helped her block out the noise of the base while trying to grab some sleep before each night's raid.

So far she'd learned Arabic, Pashto, and some Dari, and now that she was back stateside, she was delving into the languages of the exotic lands she'd always dreamed of visiting. Hell, if it helped her sleep at night, she'd learn Klingon.

She moved around her tiny room above the gym,

collecting her gear and efficiently sorting it into her ruck. TK had pretty much been on her own since she left high school to join the Corps almost nine years ago. In many ways, even long before then. Her parents had tried their best, but...well, sometimes your best just wasn't good enough.

The Corps had been her home. Supporting not just TK, but with the wages she sent back to her parents, her entire family. After leaving the Marines, she'd drifted in the general direction of her hometown—Weirton, West Virginia—but ended up stalled here in Pittsburgh, unable to finish the journey back to the home of her youth. There was nothing left for her in West Virginia. She'd be just as homeless there as she was here.

The problem with being homeless wasn't so much the lack of a place to call home. The main problem with being homeless was that there were so many damn people. Especially in the shelters, making it impossible to sleep anyway. So what was the point?

TK preferred to bivouac in the open air, but again...people. Crowding the alleys that were safest and provided the best shelter, camping out under the bridges or in the city's parks, attracting more people: street thugs, cops, the church folks.

The people were the problem, not her lack of a roof over her head. How was she supposed to get any rest when she couldn't trust who was at her back? How was she meant to "resolve her issues," in the words of the transition counselor who'd evaluated her prior to her separation from the Corps, when she couldn't find ten minutes of peace and quiet to just stop thinking, stop waiting, stop anticipating the next attack?

Sal's gym had been the ideal solution—she could work

out, chat up guys like Wilson who'd been there, done that, had the same scars she had. Share a few laughs at the expense of the suits who had no idea what a Hesco was, much less what it felt like to have thirty-nine inches of sand all that stood between you and the enemy. Hell, it even had a freaking whirlpool and a view of the river. Sal's leaky, saggy-roofed, should've-been-condemned gym had saved her sanity, if not her life. First time in years she'd felt human.

Not for long. Thanks to the demands of his new fancy-pants clientele, Sal was closing the gym for a complete reno. Leaving TK back on the street.

She'd saved up enough money to buy a bike, an old BMW R80 a Vietnam vet had given her a fair price on. But now it made things worse. Because where could she go where the bike would be secure?

If she got a permanent gig with Beacon, she could maybe afford a cheap apartment. Probably up in the Southside slopes and flats, where the developers hadn't hit yet.

She didn't care where it was as long as it was hers and hers alone. Running water and a working toilet would also be nice, but optional compared to her need for security.

Yeah, the counselors at the VA would have a field day with that, wouldn't they? Maybe it was a good thing her benefits had dried up after they decided her PTSD and anxiety weren't a result of her service. She'd been in the Corps since she left high school, so where the hell else had it come from?

Not like she'd been shot at, blown up, or attacked back home in Weirton. Or the other thing...although, that could have happened anywhere, to any woman. Didn't make it right. Especially not when it was someone who was supposed to have your back.

Leave no man behind. But what about women?

She cinched her ruck tight, slid the concealed knife free from her belt then bent to remove the knife from her boot—stupid TSA, they didn't trust anyone. The blades went into a metal lockbox secured to the wall, followed by her Beretta.

"I carry that same model," Lucy's voice came from behind her.

TK whirled, pistol in her hand, settling automatically into a shooting stance. Lucy didn't move, simply held both hands out wide, away from her body. She met TK's gaze, gave her a small nod of understanding. "Sorry. Didn't mean to startle you."

TK blew her breath out, adrenaline jangling through her entire body, returned the Beretta to the lockbox, secured it, and yanked her ear buds out. "Didn't hear you."

"Obviously. What are you listening to? Pucifer?" She nodded to TK's tee.

Ignoring Lucy's attempt at chit-chat—how the hell would someone her age even know who Pucifer was?—TK hoisted her ruck and marched through the door without looking to see if Lucy followed. She jogged down the steps and over to where Wilson worked the speed bag.

"Watch my bike for me?" She tossed her keys so they landed beside his water bottle.

"Sure. Where you going?" He looked past her to where Lucy was emerging from TK's cubbyhole of a room, pulling the door shut behind her. "Who's your friend?"

"Texas. And she's not my friend. She *might* be my new boss if I don't fuck this up."

Lucy's gait down the steps was uneven; the problem

appeared to be with her left foot. Great, that's all TK needed. Bad enough Lucy would be dogging her heels, now she was going to have to slow down for the privilege.

"Good luck," Wilson said.

"Thanks." TK headed to the door, making it there at the same time as Lucy. She pulled it open and went through first then stuttered to a stop, uncertain if she should hold it for Lucy. Technically, Lucy outranked her, plus she was older and obviously somewhat disabled. It would have been the proper thing to do.

By the time she turned back, it was too late, Lucy was already through. She clicked a remote, popping the trunk on a bright blue Subaru. TK stowed her gear and climbed into the passenger seat, surprised by the music blasting when Lucy turned the engine on.

Pucifer. TK leaned back, taking a good look at her new boss. Lucy mouthed the words to "The Humbling River," obviously familiar with them, not putting on a show for TK.

Maybe there was hope for this mission not to be a complete disaster.

All she had to do was pretend to be normal for a few days, try to act like she knew what the hell she was doing, and not let Lucy witness any of her almost-nightly freak-out sessions.

Piece of fucking cake.

CHAPTER 6

LUCY TOOK ROUTE 60, avoiding the congestion on the interstate. They were in no rush as their flight didn't leave for another hour and a half. TK sat in silence beside her and Lucy wasn't ready to push. Not yet.

She'd noticed from the schedule posted on the gym's bulletin board that TK taught classes there: mixed martial arts fighting, self-defense, and parkour. Now there was a sport that Lucy wouldn't dream of ever attempting. The thought made her feel old. She wasn't sure if the feeling came from her age—although thirty-nine wasn't that old, not really—or the fact that she'd retired from the one job she thought she'd never leave, or the pain tap-dancing along the frayed nerve endings in her foot.

TK's living quarters had been...Spartan was the only word that fit. The room had obviously been repurposed from some kind of utility closet. But it was clean, neat; clearly its occupant craved simplicity. Monastic was another word that came to mind. A place of reflection.

The room wasn't what bothered Lucy, made her wish she could call Nick to ask for his advice. It was the door's clasp and stout padlock. Shiny and new. And on the inside.

From her interactions with the man in the gym, it was clear TK felt at home, wasn't afraid of him. So who was she afraid of? Was she locking someone out? Or herself in?

"Valencia told me you were a Marine MP." A neutral conversation starter, she hoped.

"Yeah, well obviously, we're rank amateurs compared to the FBI."

Okay, maybe not so neutral after all.

TK glanced into the back seat at Lucy's cane. Lucy braced herself; she hated telling the story of the night she almost died, the night her family almost died, the night her mother had been killed. Somehow, almost losing a leg was the least important thing she'd lost that night.

"Hope you didn't bring me along just to carry your bags." TK clipped the last word short, obviously realizing she'd crossed a line. "I mean—"

"You mean it's difficult to know what someone new whom you haven't worked with before expects from you. Or what you can expect from them." Lucy glanced at the younger woman, making it clear that the sentiment cut both ways.

She expected TK to meet her head-on, but to her surprise, TK fumbled with her seatbelt and looked away. "Just saying, that isn't my job."

"No, it isn't." Okay. Pretty clear that TK's trust would need to be earned. Lucy had a feeling if she won over TK, the rest of the team would follow. "So, what is? How do you guys work at Beacon Group? Are there any established protocols?"

TK sat up and shifted in her seat, leaning toward Lucy as if finally interested in the conversation. "No protocols, and we sure do need them. I mean, you'd think it was a simple division of labor, right? I handle the interviews, Wash does all the computer shit, and Tommy takes care of the medical stuff. Simple, clean. But no, those two, they'll do whatever they damn well please. Say Tommy finds something hinky in a pathologist report—that happened the first case we worked. He figured out some dental records had gotten switched, honest mistake, the patients were both named Jones. But instead of telling me so I could follow up with the dentist or the family, he goes and does it himself. Meanwhile, I figure out the same thing, that these two Jones maybe had their identities crisscrossed, I look the fool following behind him, asking the same questions."

"You felt foolish." Lucy borrowed one of Nick's favorite counseling ploys and reflected TK's words back to her.

"Yeah, of course. But that wasn't what bothered me. Not really. It was that we got the family's hopes up and we should have held back, not gotten them involved until we had the real story. Tommy felt awful about it. But that kind of thing happens all the time. I tried to establish some rules, but they never listen to me because I'm so new. Wash and Tommy, they've been working with Valencia for years."

"Yet, they obviously respect you. Look to you for leadership."

"More like they look to me to kiss their booboos when they screw up. I'm not there to be anyone's mother. I don't want to lead. I just want to get the job done and close cases."

"Are Wash and Tommy the only other investigators you've partnered with?"

"No. I kind of float around, whoever needs boots on the ground. A lot of the people at the Beacon Group are part-time, like Tommy, or don't like face-to-face interviews, like Wash. But I've worked with them a few times."

"Do the other teams have the same problem with lack of discipline?"

"That's the thing. There really are no teams. Valencia assigns cases as they come in—only if they look like they'll need specific expertise like this one, does she have more than one person working it. But I wouldn't call it a team."

That had been Lucy's impression as well. That Valencia, although she'd built the Beacon Group into an organization that was highly successful in many ways, she now needed more structure and organization to continue growing the Group's effectiveness. Exactly why she'd hired Lucy for this new endeavor.

"If I form a field investigation team—a real team, with SOPs and a hierarchy—is that something you'd be interested in? Or would you rather pursue solo office-based investigations like the rest of the Group?" Lucy couldn't bring herself to tell the younger woman that if TK didn't work out, she'd probably lose her job.

TK was silent for several moments. She turned back in her seat, facing front once more as they turned into the airport. "Guess that all depends on how well you do on this case."

Lucy chuckled, glanced at TK, and met her smile. "Touché."

She navigated to the long-term parking. Since US Air

pulled out, the airport was almost always empty—at least compared to the cavernous terminals and parking structures—so it made no sense to pay premium prices when it was just as easy to find a space in the cheaper garage. "What about this David Ruiz working for the Justice Project? Do you know him?"

TK shook her head. "I read his report summarizing the case this morning after Valencia gave us the assignment. Good writer—gets right to the point, but also makes you feel like you're there with him. Never spoke with him, though."

They grabbed their luggage. Lucy tucked her cane over the handle of her lightweight, carry-on-sized roller. She'd been tempted to leave the cane in the car, but since odds were that she would need it—her foot was already throbbing—it seemed best to bring it. She stopped TK as they entered the terminal, heading toward the ticket counter rather than the security line. "I have to check this bag."

TK frowned. "I was kidding about not helping you—"

"No. My weapons are locked inside." Lucy grabbed a sheaf of TSA paperwork from her computer bag. Traveling with weapons always meant paperwork, even when she was a FBI agent.

"You should have told me you were checking weapons through. I could have brought my own."

Lucy said nothing. Bad enough to partner with someone she didn't know or trust, but to have them armed? "Do you have a permit to carry across state lines?"

TK shrugged. "It's Texas. They probably have vending machines at the airport. Or we can stop at a cash-and-carry gun show on our way."

Right. Like that was a comforting thought. "Hopefully we

won't need them. After all, isn't that Valencia's whole point? That the Beacon Group doesn't need trained law enforcement for its field team?"

"Don't have to be law enforcement to know how to use a weapon. Besides, be honest. Don't you feel kind of naked without one? After all, you're retired and you still carry."

"My husband says it's hypervigilance. But he's a psychologist. His specialty is PTSD, sees it everywhere. Just like I look around and see potential threats everywhere."

"I say, better safe than sorry."

Lucy couldn't disagree. "More like, better safe than dead."

"Hoo-rah."

CHAPTER 7

THE FLIGHT TO Dallas wasn't crowded, and they had relative privacy. Lucy gave TK the window, surprised to see the former Marine do a white-knuckle armrest clench during takeoff.

"Not a fan of flying?" she asked once TK's jaws had relaxed enough to allow her to answer.

"Not in planes. Don't mind helos much, which is strange since I've walked away from three hard landings. I think maybe it's because I can see the pilot or something." TK turned to Lucy. "What about you? Did you have to fly much in the FBI? Did you have a fancy Gulfstream like on TV?"

Lucy laughed. "No. We mostly drove wherever we needed to go. And when I was with the Critical Incident Response Group, working with the Hostage Rescue Team, we flew in the back of C-130s. Compared to them, I'm with you, would much rather be in a helicopter."

TK nodded. The plane leveled off and she released her

grip, took a breath. Lucy was surprised by how much more amiable the younger woman was now that they were alone. As if TK had let her guard down. A smidge.

"So," Lucy said, wanting to continue the forward progress, "tell me about this Martin case."

"Not sure there's much to tell—Valencia only assigned us to it this morning. Home invasion gone wrong. Two brothers, both confessed, pled guilty to avoid the death penalty. Older one was high on PCP and peyote, put two cops in the hospital when they came to arrest him. The other apparently walked in on the homeowner confronting his big brother with a gun—there was a struggle and the man ended up dead. Cops had the gun with the younger brother's bloody fingerprints, eyewitness saw them driving away from the scene, and like I said, they both confessed." She flicked her hand in the air as if whisking a fly. "End of story."

"Then why are we here? They must have some grounds for appeal, some reason they need us to re-investigate."

TK rolled her eyes. "The guy working with the Justice Project, that David Ruiz, he says the confessions were coerced. That the public defender took the plea without even checking the evidence. The older brother—the druggie, the one supposedly too high to know what he was doing as he stabbed a woman and her seven-month-old baby girl to death and tried his best to kill her son—he died in prison last year. So now the younger brother, Michael Manning, he's recanting his confession, asked the Justice Project to help him with a *habeas corpus* appeal."

"Tough sell. Especially after this long."

"Exactly. The Justice Project is handling the inadequate defense counsel part of the appeal, but they want us to re-examine everything, try to build a case for this guy's innocence."

"Which you don't believe." Hard to ignore the skepticism in her tone.

"Look. I like working for Valencia and her group. Love it when I can solve a puzzle no one else can. I'm not sure why she's wasting our time on this one. Seems to me it was an open-and-shut case twenty-nine years ago and it's an open-and-shut case now. But I want to go full-time with the Beacon Group, and the only way to do that is to go where Valencia tells me. And," she glanced at Lucy, "I guess, impress you. How am I doing so far?"

"You're honest, I'll give you that."

"Unbiased, too. I'll give this job everything I have. If that means proving myself wrong about Manning and his brother, that's cool. My ego isn't tied to anything except finding the truth and knowing that if I can't find any evidence to prove Manning's innocence, then it simply does not exist."

"Good to know," Lucy said with a laugh. She had to admit TK was refreshing in her attitude—so different from the office politics that contaminated most cases over at the Bureau. "Did you work investigations while you with the Marines?"

TK shook her head. "No. I was a straight-up MP—pretty much busting up parties and fights, guard duty, maintaining discipline. Then I did FET deployments, two to Iraq and four to Afghanistan, and after that they sent me to work with Cultural Affairs."

Lucy had no idea what FET or Cultural Affairs duties entailed—planning parties? No, TK had the body language and command presence of someone who'd seen real action. She'd have to ask Nick next time they talked; most of his patients were veterans. "Valencia said you were awarded a Bronze Star. What's the story there?"

To her surprise, the younger woman flushed and looked out the window, away from Lucy. "Not much to talk about. Operational security."

Military speak for "mind your own business." As in classified information above Lucy's clearance level. She changed the topic. "Where do you think we should start?"

"Me? I'd start with the scene of the crime, work out from there. Reconstruct the crime, focus on any forensic evidence we could retest with modern techniques. In 1987, they wouldn't have used DNA, so that's an option."

"If any evidence still has viable DNA and wasn't contaminated," Lucy put in. "Think how many cops and crime scene guys—hell, evidence clerks and the DA's people—would have handled any evidence, left their own DNA."

TK nodded, conceding the point. "There were no signs of any sexual assault according to the state pathologist, so you're right. It might be a long shot."

"Not to mention time-consuming and expensive. Unless..." Lucy thought about the short summary of the crime that she'd skimmed before leaving for the airport. "Did they check that all the blood at the scene came from the victims? This kind of explosive, frenzied attack—especially if drugs play a role—you'll often see the perpetrator with cuts on the hand wielding the knife."

TK straightened, her interest piqued. She pulled her laptop out and opened it on her tray. Lucy was glad it was only the two of them in this row. Hopefully no one else could see the gruesome images as TK flicked through them. "I thought only victims got defensive wounds on their hands?"

"These wouldn't be defensive. They're from slipping on the victims' blood as the perpetrator grips the knife's hilt. The force of the strike—"

"Slices into his palm. Probably near the base of the thumb, right?" TK asked, twisting her own hand as if she held a knife. "No reports of blood, not from the victims, but look at the scene. No way in hell could they have tested every blood spatter—"

Lucy gave the photos only a glance—she wanted time to study them in depth and would prefer to do it alone. A scene like that, she knew she'd need a moment to shed her emotions before immersing herself in it and she didn't need TK seeing that—or reporting back to Valencia. Who was Valencia testing with this case? The justice system? Or Lucy and her potential future team?

"What about the brothers? Any injuries should have been recorded when they were arrested. Hopefully photographed as well."

"Nothing on the younger one, Michael Manning." TK clicked a few more keys. "Hmm...His brother's initial booking photos are missing. Only one we have is dated two days after when he was officially charged, so three days after the crime. Guy looks in pretty bad shape." She swung the computer so Lucy could see.

Understatement. Richard Manning appeared barely able to stand and had obviously taken a severe beating.

"He did resist arrest," TK said, playing devil's advocate. Lucy got the idea it was a role the young woman relished, even if it meant arguing against herself. "Sent two deputies to the hospital when they picked him up."

"They must have gotten some kind of medical clearance,

even if only to cover their ass. Any mention of cuts on his hands in that?"

"Let's see...Here's a doctor's note. Also dated two days later. Mention of a mild concussion, cracked and bruised ribs, no evidence that prisoner requires further medical treatment. Doesn't say anything about any cuts. But also doesn't say he doesn't have them."

"We'll need the complete medical record."

TK nodded, made a note. "What else?"

"Full transcripts of the interviews that led to the confessions. Have you seen the actual confessions submitted to the court? Less than three pages long between both brothers. And that's longhand, not even typed."

"You're buying into this whole coerced confession thing?" TK sounded doubtful. "I just can't see anyone sane confessing to such a heinous crime if they're innocent."

"You should have that discussion with my husband some time. Turns out there are all sorts of psychological manipulations that can convince someone they did or saw something they didn't—it's a fascinating area of study. If you're not a law enforcement officer depending on accurate statements, of course."

"So even if they confessed, we can't rely on those statements?"

"Who knows what went on in the two days between their arrest and their confessions? The police did things differently back in eighty-seven, might have used coercive techniques without even realizing what they were doing. I'd feel a lot more comfortable if I could read the full transcripts or better yet, get actual video or audio tapes of the interviews."

TK used the plane's Wi-Fi to email Wash and Tommy Lucy's requests. "They're working on it. Anything else?"

"I'd love to nail down the timeline. The day before the killings as well as everything that happened after."

"You looking for more alibi witnesses? Because the one they have is dying?"

Lucy shrugged. "This early in a case I try not to look for anything specific. It's more about getting a feel for where any holes are, things that don't line up and need clarification."

"So it's like we start over, a whole new investigation? Fresh eyes and all that?"

"It's how I prefer to do things. My motto when it comes to cases someone else started is: trust no one, assume nothing."

TK smiled at that. "No problem. That's pretty much how I live my entire life."

CHAPTER 8

THANKS TO THE time difference, they landed only an hour later than they'd taken off. Lucy let TK collect their rental—a silver Tahoe—while she checked in with Tommy and Wash back at Beacon Falls. It was the first time she'd flown since her leg injury and her ankle was swollen and throbbing, the damaged nerves shooting sparks of pain.

"How's it coming?" she asked Wash, certain they wouldn't have much to report. She'd been spoiled by having the cyber-wizards from the FBI's High Tech Computer Crimes Taskforce at her beck and call.

To her surprise, both had already made progress. "The Justice Project has already gotten a court order for both brothers' medical records and just sent them," Tommy answered first. "I'm not seeing any evidence of wounds on either brother's hands, but I'm really surprised the older brother was allowed to enter a plea at all. From his intake physical at the jail, he suffered from some pretty severe cognitive dysfunction—probably a combo of the drug use and multiple head injuries."

"Interesting. See if you can pinpoint exactly when he began to have problems. Could it have been from the beating he took around the time of his arrest?"

"Maybe, yes. I'd need to see CAT scans and earlier reports of his functioning to even hazard a guess. Not sure how helpful it would be in any case since it wouldn't clear the younger brother, Michael."

"You never know. What about you, Wash? Were you able to create a timeline of everyone's movements?"

"Yes and no. There are a lot of gaps—we simply don't have the answers in the material we were given. It might be in the prosecutor's files and was not turned over to the defense. Or the questions were simply never asked."

"The lawyers at the Justice Project are supposed to be getting us access to all the evidence from the sheriff and the prosecutor." Without the go-ahead to examine the original evidence, they'd be limited to witness interviews—witnesses from twenty-nine years after the events.

"They're working on it. Said they'll have an answer from the judge by the end of business today. In the meantime, I'll send you what I have."

"Good job. Thanks, guys." She hung up just as TK approached, a set of keys dangling from her fingers.

"Canterville, here we come. The clerk gave me a map—said GPS always gets it wrong because there's limited satellite coverage and cell towers out there."

Lucy had to smile. So many of her cases took her to places where modern communications were hampered by geography.

"No problems, I love good old-fashioned maps."

"Great. I'll drive, you navigate."

Once they got out of Dallas, the drive down the interstate went quickly, but then they turned off onto the county road leading to Canterville, population 3,718. From the map, Canterville was at the heart of Blackwell County, which only had three thin squiggles of roads and one county highway traversing it. Large swaths of blank space filled up most of the county and only two other towns were marked on the map.

Lucy glanced out the window. Apparently, the blank space was filled with fields, crops, and cattle. Finally, they arrived at the only hotel in Canterville, an old-fashioned, one-story stucco building, U-shaped with a pool at the back and a cracked blacktop parking lot out front.

"You were smart, checking in before the auction," the clerk said as she registered them. "Come Thursday, every room will be taken."

"What kind of auction?" Lucy asked as she fished for the Beacon Group credit card Valencia had given her. "Livestock?"

"No, the forfeiture auction." She raised her left hand, a surprisingly large diamond on the third finger. "My guy got our ring there. Of course, he's local, so we get a preview on the items and he put the word out for no one to bid against him." She slid a sheet of paper across the counter to Lucy.

It was a list of items below the Blackwell County Sheriff's Department letterhead. "A RV? Two speedboats?" Lucy read. "Do you guys have that big of a drug problem around here?"

"Not drugs. That's the beauty of it." The clerk leaned forward. "Old sheriff began doing it years back, but just here and there. It took our new sheriff to realize how good this could be for the county, make a system that was fair to everyone. That's why this place even exists." She spread her arms wide to indicate the motel.

TK wandered over to join them, glancing at the list. "There are a lot of cars on here."

"Exactly. You break the law in Blackwell County while in your motorized vehicle, you lose said vehicle, and..." She snapped her fingers. "You'll need a place to stay. Here we are, conveniently located across the street from the sheriff's department. Is that genius or what? I'm telling you, it saved this town. The whole county for that matter."

Lucy exchanged a glance at TK, who shrugged. "Guess we better not break any laws while we're here."

"That's right, ladies." The clerk laughed.

"Any place to eat nearby?"

"We offer a continental breakfast and coffee in the morning. Got the usual fast-food places on the highway—you would have passed them on the way in. And we have the Sweetbriar—serves a decent breakfast and lunch, great steaks, but just to warn you, evenings it's not exactly family-friendly. Most of the ranch hands go there to blow off steam, shoot pool, drink their paychecks."

TK perked up at that. "Where's that?"

"Block west of here. You can't miss it—only neon sign in Blackwell County." She said it as if it were a badge of pride.

They collected their keys—real metal keys on large key chains shaped like cowboy boots—and turned to leave the lobby when the clerk called them back. "Almost forgot. You have a message. David Ruiz with the Justice Project asked if you'd meet him when you got in. He's in room one-twelve but is working out of the Sweetbriar."

Both TK and Lucy had missed lunch thanks to the flight. "Can't come all the way to Texas without a steak," TK said as they strolled through the heat to their rooms.

Lucy nodded, glancing around their surroundings. So different from small towns back in her Pennsylvania mountains, yet also very similar. The countryside transitioned from flat to gentle rolling hills in the distance, alternating brown and green fields extending to the horizon. Across the street was a small government center that included administration offices and a post office. Separated by a parking lot from the government center was the county jail and sheriff's department.

The jail itself was typical cement and steel, constructed more for security than aesthetics. Two stories high, it appeared to be the tallest building in view—although, when Lucy glanced down the street in the other direction, she saw it was not quite as tall as the Sweetbriar's neon sign with its ten-gallon hat, lasso, and cowboy boot.

TK gestured with the asset forfeiture auction list she still held. "Says here they hold these auctions every two weeks. That's a heck of a lot of stuff they've seized. Is that legal?"

"The federal laws go back to the nineties, but after nine-eleven, local police began to use highway interdiction and asset forfeiture to help their budgetary deficits. It's all done in the name of preventing terrorism and stopping organized crime, but unfortunately some departments get carried away."

"I don't get it. If no one's actually charged with a crime, only pulled over because they're suspected of something, then how can the cops keep their stuff?"

"A person is innocent until proven guilty, but an object is

presumed guilty—the product of a criminal enterprise and therefor subject to seizure—until a person can prove they've obtained it legally."

TK gave a small whistle. "Holy heck. This is the freedom I spent eight years fighting for?"

All Lucy could do was shrug. When they dropped their luggage off and regrouped outside on the sidewalk once more, her blouse was already soaked through with sweat and more had gathered around her foot swathed in its plastic brace. She was relieved when TK didn't even suggest walking as an option.

They climbed back into the SUV, the equivalent of climbing into an oven. By the time they made it down the street to the Sweetbriar, the AC had barely made a dent in the heat. They each grabbed their computer bags and strolled into the wood-frame single-story building designed to look like a log cabin.

On the inside, it was typical of family-style restaurants across the country: large wooden tables in the center; high-backed booths lining one wall; a long polished bar on the interior wall; a variety of mementos hanging from the exposed rafters and tacked to the walls. There were signed cowboy hats, a pair of horns that spanned at least six feet and could only have come from one of the state's famous longhorn steers, and a variety of horse shoes, spurs, bridles, and branding irons.

The place seemed empty of customers. Made sense since it was too late for lunch and too early for dinner. A woman stacking glasses behind the bar glanced up. "Can I help you?"

"We're looking for David Ruiz," Lucy told her.

She nodded her chin to the corridor leading behind the bar. "He's set up in our back room."

They followed her directions, past doors labeled BULLS and HEIFERS, to a windowless room with tables arranged in an open circle to accommodate larger parties. The sole occupant was a dark-haired man in his late twenties who sat at the far end of the tables surrounded by boxes of documents and files.

"David Ruiz?" Lucy said as they entered. He glanced up, blinked as if not sure where he was, and ran a hand through his hair.

TK strode forward. "We're from the Beacon Group. TK O'Connor, and this is Lucy Guardino. We're here to help."

He nodded and took TK's hand. "Glad to have you."

His voice grated through the air, lifeless and monotone. It sounded mechanical, devoid of any inflection or emotion. TK dropped his hand and stepped back. "Uh, pleased to be here."

"Whoops. Should have used this." He held a small black cylinder to his throat. It resembled the artificial larynx that Lucy's dad had after his tracheotomy. "Is that easier? I'm still figuring out the best way to put people at ease."

TK winced at the strange voice, but nodded. "I guess. Gives me something to focus on besides—"

"Exactly," he said, nodding. Without his body language it would have been impossible to discern any emotion. "Sometimes a prop saves time, right?"

Lucy stepped forward. "Are these the case files?" It was obvious they were, but she wanted to get started, figured the social chitchat could wait.

"What the defense had. The judge signed off on our court order compelling access to everything the police and prosecution have. We can start tomorrow."

TK sat down and opened her laptop. "This place got Wi-

Fi?"

"Yep, that's why I chose it."

TK quickly had them online with Tommy and Wash back at Beacon Falls. "David Ruiz of the Justice Project, meet Wash, our resident white-hat hacker."

Wash did a flourish with his hand in acknowledgment.

"And Dr. Tommy Worth, pediatrician, our medical and forensics expert."

"Nice to meet you," Tommy said.

Lucy glanced through the files David had organized. "So, David, you have no law enforcement background?"

"Investigative reporter."

Wash chimed in. "Right. I knew you looked familiar. I remember seeing you on the news. Before..." He gestured to his face, sliding a palm over half of it.

"Funny thing is, I actually get better stories now than I ever did before..." He mimicked Wash's gesture. "After, I decided the truth shall set me free, so that's all I care about. Not ratings or Q scores or any corporate BS. All I want is the truth."

"Can I ask what happened?" Lucy said. "I'm afraid I don't watch the news, so I'm not familiar with your work."

"He was embedded in Afghanistan," Wash answered. "Covering the troop drawdown and the dangers it posed. His Humvee blew up."

"Not mine. The squad I was working with. IED. Shrapnel."

"Like from the Humvee?" Wash sounded both excited and horrified.

"Bones," Tommy muttered as if by reflex.

"Bones?"

"Baby Doc's right—best shrapnel any suicide bomber ever devised. Bits and pieces of the guys around me—the ones who didn't make it. Which was everyone except me. Human bone splinters are sharp, jagged, and cause secondary infection, prolonging the healing process, and tying up more of the enemy's resources."

It was an eerie disconnect, his voice so flat, reciting facts, while his face filled with anguish and his shoulders hunched with the memory.

"I don't like it," TK said. "A reporter? What's to keep him from posting or Tweeting or Snapchatting everything we do?" She seemed to realize her faux pas and turned to him. "No offense."

"None taken. I told you, I'm not here for a story. I want the truth. All of it. Nice thing about my screwed-up brain is just like you can't hear any emotion in my voice, I can't hear yours. Which frees me to focus on your body language. Words lie, but body language doesn't. I can tell when someone's hiding something."

"Tonal agnosia," Tommy diagnosed. "The language center that processes verbal emotion was damaged."

The term was vaguely familiar. Lucy remembered watching a documentary with Nick—his turn to choose the entertainment, but she'd been just as fascinated by the strange permutations of certain brain injuries.

"Right." David beamed at TK. "See? Tell her, doc. I'm an open book—can't help it." He raised his right hand as if swearing on a stack of bibles. "Funny thing is...now that I can't lie anymore, people actually open up to me more. I get far more truth than I ever did before. Just not the kind of truth that grabs ratings."

"Let me get this straight." TK didn't sound convinced. "Upside is you're kind of a walking lie detector? But downside is you can't actually lie?"

"Not verbally. I can say the words but I can't sell the lie, if you get my drift. Can't communicate emotion with my voice anymore either.   This," he gestured to his lips and mouth, "stripped-down Tin Man robot voice is as good as I get. Shame too," he grinned at TK, "because used to be I could sweet talk a pretty girl like you out of your panties before—"

"I think we get the picture," Tommy said through the computer.

"Guess you weren't lying about telling only the truth," TK said, smiling at David.

"Pretty much talked the same before, only it would cost you a few shots of tequila first. Just now, people don't hear me the same—without emotional context coloring the words I use, unless I add dramatic body language to emphasize phrases, it all sounds flat. Spent months with a vocal coach to make it this far— should have seen me in rehab, sounded worse than a robot."

"Okay, let's get back to the case," Lucy said, trying to regain control of the conversation.

"Wait," Tommy said from the screen. "I just have one more question for Mr. Ruiz—not medical-related, if that's okay."

TK had warned her that the pediatrician would stray from his area of expertise. "Go ahead, Tommy."

"When were you going to tell us that the killer we're working to get out of prison is your father?"

CHAPTER 9

DAVID LOOKED UP at the two women in the room staring at him and then at the computer screen with the image of the two men back in Pennsylvania. "Sorry. I thought you knew. My mother was the girl with Michael Manning on the night of the killings. She's his alibi witness."

"Whose testimony was discounted," Worth, the pediatrician, added. Hostility radiated from the man although he'd never met David before. But Worth's gaze through the computer monitor was directed past David to TK. Did the two of them have a relationship?

"Yes," he answered Worth's accusation. "My mother's family has lived in the area for generations. Longer than the Mannings—or the Blackwells, for that matter. But an under-aged, brown-skinned girl with relatives who speak with an accent and a funny last name? No one will listen to a word you say."

Lucy pursed her lips and then relaxed, turned to face him, her body posture open. "We're listening now. What does your mother have to say?"

He blew out his breath, exasperated. If only it were that easy, proving Michael's alibi. "Not a hell of a lot. Except she's sure he didn't do it—even though he could have left her while she slept. That much she will admit. And the other witness puts my father and uncle at the scene of the crime after my father took her home."

"Which the brothers both admitted, being in the area that morning. So she's really not much of an alibi, then, is she?" TK said in her blunt fashion. She was by far the easiest of them to read.

"She wants me to go talk to him. In person. Make peace or some such thing. Says it's important." David felt as if he were making a confession, admitting his own emotional involvement. As a journalist, he'd always prided himself on being able to maintain a professional detachment from his subjects. One more thing lost in that Humvee explosion.

"Tell me you didn't drag us all the way across the country just because you're too chickenshit to face your daddy." This time Lucy sliced a glare at TK that made the other woman flush. But David didn't mind. He was quite enjoying TK's refreshing honesty.

He sighed. How to explain? All this, everything he was doing wasn't for Michael Manning. It was all for Maria. Keeping his promise to her, leaving no stone unturned.

"My mother raised me by herself, dragging me all over the state as my father was transferred from prison to prison. Somehow, along the way, she managed to save enough money for me to go to journalism school. She's the one who got the Justice Project involved in Michael's case last year after my uncle died in prison. I haven't spoken to the man since I graduated college and began my career as a reporter eight years ago. But the Justice Project has arranged for me to visit with him tomorrow."

"Whatever. We're here now." TK shrugged as if conceding a point.

"I asked for the Beacon Group's help because the appeals process is going slowly and my mother is dying. The doctors say she's already hung on weeks longer than they expected. All she wants is to see my father set free."

"You're not giving us much to go on," Lucy said. "I thought you told Valencia you found a hole in the prosecutor's case? A maybe-sorta alibi witness who can't account for the entire night doesn't really count."

"That's the problem. I've always believed my father was guilty and my mother was chasing a pipe dream with her delusions of his innocence. But when I began re-investigating his case, I found more than just one hole in the prosecution, I found a whole slew of them. Too many for me to handle on my own. Which is why, given my mother's condition, I need—we need—your help."

He hauled a box across the table and began throwing folders down, each smack of paper against wood releasing the pungent odor of decay. "Coroner's notes that didn't make it into the final, official report, scant as it was. And yes, it was a coroner, a funeral director, but he did a half-decent job and was the first to examine the bodies. It was a week before the state pathologist did his examination. No rush, they had their men, signed confessions."

"Except?"

"Except the coroner said the man my father supposedly killed, the husband, was actually the first victim, not the last. And he died late afternoon to early evening, *not* the next morning."

Lucy glanced up at that. "So, Friday night? When your father was in front of thousands of high school football fans."

"Exactly."

"But your uncle had no alibi for that time, right?" TK put in.

"No, afraid not."

"And the other victims?" Wash, the man in the wheelchair, asked via the computer linkup.

"The baby and mother both died several hours later. According to the coroner, the outside estimate of their time of death was midnight or thereabouts."

"When your father was with your mother." TK moved to join him.

Tommy chimed in from the computer screen, finally fully engaged. "Can you send me a copy of the coroner's notes? Even with modern methods, time of death is never cut-and-dried, but maybe I can give you some idea of what our widest window of opportunity is."

"What else do you have?" TK asked David, craning to look into his box.

"The knife was never recovered despite searching the house, the truck, and my father's trailer."

"So they ditched it." TK shrugged, leafing through a file and setting it down. David retrieved it and returned it to its proper place.

"Why ditch the knife and not the gun?" Lucy asked.

"Was the gun's ownership ever traced?" Wash put in.

"No. I was hoping maybe you could help there."

"And what about your uncle's alibi witness? This Ronald Powell he was doing drugs with. Did they ever locate him?"

"No. Apparently he hid out in Mexico until things calmed down—he was growing marijuana on federal lands."

"Wash," Lucy said to the screen.

"On it, boss."

David liked the way she smiled and sat back, letting her team run with ideas and suggestions rather than micromanaging.

"What about the lone survivor, Alan Martin?" Worth asked. "Was he ever able to give a statement? He could maybe narrow the gaps in the timeline, provide basic descriptions of the perpetrators."

"He never recovered fully from his injuries. Had permanent brain damage, the doctors said. Never spoke again."

Worth frowned at that, his skepticism about the competence of the doctor's prognosis evident. "He's still alive?"

"Last I heard, he lives in a group home outside of Dallas."

"Let me make a few calls, see if we can get permission from his guardian to speak with him. Or at least to talk to his attending physician."

"Thanks, Tommy," Lucy said. "But I'm most interested in the man who did the initial interviews. Any chance of meeting him? Andrew Saylor, he was sheriff."

"Don't see why not," David answered. "He retired five-six years back, lives out near the river, not far from the Martin place, actually."

"Good."

"But there's one more witness I need your help with," he

told them. "The boy who placed my father and uncle at the scene of the crime the morning they were arrested."

"Right," TK said. "Caleb Blackwell. Any idea where he is now?"

"Yeah. Right down the road. He's the new sheriff of Blackwell County."

CHAPTER 10

LUCY WANTED A chance to absorb the mountain of information from the case files and she did her best thinking alone, so, after their initial session exploring the case, she ordered a steak and potato to go, and left TK and David at the Sweetbriar.

It would still be light for a few hours and she couldn't face being trapped inside her hotel room, so she found a cool corner beneath the shade of an umbrella at the pool behind the motel to eat her dinner while reading twenty-nine-year-old police reports on her laptop. The pool was empty except for two boys, both preschool-aged, splashing in the shallow section and a mother who watched them from a deck chair.

"Are you trapped here as well?" asked the mother, a pretty woman in her twenties with Asian features. She moved to join Lucy. Lucy suppressed a sigh. So much for some alone time.

"It's been almost a week for us." She eyed Lucy's laptop. "The police let you keep that?" Her tone was colored with suspicion. "How'd you work that out?"

Lucy chewed on her bite of steak as she pieced together what the woman was asking. The boys weren't in swimming trunks, just regular shorts, and the woman's capris and blouse appeared rumpled as if she'd worn them for more than a day. But it was the abject despair rimming her eyes that said it all.

Forfeiture.

"Lucky," Lucy answered. "What did they take from you?"

"Everything. The station wagon, all our stuff, traveler's checks, phones, even the kids' Gameboys. I don't care what their damn radar said, we weren't speeding. And they lied, no one resisted arrest. All Paul did was ask why we were pulled over. How's that resisting?"

"Is he in jail?"

She nodded, glancing at the boys and dropping her voice. "Until my folks can bring us the money to get him out. The police said they'd drop the charges once we pay the fine, but I don't know what we're going to do without a car. We were on our way to Dallas to start his new job, but now they'll probably fire him and get someone else." Her voice broke and she covered her face.

Lucy left her dinner and closed her laptop, then moved to sit beside the woman on the chaise lounge. She positioned herself between the mother and her sons, hoping the boys wouldn't see their mother's breakdown. She wrapped an arm around the woman's shoulders and let her sob it out. Finally, the woman looked up, wiping her face on the sleeve of her blouse. "I'm sorry. I don't even know your name."

"Lucy."

"Hi. I'm Augusta. Those are my boys, Henry and Philip."

Augusta beamed proudly at her sons.

"Nice to meet you, Augusta. A week is a long time to be cooped up here, no one to talk to, worrying."

"Nothing like this has ever happened to us before. Paul is so ashamed—I can only visit him once a day and he won't let me bring the boys, says he doesn't want them to see their father like that, behind bars. I don't know how he'll ever face my parents. He hates owing money to anyone. But without a job—"

"When was he supposed to start?"

"Next week."

"You'll be there by then. You said your parents are coming to get you?"

She nodded. "My father. He should be here tomorrow—had to drive all the way from Florida."

Lucy hugged her. "See? It will work out. When's the last time you and the boys had a decent meal?"

Augusta flushed and looked away. "They get breakfast here and I take them to the place down the street for lunch—kids eat free for lunch—then I bring home a doggie bag for their dinner."

Translation: she was feeding her sons but not herself.

"No leftovers tonight," Lucy declared. "How about if you do me a favor and finish my steak—it's way overcooked for my taste—while I go get us all a pizza? I hate to see food go to waste and I'm starving. Would you do me the favor of keeping me company? It's hard being so far from home."

At first Augusta looked as if she'd refuse but Lucy kept on talking until the younger woman finally nodded.

"Good. I'll be back in a jiff." Lucy grabbed her laptop while the mother called her boys over to attack the huge rib-eye.

As she drove out of town to the fast food establishments that lined the highway, she wondered about Sheriff Blackwell and his forfeiture policy. It was a legal gray area that many local jurisdictions had turned to their favor, but it sounded as if Caleb Blackwell might have edged into the realm of extortion. Maybe even a RICO enterprise if others teamed up with him in his profit-making scheme.

After she returned with an armful of food for Augusta and her family, Lucy retreated to her room. She emailed Wash and asked him to compile a list of all the forfeiture auction items since Blackwell became sheriff as well as a list of their original owners. If Blackwell was extorting people traveling through his county, they'd need affidavits. How many had been arrested and had their property seized unjustly? And where was the money going? She had a friend who was a former IRS investigator and now worked for the FBI. Maybe he could help.

Not her job, not any more, but still, it might give her some leverage on the sheriff. At least that was how she'd justify it to Valencia if need be. And if they did find that Blackwell was corrupt, it would be a coup for the Beacon Group, facilitating the FBI or IRS investigation that would be sure to follow.

Finally, she curled up on her bed with her laptop propped up on a pillow before her. She pulled up the police reports Wash had emailed her—scanned versions of the originals, which had been typed and photocopied. So different from modern policing, where officers could enter notes from the mobile terminals in their vehicles or smartphone apps.

But the language remained the same: sparse, painting a picture without coloring it with emotion, drawing no conclusions, merely presenting the facts. At least that was the

LAST LIGHT

idea, but there was an art to writing a good report: it told a story, a story subtly shaped by the reporting officer.

The report on the Martin crime scene had been written by the former Blackwell County sheriff himself, Andrew Saylor. Lucy scanned the terse wording, imagining the actual event.

Second on scene after Deputy Prescott, Sheriff Saylor detailed the deputy to maintain a perimeter then proceeded to secure the scene. Two vehicles were unattended in the driveway (see attached photos and sketch), one a Ford pickup (see attached registration), one a Subaru wagon (see attached registration). Neither had its lights on and the Subaru's driver's side rear door was open. Several bags of canned goods were on the drive near the open door (see attached inventory and photos).

Sheriff approached the residence. Lights were visible in all front-facing windows and the front door was noted to be ajar. On entry the body of a Caucasian male was found to be partially obstructing the door's opening (see photo and sketch attached), victim was subsequently identified as Peter Martin, homeowner.

Living room and dining/kitchen areas appeared undisturbed. Grocery bags were on the kitchen table (see attached photos and inventory) and there was evidence of recent consumption (see attached). All windows and exits were intact with no signs of disturbance.

First bedroom entered revealed the presence of two deceased identified as Glory Martin (age 7 months) and Lily Martin, wife of homeowner and mother of Glory (see attached sketch and photos) along with multiple areas of blood spatter evidence. The scene was left intact once it was determined that no living occupants were present and that both mother and child had expired.

November 14, 1987

DESPITE THE FACT that it was barely sunup on a Saturday morning, Sheriff Drew Saylor was already in his office. He'd been elected less than two weeks ago and was still trying to get a handle on the administrative duties that came with the job. When Roscoe Blackwell suggested he run for office, Drew had agreed, eager to leave the boring life of a patrol deputy behind. After all, he knew the job, knew the people, knew the land. Blackwell County was a tight-knit community where the only strangers were the migrant workers and few crimes reached the level of felony offenses.

Turned out, it was also a county where the money going out was far more than the money coming in. Going over the books, Drew wondered how the hell he'd make his payroll, much less budget for badly needed repairs to the station with its small cell block that served as the county jail. Or get the new equipment his men—and one woman—needed.

He was spending his Saturday working the adding machine and highlighting an obscure statute he'd heard about from one of the old-timers over in Abilene. Forfeiture. Allowing his department seize any property used during a commission of a crime—including minor ones like traffic offenses. Even if the defendants were innocent or never went to trial. It was a potential game changer for his underfunded department.

Given how many outsiders passed through the corner of Blackwell County where I-20 ran, many of them wealthy gas-and-oil types headed into Dallas, it might be the answer to their prayers. If he could wrap his head around the legal language. Last thing he needed with his first official act in office was to get them in trouble with the Feds.

His phone rang. Velma in dispatch. "Call just came in. I think you'll want to handle it, Sheriff."

Drew straightened, still unused to the thrill of being the top law enforcement officer in the county. "What is it?"

"Carole Blackwell. Says there's some kind of trouble out at the Martin place. Said her little boy was already there and her husband was heading over, told her to call you and EMS."

Not a lot of helpful info, but it was enough to get Drew's adrenaline surging. Roscoe Blackwell handled most anything on that end of the county himself—after all, he owned everything out there except a few scattered homesteads and the strip of federal agriculture study land. Must be serious for him to be calling for help. "EMS rolling?"

"Just sent the page and alerted the guys in the firehouse." Blackwell County had a volunteer fire department that was as good as any you'd find in a city—they had to be, as it was their own land, families, and livelihoods they protected.

"Send the nearest patrol unit—" He hesitated, grabbing his portable radio and clipping it to his belt. "No, cancel that. Send Ortiz, the others can cover her territory." Ortiz was the only one of them, Drew included, who had completed the state's crime scene course. "I'm on my way."

"Yes, sir."

A thrill ran through him as he left via his private door and headed to his patrol unit. What could it be? The Martins lived between the Blackwells and the federal land that Ronnie Powell, the county's main drug dealer—a Vietnam vet who lived rough but never had been arrested for any violent offenses—squatted on. Maybe the Mexicans had finally decided to take over Powell's tiny drug enterprise? Or an outlaw motorcycle gang? There were several in the area, although they'd never dared to cross into Blackwell County before.

Maybe they were testing the new sheriff? If so, he was up to the task. Drew yanked open the door of his official Jeep Cherokee and climbed into the driver's seat, automatically adjusting his weapon and radio. He had a pump-action Remington loaded with double-ought and slugs racked and ready, clipped below the dashboard beside him where he could reach it with one hand.

He sped out of the lot, lights and sirens streaking through the empty street, hunched over the steering wheel, ready for a fight.

Prescott, one of the deputies on duty, was already at the scene when Drew arrived. Barfing his brains out in the hydrangeas. He looked up sheepishly when Drew approached. "It's bad, boss." He wiped his mouth with the back of his hand. "Real bad. I ain't ever—"

"Is the scene cleared?" Drew asked.

"I—I think," Prescott stuttered. He was Drew's least experienced deputy, hired a few months ago by the old sheriff. Second cousin's son or some such thing. "The boy's who found them. He and his old man are waiting for you." He nodded to a large black Dodge Power Ram with the Blackwell logo emblazoned on it.

Drew left the deputy and approached the crime scene. Lily Martin's Subaru sat on the right hand side of the drive. Two bags of groceries were spilled onto the gravel and one of the rear doors was open. Peter Martin's rusted-out pickup stood beside it.

No signs of any blood out here. Drew crept toward the house, avoiding the main walk in case there was any evidence left behind. The front door was ajar. He drew his weapon—first time he'd ever done that as sheriff. Never had much need for it as deputy either, maybe a handful of times had even thought of taking it from his holster. Never discharged it off the range, certainly never shot at a real living person. But he couldn't take any chances. Someone needed to clear the scene.

He kicked the door open. It hit something, bounced back. He startled, then tried again, this time easing it open with his foot and peering around it. The first thing that hit him was the smell—there was nothing else like it, not in this world. It raised hackles on the back of his neck as if every fiber of his being was warning him to turn back before it was too late.

Peter Martin lay facedown in front of the door. Most of his skull was blown apart and there was blood on the back of his denim jacket.

Gingerly, he stepped around Peter into the foyer that separated the living room from the dining room and kitchen. It seemed as if every light in the house had been left on. So whatever happened must have happened last night.

The TV was on but the sound was off. He wondered at that but only for as long as it took him to make sure there was no one in the hall closet or behind the couch. Next he cleared the dining room, kitchen, and laundry room. Only thing unusual were the groceries left out on the table and some dishes left soaking. An empty carton of milk and empty box of cookies sat on the counter.

Had whoever killed Peter stopped for a snack? Or was it left over from the son, Alan? The Martins had a baby girl as well. Where were they?

He crept down the hall to the bedrooms. The first was painted pink with a rainbow on the far wall. The baby's room. But it was Lily Martin he found first. Tied to a rocking chair with clothesline, her face contorted, slashed, gouged, her mouth slit wide in a parody of a clown's grimace. Blood covered her dress, dozens of slashes and cuts. Her skin was a dusky shade of blue, cold to the touch. She hadn't gone quickly, that was for sure.

Why here? In the baby's room? He almost wished he hadn't thought of the question. First, he cleared the closet. Finally, he turned to the baby's crib. There was a puddle of blood below it and more sprays of blood on the pink crib bumpers.

One look was all he needed. The baby had fared even worse than the mother. Christ almighty, what kind of sick bastard had done this? He could almost forgive Prescott for losing it.

Backing out of the room, taking care not to step in any of the many puddles of blood, he turned to the other room across the hall. Alan Martin's. He'd be, what? Six?

He hesitated, his hand hovering above the doorknob. If they didn't spare the baby, no way in hell would they have spared the boy. Grimacing, bracing for what lay inside, he opened the door.

The room was decorated with racecars. No body that he could see, but there was blood—a trail of it leading from the bed as if someone had been dragged out from underneath it. A small palm print against the bed rail, the blood bright against the white pine. Twin smears across the floor. A larger puddle on the floor near the closet surrounded by crimson sprays. Someone had been there, bleeding. He could about make out a boy-sized void.

But no body. He peered under the bed. A stuffed rabbit and some dirty shoes. No boy. Which left only the closet.

He stood, yanked the door open before he could have second thoughts.

A small body rolled out, limp. Aw hell. Drew crouched, touching the boy's arm. Unlike his mother, his flesh was still warm.

He was shirtless, the skin on his chest and back hung in strips, flayed as if someone had tried to peel it off him. There were defensive wounds on both hands and forearms. His face was intact, his blue eyes staring at Drew.

Drew knew better than to touch the body more than he had to, but he just couldn't let this poor boy lie there, his lifeless eyes staring at his own murder scene. He holstered his weapon and reached his hand to close them one final time.

They blinked.

Drew scuttled backward, hand grabbing at his gun.

They blinked again. The boy's mouth opened, a low moan emerging along with frothy bubbles of blood.

"Prescott." Drew had to try twice to create any sound higher than a mouse squeak, his throat choked tight. "We've got a live one!"

CHAPTER 11

"So," TK SAID after Lucy left and she and David had locked up their makeshift office and were enjoying beer and the final bites of their steaks, "is it weird knowing that you must have been conceived right before the night your father was accused of murder?"

He laughed. It was a relief that it was normal, so unlike his speech. But she kind of liked that he said what he meant without wasting time on verbal misdirection. "According to my mother, their only time together was that night. They'd planned on waiting but she was sixteen, he was seventeen, and nature took its course."

"Wow. How sad is that? I mean, she spent the rest of her life—"

"Chasing after the one man she could never have. I know. When I was in high school, I once told her she should just join a convent, at least then she'd have guaranteed room and board. I was trying to make her angry—typical, stupid teenager. But you know what she said?"

"What?"

"She said she couldn't lie to God, that Michael would always have her heart. I mean seriously, there's something wrong with both of them. Her for believing in him for all these years and him—"

"Because he sacrificed everything to save his brother?"

"If you'd asked me last week, I would have said him because he's a stone-cold killer." His pause had weight to it, as if it was anchored to the past. "But now…" He shook his head. "Now, I honestly don't know what the truth is."

She glanced up at that. "But…all those holes in the case that you found. And we've barely even begun."

"My mother's dying. Her last wish is for Michael Manning to go free. To do that, we need to tear apart the original case. But overturning a conviction is a matter of law, not the truth."

"You mean, even if we find enough to set him free, you still think he might be guilty?"

"My first job was working the crime beat in Baltimore. It was then I realized that every case has holes in it—it's the nature of the universe. Nothing is ever for certain."

"Then it's just as likely to put innocent men behind bars as it is to have guilty ones walking free. What kind of justice is that?"

"Justice doesn't exist. It's a delusion—one that my mother has been chasing her entire life."

"You're fine with the fact that we might be working to set

a guilty man free?"

"No. Of course not. I wish he was innocent, this man my mother has put all her faith in. I mean, he's not my father, not really. Innocent or guilty, he never will be."

It was strange, his voice was totally devoid of emotion, yet a dozen of them collided on his face. Everything from frustration to rage to despair to hope.

"As a reporter, it's my job to be objective, look at all the facts. And unless we find new evidence, the facts say Michael Manning is guilty. Hell, that's what he said himself in his own confession. But it's my mother's dying wish. How the hell was I supposed to say no to her?" He glanced up at TK. "Wouldn't you do anything if it was your family?"

That stopped her in her tracks. Because she had done worse, much, much worse, for the sake of family.

"What if he is innocent? And we don't find enough evidence to set him free?"

His lips tightened as if both denying the idea and steeling himself for it. A man of contradictions, this David Ruiz. Intriguing.

"Then I have to face my mother with the truth. But at least I'll have tried my best."

TK couldn't resist the urge to press the issue. "But what about you? To know that the man you've been so angry at all these years, that you blamed for so many crimes—not just murder, but what he did to your family—that he wasn't guilty?"

"He confessed. He chose to go to prison. Even if he's innocent of murder, he's still guilty of the rest. Including abandoning my mother and ruining her life."

Without the force of his anger behind them, his words

sounded hollow, and she wondered if he really, truly believed them or if so many years of blaming his father had become so ingrained that he couldn't kick the habit.

He touched her arm. "Sorry," he said, his expression contrite. "I don't know what came over me. I never talk this much, not about myself. Believe it or not, I used to be good at small talk. How about we get two more beers and maybe play some pool? Less talking, more drinking. Good for the soul, I always say. Or," she liked the unexpected twinkle that sparked in his eyes, "karaoke. Funny thing about this kind of head injury—it messes with talking but not singing. Up for a duet?"

Now it was her turn to laugh. "Only if you want to start a stampede. Sorry, no singing, not for me. But pool sounds good. I'll play you for the tab."

The one more beer turned into three, but TK didn't mind, as she wasn't the one drinking them. When she'd first returned stateside, she used alcohol as a sleep aid, but she'd weaned herself off of it, substituting various forms of aerobic exercise and, when the voices of her memory grew too loud, her language tapes.

"Where'd you serve?" he asked after missing a shot and handing the rotation back to her.

"What makes you think I served anywhere?" She chalked her cue and considered her options. He leaned against the table, facing away from the felt, nursing his last beer. She could tell he wasn't sloppy-drunk, liked that he'd turned away the waitress's offer of another drink.

"I know the look. Was over there the better part of four years—not on base, out with the guys. Bedding down at COPs and observation posts that didn't even have official names."

COPs, combat outposts. Usually named after soldiers who'd died defending them, like the smaller, more remote forward observation posts. Names that often didn't make it onto the military's maps and certainly would never be remembered by the locals.

"I was there," she finally acknowledged. "Two tours Fallujah, four Afghanistan."

"MOS?" Military operational specialty.

She leaned forward and took her shot. A smooth bank sending her target exactly where she wanted into the side pocket. When she glanced up, she noticed a trio of burly men gathered around one of the tables near the bar, two empty pitchers of beer on the table before them along with assorted shot glasses. All eying her. Laughing and elbowing the youngest of the bunch, a kid who couldn't even be drinking age.

"I had several," she finally answered Ruiz's question after the men were distracted with the arrival of a fresh pitcher brought to them not by the waitress, but an older man in his forties who stayed to talk with the trio. Their attitude shifted immediately to one of respect, all three nodding to something the older man said. She relaxed a smidge now that their attention was off her and David.

He squinted at her. "There was an O'Connor. Marine. Worked as an enabler for a SEAL team I did a story on. That wouldn't be you, would it?"

Enabler. She hated the term, the military's way of weaseling out of the fact that they needed women on the front lines but legally were forbidden from ordering them there. Which meant she and her teammates took the same risks, did much of the same job, but weren't given the same training as her male counterparts in special operations.

She shrugged away his question and lined up her next shot. He stayed where he was, his posture relaxed, not looking at her, as if they were discussing someone else's life. In a way they were.

"That O'Connor, she won a Bronze Star. Was roping out of a helo with the SEALs when they came under fire. One of the men took a round, fell near where she was providing cover. A string of daisy-chained IEDs blew, separating her and the downed SEAL from the rest of the team. She KIA'd three insurgents and secured their flank until the SEALs were able to regroup."

She missed her shot, not because she couldn't make it but because she wanted him to shut up and focus on something else. "Your turn."

"They said that O'Connor was one of the finest Marines they ever had the pleasure of serving with," he finished, turning to look at her. "Coming from Navy SEALs, that's probably the greatest compliment a soldier could earn."

"Sure they were real SEALs and not just wannabes? Sounds like they don't know how to keep their mouths shut— unlike us Marines. Take your shot."

"Didn't just hear it from the SEALs. I did a profile on the helicopter pilots who flew those missions. Fun stuff—even got my hands on the stick a few times. Two of them were on station that night. Saw everything."

She shot him a glare that even a reporter who couldn't understand verbal nuances would not mistake. "I said, take your shot."

He considered her for a long moment before turning his

attention to the balls on the table. While he set up his shot, she looked past him to the table with the three cowboys who'd been eying them earlier. The two older ones were pushing the third toward the pool table. She touched his elbow before he could take his shot. "Maybe we should call it a night."

"Why?"

She nodded to the trio approaching them. Both older men held beer mugs in their hands. Heavy glass. Which meant two armed and drunk; only the youngest being steered by the two older ones wasn't a threat.

"I see what you mean." Ruiz balanced his pool cue against the table.

TK assessed the crowd behind them. Gone were the families; the restaurant was now filled with a more rowdy clientele, the men outnumbering the women by three to one.

The first man stepped sideways, blocking their path. His two companions circled around the other side of the table, outflanking TK and Ruiz. Leaving them trapped with their backs to the narrow end of the table.

Ruiz played the gallant, stepping forward, hands raised in surrender. "We don't want any trouble."

The drunk cowboy frowned at his robotic tone. "Hear that?" he called to his companions coming up on TK's strong side. "Hear the disrespect in his voice?" He sneered at Ruiz. "Where you from, boy?"

She reached for her pool cue in a casual movement, pretending to be focused on chalking it. A heavy pool ball would be a better weapon if she actually wanted to hurt anyone, but she was hoping to simply clear a path to the exit.

Adrenaline hummed through her veins, a familiar friend.

The noise of the crowd dimmed to a hushed hum, allowing her to focus on the three threats. She watched their hands, not their faces. Hands told you so much more about a man's true intentions.

"No disrespect intended," Ruiz said, still trying to salvage the situation.

The young cowboy grinned drunkenly, stumbling near to TK. "Ma'am," he said, the syllables smushed together and carried on a wave of alcohol, "we were—I was—wondering if you'd like to dance?"

As he finished his request, his friend shoved him into TK. She almost felt bad for the kid—until he used the encounter to squeeze her breast. His breath was hot against her face; there was no escape from it. Something sparked, an old memory, old fear she couldn't evade took over her body and she felt as if she watched from a distance.

In a blaze of movement TK kneed him in the groin. When he bent over in pain, she grabbed his wrist, spinning him back into Friend One, sloshing beer over them both.

"Hey, we paid for that beer. You owe us!" Friend Two said, stepping forward, beer mug raised high, ready to strike. Until TK flicked her pool cue up as if it were a bo, hitting him in the crotch, then swinging it to sweep his leg out from under him. He landed with a thump on the floor. Ruiz stepped forward, between TK and the men, but by then it was all over.

The noise and movement attracted the attention of the rest of the clientele—probably all locals and probably all friends of the trio. TK shifted into a fighting stance, gripping her cue stick. The sounds around her were muffled as if coming from a distance; all she heard clearly was her breathing and the pulse pounding through her skull.

David touched her arm. She shook him off, searching for danger, for new enemy combatants. But he persisted, sliding the stick from her hands. His lips moved but she didn't register his words.

"Can't a man eat his steak in peace?" a voice filled with command authority cut through the noise in TK's head.

The onlookers who'd scraped back their chairs and risen to their feet, ready to defend their buddies, suddenly sat back down, engrossed in their beers.

In the wake of their sudden silence, a man strode forward, the same one who'd been talking with the cowboys earlier. He was mid-forties, dark blond hair, a little less than average height but with a greater than average swagger. He wore jeans, black cowboy boots, and a khaki shirt with no insignia on it. Could have been a ranch foreman or head of a crew of oil workers.

Could have been. But of course, that wasn't how TK's luck worked.

"Howdy, folks," he said, touching two fingers to his forehead as if tipping a hat. "Welcome to the Sweetbriar. I'm Sheriff Blackwell and you all are under arrest."

Chapter 12

Lucy looked up from her computer, rubbed her aching eyes—Nick kept telling her she needed reading glasses, but having to keep track of the cane was bad enough—and glanced around the empty hotel room. Being alone here was so different than being alone back home. Despite the lack of ambience, it felt...exotic.

During her fifteen years with the FBI, she'd never traveled very often. Her usual fieldwork had entailed driving to interviews then back to the office. Even then she was considered old-fashioned for wanting to interview subjects in person in their own environment instead of relying on the phone or Skype.

It was so quiet here. No skitter-skatter of the cat chasing the dog around the hardwood floors, no grunt and whine of the refrigerator defrosting, no leaf blowers or lawn mowers running in the distance. She couldn't remember the last time she'd felt this alone.

It was only 9:12. Too early to go to bed even with the time-zone difference. Yet she was exhausted. Her foot screamed to be released from the confinement of her AFO brace and her back ached from the unaccustomed sitting for so long on the plane. Despite her injury—or because of it—Lucy had gotten into the habit of spending most of her days in motion. She'd start the morning doing her rehab with either Nick or their mutual former Marine friend, Andre Stone—himself a survivor of burns over sixty percent of his body, courtesy of a bombing in Afghanistan. Andre had to do physical therapy every day to keep his scars from contracting and limiting his mobility.

After rehab, she'd spend the rest of her day doing all the things she never had the chance to do while working full-time: she'd finally planted the vegetable garden she'd always wanted, repainted her and Nick's bedroom, cleared out the garage which still had unopened boxes from when they moved from Quantico almost three years ago, and she had even dared to tackle organizing Megan's room—after much protesting, of course. She'd cooked, cleaned, ran errands long overdue, shuttled Megan from karate to soccer to home, walked the dog, did a second round of physical therapy in the afternoon, and had even dared—once—to go to the mall.

Everything a "normal" parent did. It had about driven her crazy. She didn't know what to talk about with the other moms and dads at Megan's activities. She couldn't stand being trapped inside the shooting gallery that was the mall, with all its sound-distorting echoes, lack of cover, and multiple perches for potential snipers. And if she had to smile politely and nod to one more neighbor's suggestion about how to properly mow their lawn and get rid of their crabgrass, she'd probably pull out her weapon and silence someone permanently.

A nice long bath. No one pounding on the door and calling for "Mom!" as if a lost pair of soccer cleats was a DEFCON Four emergency. No dog or cat nosing their way in to try to join her. No rush because she had to get dinner ready or pick up Megan. Heaven.

The bathroom was remarkably clean—more so than her one at home. Nick was by far a better housekeeper than Lucy would ever be, no matter how much time she had on her hands. He noticed dirt in the nooks and crannies that she was oblivious to. She ran the water as hot as she could stand it, used some bath gel to make a few bubbles, rolled up one towel to use behind her neck, grabbed a washcloth to use as an eye pillow, and climbed in.

Her cell rang. Shit. She lurched halfway out of the tub and grabbed it from the vanity. Nick.

"How's Texas treating you?"

"So far, so good," she answered, sinking back into the warm water, except for the hand with the phone. "Is Megan mad about my leaving?"

"So far, so good. You made it through TSA and everything?" It was the first time Lucy had traveled as a civilian with her weapons. As much as Nick hated guns, he hated Lucy being unarmed even more.

"Surprisingly little hassle, actually."

"How's the case going?"

"Turns out the man working with the Justice Project, the one who got us here in the first place, is the defendant's son." She told him about David Ruiz and his strange head injury.

"Tonal agnosia," he diagnosed from her description.

"That's what he called it."

"I've seen it a few times. Don't put too much stock in his human lie detector abilities," Nick warned.

Hah. She knew it. "Or the fact that he can't lie as well?"

"It's not that simple. It's like when you listen to a politician's speech. Even if you don't like them, don't believe anything they say, after awhile you find yourself nodding and agreeing with them. That doesn't happen with patients with tonal agnosia—not if they can see the speaker. The words to them are empty. There's no emotion behind them, so they cue in on the body language. And since most politicians aren't one hundred percent sincere, they can detect the disconnect between the two."

Lucy was intrigued. "So what about someone who believes their lies, like a psychopath?"

He laughed. "It's not like there have been enough of these cases that there have been studies done like that. I'm just saying while it might indeed be a good BS meter, it's not something he should stake his life on or anything."

"Have to say, I think the poor guy actually believes it. Like he needed something good to come out of his trauma."

"Sounds like he still has a lot of healing to do," he said in his counselor's tone. "And your team from the Beacon Group? What are they like?"

She paused. "Not sure. I'm here with TK. She's former Marine, was an MP—but not an investigator. Most of her file has been redacted. Classified. Way she handles herself, I think she spent some time outside the wire, as Andre would say."

"Not a Hobbit, then."

"Fobbit," she corrected, knowing he'd fumbled the

military slang on purpose to make her smile. Fobbits were military personnel who never left the safety of their base to go past the razor wire perimeter. "No. She's seen real action. Do you know what Cultural Affairs does? Or what a FET is?"

"Cultural Affairs works with human intelligence, not spies per se, so much as working with the actual native civilians living in war zones. Soothes things over with local leaders, tries to leave places better than before we arrived."

"Building schools, winning hearts?"

"Right. And FETs are Female Engagement Teams. They embedded women with the guys on the front lines, usually Special Ops, raiding suspected insurgent strongholds."

"Makes sense. Afghani women would talk to another woman before a man."

"Not just that—the women could search women and their quarters without offending the males in the family. And often the tribal leaders had more respect for our warrior women than for the guys. So the women in the FETs could gain valuable intel and de-escalate situations the guys couldn't. But sometimes they'd end up in the thick of things."

"So she probably did see action."

"I'm sure she did. FETs worked alongside SEALs, Force Recon, Marine Special Ops, and occasionally were even loaned out to the Rangers—until the Army set up their own female teams. They'd go on missions with their assigned units, in pairs or alone, the only women on a team of men who lived and trained together, moving fast, carrying their gear, ready for action—but without the extensive training the male operators have."

"Sounds pretty heavy-duty." And risky—thrown into that

kind of volatile environment with little to no training. Probably a good thing the military was revamping its stance on women.

"It was. Think TK might have a problem now that she's back in civilian life? I imagine since the women weren't given the full combat training their male counterparts received, it would be especially difficult for someone like her to make the transition." He sounded guarded. Worried about her not having backup.

"It's a case from thirty years ago," she reminded him. "We're just here to sort through whatever paperwork that's left and ask a few old-timers questions about anything they can remember."

"Still. I wish you were there with Taylor or Walden." Her old team.

"Me, too. TK's okay—she's just so damn young. Out at the bar now while I'm soaking my achy old bones in a hot tub. How sad is that?"

"You're in the tub? Now?" A thrill of anticipation colored his voice. "Because Megan's in her room and I'm all alone in ours."

"Hmm...What are you wearing?" she asked in a sultry tone.

Before he could reply, movement at the doorway caught her eye. Something dark against the white tile floor. "Nick," she screeched, sitting up, splashing water and not caring.

"What? What is it?"

"A scorpion. There's a damn scorpion. Coming right at me." Her gun—where was her gun?—out of reach on the nightstand, damn it.

His laughter didn't help. "Don't shoot it," he said, reading her mind. "It's not going to crawl into the tub with you."

She kept her gaze focused on the ugly creature with its menacing barbed tail. "I don't care. How the hell am I going to get any sleep knowing there are scorpions in my damn room?"

The scorpion continued its scuttling across the tiles, seemingly oblivious to the human nearby.

"Relax. They're all over Texas. Ask TK. She was in Afghanistan. She'll know how to deal with them."

Not reassuring. "I have to get out of this tub sometime."

The scorpion paused at the edge of the vanity, seemed to look back over its shoulder at her as if it had finally noticed her presence. It did not seem impressed—or intimidated.

Instead, it moved forward and vanished.

"Damn. It's gone. Somewhere under the vanity."

"That's good, right?"

"Hell no. Only thing worse than a scorpion I can see is one I can't. And who knows how many of its cousins are lurking around?"

His laughter was not helpful in the slightest.

November 14, 1987

By the time Drew closed the door on the back of the ambulance and the medics sped away with Alan Martin barely clinging to life, his hands and shirt were covered in blood. While he'd tended to the boy, Ortiz, his lone Hispanic and female deputy, had arrived, finished securing the house, called the coroner and the state crime techs, photographed the scene, and had begun taking witness statements from Roscoe and Caleb Blackwell.

"Boss, I think you're going to want to hear this," she called to him as he futilely wiped his bloody hands with a wet-wipe. "Boy saw someone leaving the scene."

Caleb Blackwell stood beside his father, his back pressed against their pickup truck. The kid was short for his age and a bit on the pudgy side. He looked scared; there was even a whiff of urine coming off him. Not that Drew blamed the boy—he'd almost lost it himself and he'd seen traffic and farming accidents that resembled scenes from *The Texas Chainsaw Massacre*.

Drew crouched down so he was at eye level. He didn't

have kids of his own, but he doubted Caleb was the kind who'd have many friends—even if his father wasn't the most powerful man in the county and his mother the biggest bitch. He'd never heard anyone in Blackwell County say a kind word about Carole Lytle Blackwell, formerly of Philadelphia, Pennsylvania. Not that it stopped her from attending every civic and social event as if she were the queen and they were her subjects.

He'd heard rumors about Roscoe sleeping around—wouldn't blame the man, but he was surprised Carole put up with it. One of those so-called modern marriages, he guessed.

"You want to tell me what you saw, son?" Drew asked Caleb.

Roscoe tightened his grip on the boy's shoulder. "You heard the sheriff. Tell him."

"Well, I was riding my bike here," Caleb began, his voice strung tighter than barbed wire. Almost as high-pitched as any girl. "Coming up the lane from the highway."

"What did you see?" Drew asked, trying to keep his patience. Hard to do with another boy's blood soaked into his shirt, stinking up every breath he took.

"Coming the other way. A red pickup. I've seen it around before. It was going real fast, swerving." Caleb's voice grew more animated and he whisked one hand through the air back and forth like a whip snake. "Almost ran me off the road."

"Tell me about the truck. Any distinguishing marks?"

"There was a dent right in the middle of the front bumper, like it'd run into a fence post or something. And the windshield had a big crack on the passenger side."

Drew straightened, a cold feeling churning through his gut. He knew that truck. "Did you see who was driving?"

"Two guys. I don't know the older one's name, but the younger guy, I've seen him play football. Mike Manning. He was the driver."

Drew turned, glanced at the house and then the road. Mike Manning. Goddamn it. He never would have guessed—kid had come so far, was so close to making it out of here, had a scholarship and everything. "I watched Mike play last night. How the hell—"

"Had to be the older brother, Dicky," Roscoe said. "I've found him and Ronnie Powell stoned out of their minds, in my fields, trying to mess with my cattle, more than one occasion. Lord only knows what kind of drugs they've gotten their hands on." He gave Caleb a little shove. "Get your bike, ride home to your mother. I've got work to do."

"Now, Roscoe, hold on there," Drew said, understanding what kind of "work" was so urgent. "You need to let me handle this. Keep everything legal. We owe it to them." He nodded in the direction of the house. "Lily and Peter and their baby."

Roscoe's eyes narrowed. He was not a man you said no to. Especially not after he'd just handed you the election. But if Drew was going to do this job, he was going to do right by the people of this county. All of the people, not just the Blackwells.

He keyed his radio and called dispatch. "I need you to send all our free units to the Mannings' trailer. Bring in both boys for questioning. And get me the county prosecutor. I'm going to need some warrants."

"Fine," Roscoe said. "You just make sure you seal this up good and tight—and fast. Because folks around here, they won't stand idle while baby killers walk their streets, believe you me. You and the justice system don't handle this, they sure as hell will."

"That's not the way and you know it. Folks here respect you. They won't take justice into their own hands unless you tell them to."

"Then you'd better give me a damn good reason not to. Understand, Sheriff?"

Drew did not like the older man's tone, not at all. Maybe Roscoe Blackwell had gotten him elected, but he was elected and by God he was going to do the job the way he saw fit. He leaned forward into Roscoe's space. "I understand this is a crime scene and you need to let my people do our jobs. Now, take your boy home and wait for me there. I'll need to get formal statements from you both."

"What are you going to do now?"

"I'm going to have a talk with the Manning brothers. After I have all the facts I can rustle up from the scene, the coroner, Ronnie Powell, and God willing, the Martin boy. This kind of case can't be rushed and you're just going to have to wait your turn, Roscoe."

Roscoe turned as Caleb wheeled his bike past the two men. "Okay. We'll do it your way. For now. But you'd better move fast, Saylor. I'm not a patient man."

"Then maybe you'd best let me get on with my job, Mr. Blackwell."

Roscoe grabbed Caleb's bike and with one hand tossed it into the back of the pickup. "Get in the truck, Caleb. Good God, you're a mess. Did you wet your pants? You ride in the back." He marched around the cab to the driver's side, barely waiting for Caleb to scramble into the truck bed before starting the engine and screeching away, raising a cloud of dust.

Drew stared after them. Bad enough he had to handle the first mass murder in the history of Blackwell County, but now he had to worry about a possible lynch mob and frontier justice forcing him to rush his investigation.

He glanced back at the house. It looked different somehow. Despite the bright sun beating down on it and all the lights still shining from the inside, it was as if the house was shrouded by shadows...or ghosts.

He shuddered, shaking off the feeling he was being watched and turned to greet the coroner as he drove up in his hearse.

CHAPTER 13

DAVID MADE CERTAIN he stayed close to TK as the sheriff called his deputy and escorted them to the parking lot. Not that he was worried about her defending herself—Sheriff Blackwell had taken control of the situation before the natives could get restless. But the way she'd snapped so quickly into combat mode, he'd seen too many guys do that both on and off the battlefield, addicts chasing an adrenaline fix, unable to stop once they'd started.

The Sweetbriar's parking lot was filled with vehicles, their colors morphed by the buzzing neon light above them. A few locals looked on from the shadows as Blackwell stood between the three men and David and TK.

"You three, sit your asses down there on the curb," he ordered the drunk men.

The kid, the drunkest of the three, was wavering as if debating whether to throw up or fall down. Finally, he settled for plopping down to the ground, resting his head in his hands. The oldest edged a belligerent glance at TK. "She started it. Don't see why—"

"Button it," Blackwell ordered, one hand on the butt of his gun. "Think I didn't see you push Junior?"

"Not our fault bitch got no sense of humor," the other man said even as he sank down to the curb.

TK tensed beside David and he grabbed her arm, stopping her lunge forward.

"Who you calling a bitch?" she demanded.

Blackwell turned his attention on them. "These boys might have started things, but you could have done some serious damage young lady."

"Then it's to her credit that she didn't," David put in before TK could say anything. Her hands were raised at chest level, ready to strike, muscles buzzing with the urge to fight.

Blackwell frowned at David's voice but nodded at his words. "Which is why I'm taking you all over to the station."

One of the ranch hands didn't like the idea. He got up halfway to his feet. "But Sheriff, you—"

Blackwell shoved the man down. "I can do as I damn well please. Besides, you all need time to calm down, sober up, sleep it off. Then we'll decide if any charges are being filed."

The man blinked, finally nodded. Blackwell turned to David and TK. "And how about you two? Want to add resisting arrest? Force my hand as far as charging you?"

David nudged TK with his hip, a silent warning. "No, sir," he answered for both of them. "Whatever you need."

"What I need is some peace and quiet, but don't see as I'll be getting it any time soon." A van with the sheriff's department insignia pulled up, two deputies in the front seat. "Let's go."

"You okay?" David asked as they waited their turn to be escorted into the van.

"I'm fine," TK muttered. "I never lost control."

"You sure as hell lost something," he replied.

Her lips tightened. "I can handle it."

A deputy separated them before he could challenge her.

Half an hour later after surrendering their possessions, being searched for weapons—turned out the cowboys were carrying a small arsenal between them, it was lucky for him and TK that they'd been too drunk to think of escalating the fight—all five of them were deposited in the holding area, a large three-sided room that faced the processing desk and was monitored by two deputies. They were handcuffed to railings that ran along the wall above mesh metal benches.

"What about our phone call?" David asked.

"It's coming. Once the sheriff decides what charges are being filed," a deputy told them. "I were you, I'd sit tight and not make any trouble. Best way to keep the sheriff happy."

TK slumped against the concrete wall behind the bench she was handcuffed to. She eyed the trio from the Sweetbriar, cuffed to the bench farthest from her and David. "Don't let me fall asleep."

He glanced across the holding area at the three men. All were snoring, the youngest drooling, his head rolling almost into his friend's lap. "I don't think you have anything to worry about from them."

"Not them I'm worried about." She didn't look at him but a shudder rattled her body. "I get nightmares. Sometimes I—"

"Wake up screaming?" He finished for her when she went

silent. "In a different part of the house and you don't know how you got there or why you're holding a knife? It's how mine go, at least."

She nodded slowly. "Something like that. Yeah."

"Okay, then you don't let me fall asleep, either." He shifted his weight down the bench toward the corner they shared, giving her room to lean against him. Not for intimacy, although it felt good, another warm body touching his. But it also brought their heads close enough together that they could speak without being overheard. "What do you want to talk about?"

"What made you become a reporter? Why not a lawyer or something if your mom wanted you to help get your dad out of prison?"

He snorted at that. "Wow. No foreplay with you, right to the rough stuff."

"You can take it, tough guy," she teased.

He wished he could hear the emotion in her voice—her body posture said she was interested, but he sensed she was also still probing his defenses, hadn't decided yet if she trusted him. "Guess you could say I was running. At the time, when I got that scholarship, my ticket out of here, I was so damn angry, tired of being lied to my entire life that I thought I was running to something. A new life. The truth. A place where I could find answers."

She arched an eyebrow. "So you became a reporter?"

"Don't laugh. I had so many questions—all my life I always had questions. When I was little, my only answers were my mom's. I believed her when she said Michael Manning was innocent. I'd come home everyday from school battered and bloodied, fighting for her and the truth she gave me."

"Until you got old enough to wonder if she was lying."

"After that, I didn't believe in anything. For a long, long time. When I went to college, I thought I was running to something, to who I was meant to be. But I was running away. Ran all the way to Baltimore, then to Afghanistan and a war that was ending without answering anything about why it really started in the first place."

He sighed, almost forgetting that he was talking to someone else. He'd never admitted half this stuff, not even to himself—but he'd also never been half-drunk, handcuffed to a bench with a pretty girl as a captive audience. "All those miles and years. I still just wanted the truth. To ask a question and be able to believe in the answer."

There was a long pause while she considered that. She rested her hand on his arm, nothing sexual, simply comforting. "Maybe you should have become an accountant? Something where there are answers."

"Or maybe I need to ask different questions. I don't know anymore."

"Where will you go after this? I mean, after your mom—"

"My old editor in Baltimore started an online news service devoted to crime. Not the flash-in-the-pan stories of the crime beat, but real, in-depth stuff. Invited me to join him."

"While your father stays here in prison?" He loved the way her frown made her eyebrows come together in a small V. "Isn't that still running away? Maybe your mother was right. Maybe, even if your father really is guilty, there's a truth you still need to face. Right here."

CHAPTER 14

LUCY FELL ASLEEP dreaming of the Martin crime scene. There was something wrong with the reports, something even her unconscious mind couldn't quite put a name to...

Her phone woke her. Adrenaline jangling through her, she sat up, reaching for her weapon, scouring the room for hidden danger.

The phone rang again. The real phone, the one with a cord and an old-fashioned blaring bell. "Hello?"

"Ms. Guardino? This is the front desk. We have a call for you from a David Ruiz. Okay to put him through?"

David? Why was he calling at—she glanced at the clock—five-eleven in the morning? "Yes. Put him through."

"Sorry," he said once they were connected. "They wouldn't let us call long distance to your cell, so had to call the hotel. Can you come get us?"

"Where are you? The Sweetbriar? What happened?"

"Um, no. We left there hours ago. We're, uh, actually, we're just across the street from you. In jail."

"You and TK—"

"Were arrested. Along with a couple of locals. They started it and the sheriff is dropping the charges but not until we pay a fine for disturbing the peace. So could you?"

She blew out her breath. What the hell? This was exactly why she did not want to work with amateurs. "I'm on my way."

Hoping to get a handle on her anger, she took her time in the shower before changing into a sleeveless cotton top, slacks, and Megan's boots. On her way out through the lobby, she ran into the talkative clerk who checked them in and another woman setting out pastries for the free breakfast.

"Any coffee ready?" Lucy asked.

"Sure thing, sugar." The clerks exchanged a glance. "Couldn't help but hearing—your friend, she's got quite the temper, hasn't she?"

The second clerk gave Lucy a wide smile that was more fake than her two-inch-long glittered nails. "Is she one of those women who just don't like men? I'm guessing she isn't used to our Southern hospitality."

"What did you hear?" Lucy asked, sipping from the foam cup the first clerk handed her. She'd hear TK and David's side of things soon enough, and it'd be nice to compare it to the natives' perspective.

"Well, now. I heard from Bobby Su who was there that three of the Blackwell hands took a shine to your little friend, but when Junior Barstow screwed up his courage to ask her to dance, she attacked him." Her eyes went so wide that flakes of mascara dropped onto her cheeks. "Hit him with a pool cue for just being nice and trying to make her feel welcome and then went after the other two."

"We got a strict family-friendly policy here," the first clerk added. "If you all are going to be causing trouble, you can just pack your bags and leave right now."

The two clerks nodded in agreement. Lucy slid her credentials identifying her as a retired federal agent from her bag. They lacked any true power but still looked damned impressive to the uninitiated.

"We're here on assignment," she said, purposely taking care not to falsely identify herself as a law enforcement officer. "Sheriff Blackwell is assisting us in our investigation. If he signs off on Ms. O'Connor's behavior last night, will that suffice?"

They pursed their lips, each waiting for the other to take charge. Lucy took advantage of their silence to top off her coffee and grab a chocolate donut.

"I thank you for your cooperation, ladies. It will be duly noted in our report. Have a great day."

Leaving the gawking clerks behind, she went out the front door and got into the Tahoe. As she adjusted the rearview mirror, she realized she was smiling. Taking on three men just to see if she could. If Nick were here, he'd say TK reminded him of Lucy back when he'd first met her and she'd been trying to prove herself to the world.

Good thing Nick wasn't here. Although she'd definitely need to channel him if she was going to make nice with the sheriff. Nick could sweet-talk Santa Claus into giving up candy canes and going on a diet.

Lucy drove the short distance to the jail side of the sheriff's offices. Up close, it was obvious that the jail had been added on more recently—expanding to make room for all those forfeiture cases?

The plight of the family she'd met last night still nagged at her. So much wrong with this town—or maybe it was her subconscious's way of trying to figure out what she sensed was wrong with the Martin case. She'd need to find time to go through the crime scene photos in more detail—and the coroner's report, the one that the defense had never received. She needed to drill down on that.

As soon as she freed her team. Sigh. She finished her coffee and left the Tahoe, taking only her cell phone, wallet, keys, and ID with her. Since no charges were being pursued, TK and David had been left to wait in the processing room. It was a large, open area with benches lined up against three walls facing the deputy's desk.

Lucy introduced herself to the deputy on duty then turned to face the room. Its sole inhabitants were David and TK, each handcuffed to separate benches at one corner of the room. TK stood, her handcuffed wrist stretched across the bench. "Thank God you're here. What took so long?"

"Sorry. Bailing out a pair of drunks wasn't a priority."

David flushed and looked sheepish.

"I wasn't drunk," TK protested. "Tell her, Ruiz."

He nodded. "It's the truth."

"So what happened? You decided to take on three men because that's your idea of fun?" The expression that flit across TK's face told Lucy she'd hit close to home with her flippant remark. Proving yourself was one thing, but violence for fun? That crossed a line.

"I didn't start it," TK grumbled as if that was any kind of

defense.

Lucy looked to David. He didn't meet her glance, instead shifted his weight and rolled his shoulders into a lopsided shrug. "It was kind of a mutually-ensured-destruction thing."

Funny, the more she heard him talk, the more she heard his real voice—or what she imagined to be his real voice, filled with wry sarcasm and emotional inflections that his ruined atonal one lacked.

"So that's why you felt obligated to jump in?" Lucy asked.

"He didn't jump in. Just tried to play Galahad and told the cops he had." TK rolled her eyes. "As if I needed any help dealing with three drunks."

"Actually, that's exactly what I was afraid of," David said. "Men around here have long memories of battles lost—memories that tend to fester until they can get payback. Figured if folks thought it was me—"

TK bristled at that until she intercepted Lucy's glare—the same look Lucy used on her teenaged daughter. Nice to see it worked on former Marines as well.

"Doesn't matter who's taking the blame. Because we're not here on vacation or to blow off steam or settle old scores. We've got a job to do and you two have just made it infinitely more difficult. Not to mention undermining any pretense of professionalism."

"Don't worry none about those boys," a voice came from behind her. Lucy turned around. Leaning against the wall inside the door was a man in his forties wearing jeans and a khaki shirt. No insignia, but given the large pistol holstered at his belt and the way the deputy was watching, she guessed this was the sheriff.

"Sheriff Blackwell," Lucy stepped toward him and extended her hand. "I'm Lucy Guardino of the Beacon Group."

His grip was firm, his smile genuine. "Pleased to meet you, Mrs. Guardino. I was hoping we could speak. When you're finished here."

Lucy edged a glare toward TK and David. "Of course. I'd appreciate a few moments of your time to explain—"

He waved away her concerns. "Like I said, don't worry none about my boys. Going to be a long time before they live down the fact that a filly took them down." He turned his smile on TK before glancing at David. "Although I'm afraid the folks over at the Sweetbriar are asking that you clear out your stuff and not return. I'm sure you understand."

The deputy approached, bearing handcuff keys and paperwork. Valencia was going to freak out when she got that credit card bill.

Blackwell touched two fingers to his forehead in a casual salute. "I'll see you soon, Mrs. Guardino. And hoping not to see either one of you two back here again." He left. The deputy released both David and TK.

"What now?" David asked, rubbing his wrist.

"David, you check in with the prison authorities; see if your visit with your father is still on for today." Special visits like the one the Justice Project had arranged were at the warden's discretion and subject to change.

"What about me?" TK asked, her tone tight with frustration.

Lucy inhaled and took a moment. "You serve the court order granting us access to the prosecution's evidence. Go through every scrap of paper they have. I want the evidence inventoried, photographed, scanned, logged, and cross-referenced with what the defense gave us. Coordinate with Wash back home. Find me the holes in their case."

TK bristled, her mouth open to protest at her sudden demotion to paper-pusher.

Lucy continued, "When David's done he can help you. If I can't get the sheriff's cooperation, our stay here might be shorter than anticipated and we can't leave without that evidence."

CHAPTER 15

LUCY WAS GLAD she'd taken the time to shower and change before meeting with the sheriff. Re-opening a twenty-nine-year-old case considered solved was difficult enough without needing to apologize for the actions of her team. Not to mention the fact that Caleb Blackwell was also a witness who needed to be interviewed.

After meeting Augusta and hearing about her family's forfeiture nightmare, she'd been prepared not to like the man, but she had to admit that he was charming. Assertive yet polite, direct without being overbearing—it reminded her that sheriffs were elected officials and thus politicians first and law enforcement officers second.

Blackwell's office was in the back corner of the bullpen, the door open. Despite the early hour, a few minutes past seven, an administrative assistant sat at a desk in front of the door, busy typing on a computer, but she stopped and smiled at Lucy when she approached. "Can I help you?"

"Lucy Guardino of the Beacon Group. The sheriff asked to speak with me."

"Of course, Mrs. Guardino. He's expecting you. Can I bring you coffee?"

Before Lucy could answer, Blackwell appeared in his doorway. For a man of such average height and build, he radiated an intensity that was compelling.

"Trust me, say yes," he said with a smile. "Anita brews the best coffee in the state."

Anita blushed and nodded, moving from her desk to the coffee station along the other wall. Blackwell stood aside, motioning for Lucy to enter his domain.

It was a typical working office that reminded Lucy of her old one at the federal building back in Pittsburgh: papers stacked on every surface, whiteboards filled with notes, calendar with almost every date filled, the obligatory framed diplomas and commendations along with a flag, photo of the president, and one of Blackwell shaking hands with the governor.

Blackwell moved behind his desk, leaving Lucy with the choice of one of two matching leather chairs. She waited for him to sit before taking her own seat. For some reason that made him smile.

"So." He leaned back in his chair. "I take it David Ruiz hired your company to convince the court to free his father? I admire you for taking on a challenge like that. Pretty much an open-and-shut case."

"The Beacon Group is nonprofit and we don't actually work with the courts—that's up to the lawyers with the Justice

Project. We're here to record the facts of the case, see if there's any new evidence that might be considered exculpatory."

He considered that. "Seems to me the facts are pretty straightforward: one brother on a drug-crazed murder spree, the other protects him by shooting the homeowner who interrupted things, and after they're caught with the murder weapon, they both confess to avoid the death penalty. Not sure how much simpler a case could be."

Anita returned bearing two mugs of steaming coffee. She handed Blackwell his first, then gave Lucy hers. "Thanks, Anita, that will be all for now," he said.

The interruption gave Lucy time to regroup and choose her approach. She totally understood why a sheriff would feel defensive about re-opening a closed case, even if it wasn't one he had closed himself. Plus, Blackwell had been an important witness, sealing the fate of the Manning brothers.

"I think maybe that's the beauty of working with an independent group like ours," Lucy said. "We can assess the evidence and let the Justice Project know if they're wasting their time."

"Except you're working with the defendant's son." He raised a skeptical eyebrow.

"I didn't know about Mr. Ruiz's connection to Michael Manning until after we arrived." She leaned forward. "Confidentially, that's one of the reasons why I'll be interviewing witnesses such as yourself personally. That way there's no chance of introducing any bias in our final report."

"And the girl, Miss O'Connor? What's her story? She seems quite the firecracker."

"I do apologize that things got out of hand last night—"

He waved a hand, dismissing her apology. "The boys were drunk. It happens. Well, hitting on a pretty girl happens. The pretty girl knocking them flat on their asses? Not so often. Might want to keep her out of the public eye for the rest of your visit—gossip spreads faster than wildfire around here."

She remembered the two clerks at the motel. "I agree. I've put her on records duty for the time being."

"Sounds like a plan." He began to push up from his chair to dismiss her, but Lucy remained seated.

"Just one more thing, Sheriff. While I have you here—I understand you were a witness in the case? You must have been very young. How traumatic. Are you okay to talk about it? We could do it now, save you time, if you like."

He frowned, squinted down at her, then resumed his seat. "Of course. I suppose you'd need to speak with me sooner or later. Might as well get it out of the way." He turned to his phone and hit a button. "Anita, hold my calls for the next fifteen minutes—except if the county commissioner calls with those budget figures, let me know. Otherwise no interruptions."

"Of course, sir."

He spread his hands wide, palms up. "I'm all yours, Mrs. Guardino."

"Lucy, please." She pulled her phone out, set it on the desk between them. "You don't mind if I record this?"

"Of course not, go ahead."

"Thanks. Tell me what happened that day—actually, let's start the day before the killings. What do you remember from that day?"

He frowned in concentration as if it was an effort to remember. "Thursday? I don't know. Went to school, came home, did what normal twelve-year-old kids do, watch TV, play video games."

Lucy didn't challenge him for more details, instead simply nodded. "And the next day, Friday?"

"Same. Except there was a football game. I was only in seventh grade so had just started going to the high school games. It was like a rite of passage, a lot like your parents letting you go trick-or-treating on Halloween with your friends and no grownups."

"So you went to the game. Who do you remember seeing there? Tell me about it. Did you eat dinner there—hot dogs, popcorn?" She tried to guide him through a basic cognitive interview, but something was obstructing the process. He wasn't responding like most witnesses. Usually, by incorporating sensory details, memories were easier to reconstruct.

"I'm sure, all that. But the main thing I remember— probably because of what happened later—was Mike Manning. He was a running back. That night he about blew away every record the school had. He was a real hero. Which is why I was so shocked the next morning when he almost ran me over in his brother's truck. He was supposed to be a nice guy and all I was doing was riding my bike. I wasn't bothering anyone."

Lucy followed his lead and skipped ahead to Saturday. "Do you remember what time you got up? Why so early on a weekend?"

"Not sure what time it was, but the sun was barely up. Saturdays I got paid to watch Alan, a dollar an hour, so the sooner I got over there, the more money I'd make. It wasn't really babysitting. Mrs. Martin was always there getting her chores and stuff done. More like practice babysitting." He smiled at her. "Do you have children, Ms. Guardino?"

"A daughter."

"Then you know how it is, trying to prepare them for the responsibilities of adulthood. My father was a firm believer in every man earning his keep and my mother believed it was never too soon to learn the value of taking charge of your life. A man has to be ready for anything, willing to do anything to protect his family. That's what I learned at the hands of my parents. Perils of being the only heir to the family empire, I'm afraid."

"Family empire?"

He gestured to the window with its expansive view of farmland. "Pretty much all the land you see and all the cattle grazing it belong to my family. The Blackwells were among the first settlers here. We kept this place and the people living here going through times of war, times of drought and famine, even economic collapse. Without my family, none of this," now he gestured to the building and the people bustling outside his door, "would exist."

Somehow he made the grandiose statements seem like simple recitation of facts rather than benevolent patronizing. Probably ingrained in him—after all, the county was named after his family.

She steered him back to the case. "Did you mind giving up your Saturdays like that? Hanging out with a kid half your age?"

"No. Alan and I played games, ran around in the woods behind their house. We'd stay out for hours. And then Mrs. Martin would call us in and give us cookies and milk, or sometimes coconut cake—she knew it was my favorite."

"So that morning you got up and got on your bike

and…What route did you take? What was the weather like? Did you see anyone?"

"It was nice, just cold enough I wore my windbreaker. I remember because later we had to throw it out—" His voice broke off, his gaze distant, before he allowed the memory to embrace him. "I could have cut across the fields if I went on foot, but that morning I took my bike. It was such a nice day. I rode down our drive to the highway along the river—I wasn't supposed to ride on the highway because of how fast people drive, but since I was going to turn thirteen in a few days, my father had given me permission to start riding there. Then I turned up the lane that led to the Martins' place. Hadn't gone very far when a pickup truck comes speeding down, zigzagging all over the road like they weren't even looking where they were going. Came right at me, about ran me off the road, then left me choking in their dust. But I got a good look at them: Mike Manning was driving and his crazy brother, Dicky, was in the passenger seat."

He stopped abruptly, his gaze shuttering as if blocking out the rest of the memory. She couldn't blame him—who would want to remember what he'd seen in that house?

"I'm sorry. I think that's all I have time for now. I need to meet with the county commissioner about the budget." He pushed back his chair and stood. Lucy got to her feet as well. "I'll see to it that your people get full access to our records, Ms. Guardino. But I wouldn't get your hopes up, I were you. Raking up all these memories twenty-nine years later, can't see that it's going to do anyone a lick of good."

She shook his hand. "Thanks for your time and hospitality, Sheriff."

"Just doing my job." He walked her to the door. She spotted another forfeiture-auction announcement.

"How long have you all been doing these auctions?"

"Drew Saylor, the sheriff before me, started. Never really got serious about them, though. Just dipping a toe in, you know. But I attended a conference that spelled out the law and procedure and realized we could really help the county out, so I began making them a regular event. The county now has its own helicopter, we've got a mobile cell phone jammer that's come in handy with barricaded persons, and we're starting our own SWAT team. Thanks to those funds, we've been able to help out a lot of people, let me tell you."

Not people like Augusta and her family, Lucy thought. "So, would there have been an auction around the time of the Martin killings?"

He tilted his head, chewing on the idea. "Not a clue. I don't remember any, but I was just a kid. Why?"

"I was thinking that if there was, maybe there would have been records of who attended. People from outside."

"You're looking for a stranger—or a pair of them—who just happened on the Martins' place even though it's way back of beyond?" His smile was that of a politician. "You've been reading too much Truman Capote. *In Cold Blood,* this was not. No. We got our killers twenty-nine years ago, that much I'm sure of."

With that, he ushered her out to the lobby, the security door closing behind her. Lucy thought about their conversation. She had no proof, not even an inkling of an alternative theory of the crime, but something just didn't feel right.

And one thing she'd learned in her fifteen years as a federal agent: always trust her gut.

CHAPTER 16

BANISHED TO THE sub-basement where evidence and records were stored, TK followed a deputy through a maze of shelves filled with boxes and smelling of mildew, stale pesticide, and the occasional whiff of decay. "You don't store biologic evidence down here, do you?"

He shrugged without looking back. "Who the hell knows what's down here? I can't remember the last time anyone even looked at any of these. There could be anything in those damn boxes."

"Really?" Maybe this wasn't such bad duty to pull after all. She'd hated the thought of reading through stacks and stacks of reports. TK was a hands-on learner, not as good with words on the page. Tell her something and she'd remember, show her how to do it and she'd do it, but give her something to read? Her brain just couldn't hold onto the words. They'd drift away, meaningless, unless she took careful notes.

But a treasure hunt through forgotten evidence? She imagined finding the clue that would solve everything—something overlooked the first time around—and a thrill ran through her. Maybe David was wrong and his father was innocent. Maybe TK would be the one to prove it and save the day.

"No. Not really." The deputy burst her dream. "Stuff down here tends to be the stuff no one needs anymore but we're mandated to store. Personal effects would have gone to the next-of-kin. Drugs would have been logged, tested at the state lab, and then destroyed. Same with biological evidence. Rape kits are stored separately."

"Wouldn't they have been tested by your state lab?"

He glanced back over his shoulder, his scorn at her naiveté evident. He was older, gray-haired, wrinkles around his eyes, sagging jowls—near retirement or past it, even. This job was probably the last one he ever had and it was clear that he hated it. "You have any idea the backlog at the lab? Not to mention the expense of testing? We send the ones that take priority. The rest wait their turn."

Now it was her turn to be scornful of his callous dismissal of victims of sexual assault. "Except they aren't just evidence kits, they're women. Who've been violated. Besides, the statistics show that rapists don't stop with one victim—testing sexual assault evidence kits, even old ones, can identify them sooner."

His cadence continued as he ignored her, occasionally consulting his clipboard for the case number she'd given him along with the court order and official request to review the evidence. Then he stopped and looked up at the boxes on the shelves surrounding them. They were at the windowless concrete wall farthest from the door, the only light a flickering fluorescent bulb above them. "The Martin case? Why the hell didn't you say so in the first place?"

"They told me to use the case number."

"Hell, everyone knows about the Martin case."

"Were you here for it?"

Finally, he stopped and turned to face her. "Lady, I was first on scene."

She squinted at his nametag. "Deputy Prescott, what can you tell me?"

"Why do you want to know? Writing a book or movie or something?" His chest puffed out at the thought.

TK didn't answer, instead pulled out her phone and notepad, juggling them as if she didn't want to miss a word. "I know you're busy, but a firsthand account, well," she gushed, "that would be invaluable. Could you spare a minute to sit and go through a few of these boxes with me? Let me record your insights? It would be super helpful."

He glanced behind her, the cavernous room silent as a tomb. She bet he got lonely, nothing to do but prowl around dead cases. She laid her hand on his arm. "I would very much appreciate it. I know how valuable your time is."

He snorted. "Not like anyone else around here does. Okay. There's a table at the end of the row. Help me get these boxes over there and I'll tell you what I know."

He grabbed one of the document boxes, hefted it easily, so TK guessed it wasn't full of paper. She put her phone and notebook away, and lifted another box. Whoa. This one definitely filled with paperwork. A good twenty pounds' worth.

She followed him to the table and plopped it down. Another trip and they had it all. It was kind of sad, the lives and deaths of an entire family reduced to four cartons.

"Do I need to sign a waiver or something?" he asked, his hands poised on the lid of the first box. "Like a release for you to use my name?"

"My boss will have her assistant take care of the paperwork later if what you tell me is valuable enough for us to use. In the meantime," she pulled out her phone and hit the recording app, "I just need you to state your full name and that you understand we're recording this conversation."

"Sure, okay." He held the phone close to his mouth. "I'm Deputy Marc Prescott with the Blackwell County Sheriff's Department. We're recording this conversation with my permission."

TK nodded for him to continue opening his box.

"Don't you want to take notes?" he asked, holding the box lid half open, still not revealing its contents.

"Oh yes. Of course." She tucked her bag between the boxes—there were no chairs at the table, so they both stood—and had her pen poised over her notepad.

"Good." Again he held the phone close to his mouth. "Here's the truth about what happened to Lily Martin and her family."

He paused. TK stared at him. Was she going to break the case right here and now?

Prescott took a breath. "The real crime is that taxpayer money was wasted on keeping those two animals, Dicky and Michael Manning, alive. Those bastards should have bought the chair for what they did. We nailed the sonsofbitches, may their souls rot in hell."

He handed the phone back to a stunned TK. "I went to school with both Lily and Peter. You're wasting your time. There are cameras watching," he continued. "You and your bag will be searched on the way out, so don't even think of trying to take any souvenirs. The rules are posted on the wall. Ring the bell when you're ready to leave and I'll come, re-inventory everything, and let you out." With that he was gone, vanished into the rows of shelves. Leaving TK alone with the dust-covered boxes.

Pretty damn obvious that no one here wanted the past brought back to life. TK returned her notebook to her bag, feeling a bit sheepish that she'd fallen for Prescott's act, wiped her phone clean of Prescott's spittle, turned off the recorder, set up the portable scanner and her laptop, then got to work.

The first box was filled with unbound sheets of paper jumbled together; a blue inventory sheet on top stated they were transcripts, crime lab reports, investigator notes, and "various memoranda." Whatever the hell that meant. The next box had sheets of old-fashioned film negatives and eight-by-ten photos, plus scattered Polaroids. Glimpses of body parts turned her away. She closed that box, deciding to save it for last.

The third box contained more records—it was amazing how much paperwork a crime generated. The last box, the one Prescott had begun to open, was filled with miscellaneous evidence: sealed bags containing the Manning brothers' personal effects from when they were taken into custody, a cardboard box that contained the revolver used to kill Peter Martin and had a variety of crime lab reports and chain of evidence receipts attached to it, an evidence bag with three bullets—no crime lab report or evidence receipts indicating that they'd ever been tested, but why would they have been?

Rattling around at the bottom was a collection of audiocassette tapes, each in its own clear plastic box, labeled with date, time and order. All from Michael Manning's interviews. Except...according to the labels, there should have been eleven hour-long tapes.

But TK could only find ten. Hour four was missing.

She switched back to the boxes with the paperwork, rustling through them until she found a binder with the interview transcripts. Hour one, two, three, five, six, seven, eight, nine, ten, eleven.

No hour four. Drumming her fingers on the table, TK thought about that as she leafed through the first three hours' worth of transcripts. Not a whole lot said—a variety of deputies checking on Manning, Manning asking questions about his brother's condition and why he'd been detained and not getting any answers, no one mentioning the Martins, more exploring whatever Manning would say on his own about his movements.

Skirting the Miranda rules, she realized. Not questioning him as a suspect. Manning either was a brilliant actor or truly had no clue about the murders, seemed more concerned about his brother's well being, along with possible drug and assault charges against Richard. The last thing on the transcript of the third hour was the deputy mentioning that the sheriff was coming to talk to Manning.

She kept reading as she fed the sheets into her scanner. None of the transcripts had been given to the defense—they were considered work product and immune from something called Brady according to a memo from the state's attorney to the sheriff that was paper-clipped to the inside of the binder.

Tape five had both the sheriff and the state's attorney present with Manning, and included the first of many recitations of his confession. But according to the time stamp, more than six hours had passed since the end of tape three.

What had happened during those six hours? And what had been captured on the missing tape?

TK grabbed her phone and called Lucy. "Hey. I might have something here."

November 16, 1987

POOR KID WAS so all alone, Drew thought as he entered the Pediatric ICU. He'd made the drive to Mercy Hospital in Abilene every night, hopeful that Alan Martin might be able to tell him something about his family's murder. The doctors said it was doubtful, that his brain had been without oxygen for a long time because of the blood loss. But they also said you could never tell with kids, especially young ones.

Resilient was the word they kept using as if it were a prayer or had magical properties. Looking around the ICU filled with children and their families and then seeing Alan lying in his too-big bed, no one to watch over him except the monitor connected to his body by brightly colored wires, Drew couldn't help but wonder if resilience might be a curse rather than a blessing.

If Alan recovered his memory, what kind of hell was that for a six-year-old kid to suffer through? They hadn't been able to find any family to take him in, but Drew hadn't given up hope. Kid already had it tough enough without trying to survive the foster system.

He approached cautiously, asking silent permission from a nurse nearby. She smiled in recognition. Nice thing about pediatric ICUs, as long as you were as invested in helping their patients as they were, they didn't worry about rules or regular visiting hours.

He paused at the foot of Alan's bed. The nurse—Beth was her name—finished her charting and came over. "How's he doing?"

"Better. His blood pressure is stable, he hasn't needed any more transfusions, and his renal function has normalized." Her tone was that of a proud mother. "We'll be transferring him out to the regular floor in the morning."

"But," he hesitated, not sure if he actually wanted an answer, "how's *he* doing?"

"The doctors weaned him off sedation, so he's been more awake. But still hasn't said a single word." She smiled at the book in Drew's hand—*Curious George*. He'd seen a tattered, well-loved copy of it in Alan's bedroom, and picked up a new one on his way here. "Reading to him is a big help."

He nodded and settled into the vinyl recliner at the head of the bed on the opposite side from the monitor and IV poles. Many parents slept in the chair, but despite the fact that he was going on three days without more than catnaps, he couldn't sleep. Not here, surrounded by all these sick children. The air reeked of desperation, made him fearful of letting his guard down.

There were only so many miracles to be had in a place

like this, but didn't a kid like Alan, after having lost so much, deserve a miracle? Then again, he thought as he glanced around the open space with its neon monitors and silent patients, didn't they all?

He opened his book and began reading.

A hand touching his shoulder startled him awake. "You've got an audience, Sheriff," Beth said. "Alan, do you remember Sheriff Saylor?"

Drew stared down at the boy in the bed who stared back at him. "Alan? How you feeling, kiddo?"

The boy's face creased with confusion as tears slipped down his cheeks. He glanced at each of the adults in turn, his frown deepening, but never made a sound. Finally, he curled into a ball, facing away from them, his thin body rocking against the mattress.

Beth shrugged at Drew and pulled him out of earshot. "He's still in shock," she whispered. "It might be a while before we see what he actually remembers."

"Should I tell him? Has anyone told him? About his family?" It was the worst part of Drew's job, but he'd rather shoulder the burden than let Beth take it on herself. "Or is it better to let him remember on his own?"

She glanced back at the boy, now still, eyes closed once again. Asleep or blocking out the world? From the way his heart raced on the monitor, Drew guessed the latter. He had a feeling it didn't matter who told Alan about his family—he already knew.

"Let me talk to the doctors," Beth said. "But you should know, he might never remember any details about that night. Or be able tell us about it, even if he does."

Drew's shoulders slumped. Alan Martin had been his last

hope to learn the truth. If it was the Manning boys, he could accept it—he'd have to if Alan verified their story. But he just couldn't get over this gnawing in his gut that it had all been too easy, that there was more to this than a drug-fueled frenzy coupled with a boy trying to protect his big brother.

"Maybe you should go home, get some rest," Beth suggested. "Come back when Alan's calmer. Last thing we want is to upset him now that he's come so far."

Silently, Drew handed her the copy of *Curious George*. He turned away then turned back, the sleepless days crashing over him, leaving him empty and too exhausted to protest. "Call me? When he's ready for visitors."

Her smile was the only warm thing in this sterile, cold place. "I will, Sheriff Saylor. Drive careful now."

He didn't make it farther than the parking garage and his Jeep. He curled up in the back seat, using his jacket as a pillow, and slept. The next day he returned to work and turned the Martin case over to the state's attorney, effectively closing the investigation.

"You're okay with this?" the prosecutor asked. "I don't need anything down the road messing with this plea bargain."

Drew's gut said the case was far from closed. But all the evidence—hell, the two main suspects themselves—said otherwise. Plus, people were clamoring for closure. Sometimes public welfare trumped gut instincts.

He guessed. Didn't mean he had to like it. But he'd have to learn how to live with it. "Yeah, we're done. It's in your hands now."

"Okay, then. I'll get a court date, and as soon as the judge signs off on the plea agreement, we'll get those two off your hands. I'll bet you'll be relieved not to have to worry about them any more."

CHAPTER 17

LUCY WAS JUST leaving the family-run funeral home that also served as Blackwell County's coroner when TK's call came.

"Hey, I think I might have something here," TK said breathlessly—it was the most excitement Lucy had heard from the younger woman since they met.

"Good, because I didn't have much luck with the coroner. The one who attended the Martin scene died eight years ago and didn't leave anything except the notes we already have."

"What would you say if a police interview went on almost thirty-six hours but only eleven of them are recorded?"

"I'd say there's a good chance some civil rights were violated if a lawyer wasn't present."

"And," TK's voice up-ticked like a game show host, "what would you say if, of the eleven hours recorded, one is missing? The one right before the suspect confesses?"

Lucy pulled off the road and onto the dusty shoulder. The fields around her were parched; cattle lay in the scant shade of a hillside, seeking shelter from the blazing sun. "I'd say that sounds promising. Any ideas who was doing the interviewing during that missing hour?"

"From the end of the last tape beforehand, it sounds like it was the sheriff himself. Andrew Saylor."

Saylor was on Lucy's list to interview anyway. She consulted her map; his house wasn't far by Texas standards, maybe eighteen miles. "Good work, TK."

"Does that mean I get out of this hellhole?"

"No. It means you're doing exactly what we need—finding those holes in the timeline and the bits and pieces the defense were never given access to."

"There are boxes and boxes of paper—"

"Ignore anything we already have. Focus on work product: detective notes, memoranda, witness interviews, and any lab reports that weren't forwarded to the defense because they weren't deemed exculpatory. Those could all give us new leads."

"You really think Manning could be innocent?"

"I think we need to keep digging for the truth."

"Is Ruiz coming to help me?" A warm undercurrent in TK's voice said maybe it wasn't the help she was looking forward to as much as seeing the man again.

"No. His visit with his father was approved. He's on his way to Abilene." Lucy pulled back onto the county road, keeping the map close at hand. "I'll talk to you after I interview Saylor. Oh, and do me a favor. Scan all the crime scene photos and upload them to our cloud drive. Feels like we're missing something from the ones we have. Call me if you need anything."

"How about a box of Band-Aids for my paper cuts?" she said with a laugh.

Lucy hung up. She had the feeling that if she'd sent the former Marine out into the sunbaked fields to do recon in the ninety-six-degree heat, she'd get less whining.

Half an hour and several wrong turns down unmarked lanes later, she drove over a lane bordered by meadows on both sides and then pulled up in front of a gate surrounding a forested plot of land along the river. Three separate signs—two written and one a simple silhouette of a man holding a shotgun aimed at the viewer—informed her that trespassers would be shot. Message received.

At the far end of the property, nestled in a clearing on the riverbank was a ranch-style house with a tin roof. Lucy leaned on the horn to announce her presence. A few moments later a man with a shotgun appeared on the porch. He waved her forward as the gate swung open to let the SUV through.

If this was Texas hospitality, Lucy wondered what her reception would have been like if she wasn't welcome. But Saylor had been sheriff for twenty-three years; she was sure he'd made his fair share of enemies in that time. Even so, she couldn't envision Nick and Megan ever agreeing to live in an armed compound.

Lucy parked behind a pickup truck and SUV sheltered beneath a carport. She slowly exited her vehicle, leaving her bag inside, keeping her hands visible. "I'm Lucy Guardino. We spoke on the phone?"

The man on the porch was average height, in his fifties, with salt-and-pepper hair and a lanky build. Despite the heat, although it was cooler here near the river and beneath the trees, he wore jeans and a khaki work shirt with the sleeves rolled up. Now she knew where Caleb Blackwell had gotten his fashion sensibility.

Saylor scrutinized her from his high ground eight feet up on the porch, then set his shotgun beside one of the canvas chairs and nodded for her to approach.

"Drew," he said as she mounted the steps. "Drew Saylor." He greeted her with an outstretched hand. She shook it and took the canvas folding chair he indicated with a minuscule nod of his head. "What can I do for you, Mrs. Guardino?"

As he settled into his own seat, the one beside the shotgun, she scooted her chair around so she could face him and the windows behind them. The curtains rustled; there was someone in the house watching. No doubt also armed.

"Maybe your wife could join us?"

"Don't see that's necessary. She runs the pediatric ICU at Mercy in Abilene, is getting ready for work."

Lucy didn't comment on the fact that it was already past nine in the morning, and with Abilene being over an hour away, it was a strange time for a nurse to be leaving for work. When she was still with the FBI—just a few weeks ago—she could have reminded a subject that under Title 18 it was a crime to lie to a federal agent during the course of an investigation.

Now she was just a civilian. And people like Saylor could feed her lies for breakfast, lunch, and dinner and there was nothing she could do about it.

Didn't mean she had to like it.

He smiled at her—knowing she knew he lied. Lucy smiled back. "Thank you for taking the time to speak with me, Sheriff

Saylor."

"Call me Drew. I haven't been sheriff for a long, long time. I know who you are, Mrs. Guardino. Hunted down serial killers, saved a bunch of kids from a kidnapper—hell, you even took on the Zapata cartel and sent them running with their tails between their legs when they dared show up in your hometown. You're at my home now, so do me a favor and cut the bullcrap. Why the hell are you trying to get Michael Manning out of prison?"

Lucy answered his question with one of her own. "What happened during the missing hour while you interviewed Michael? What happened during hour four that made him suddenly confess?"

He pursed his lips, narrowed his eyes, as if considering exactly how much of a threat she posed. "You know about that, do you?"

"That and the other over twenty-odd hours you didn't bother recording. What was happening? Were you and your deputies taking turns beating Michael and his brother? When did you realize the only way you'd be able to keep your job was to find a couple of fall guys fast?"

Now he flushed and stood halfway out of his chair, fists bunched. Before he could say anything the door behind him burst open and a sandy-haired, reed-thin man ran through it. He hugged Saylor from behind, gleefully.

"Alan, no!" a woman cried as she followed him out. She glared at Lucy as if this was all her fault.

Saylor turned his back on Lucy to embrace the younger man, pat his hair. When the man looked up at Lucy, she saw he was at least in his mid-thirties, yet had the face of someone much younger. No lines or creases, and a smile so wide and toothy that it reminded her of Megan on Christmas morning years ago, when she still believed in Santa Claus.

"Alan?" she asked, getting to her feet. "Alan Martin lives with you?"

The woman bristled at that. "Alan *Saylor*. Come along now. Let Dad talk in peace." She took Alan's arm and led him back inside, sending one final glare in Lucy's direction.

Saylor stared after his wife and son, his back still to Lucy.

"I thought he was in a group home in Dallas," she said.

"Was. Three years of hell. Took Beth and me that long to get him out, adopt him." He turned back to Lucy. "I didn't steal that transcript and tape to protect my career, Mrs. Guardino. I took it to protect my family."

CHAPTER 18

THANKFULLY, DAVID'S FATHER had been incarcerated at the Robertson Unit for the past eleven years. The drive to the facility on the east shore of Lake Fort Phantom Hill was much easier than some of the childhood trips his mother had dragged him on when Michael had been housed in the Polunsky Unit over in Livingston or the Connally Unit near Kenedy. On those trips, they'd leave as soon as his school ended and drive all night to get in line and wait hours for visitation.

Growing up with a father who was a prisoner in a maximum-security facility definitely did not provide the same developmental milestones that most children enjoyed. It wasn't until David was four that he'd had his first contact visit with his father—a reward for Michael being a model prisoner.

First time he'd ever been held in his father's lap. Almost made it worth the trips that ended in disappointment when they'd arrive only to find a lockdown had occurred or someone before them in the queue stirred things up, canceling visitation for everyone else.

Even when they did get in, it meant eating from a vending machine—after their food was inspected by guards, of course—and sitting at a cafeteria-style table, barely able to hear each other over the sound of all the other families that had been granted contact visits.

Yet Maria kept dragging him to one prison after another, week after week, month after month, until finally, when he was sixteen, David refused to go anymore.

He only went one time after that—alone, without Maria—after he'd graduated from high school and was ready to leave for college. One last time to tell his father he thought he was a low down sonofabitch for keeping Maria's hopes and love alive, and that the next time David saw him would be at his funeral.

Guess he spoke too soon, David thought as the guards ushered him into a private consultation room—courtesy of the lawyers at the Justice Project pulling some strings.

The room was about what you'd expect: cameras monitoring and a window at the door for guards to observe; table bolted to the floor, a steel railing to secure restraints running across the top of it; two lightweight vinyl chairs, cinderblock walls, a caged light bulb overhead; and the stink of a thousand men who came before carrying their desperation like shackles.

David took his seat facing the door and waited. What the hell was he going to say to the man? He was only here for Maria. Only thing he wanted from the man was the truth. Could Michael Manning give that to his son?

He doubted it.

Finally, the door opened and the guards escorted Michael in. David was amazed at how little he'd changed in eight years—still the same bland expression, same stooped shoulders, same wrinkle-free face. David was only twenty-nine to Michael's forty-six, yet he felt decades older than how his father appeared.

Michael had been a model prisoner for so long they removed his restraints once he was inside the room, although David was certain he'd undergo a strip search before and after the visit, just as for any visit that allowed contact.

Michael sat, his face a stone wall, devoid of emotion, until the guards left and the door closed behind them with a click. With the sound, his facade broke. His face twisted and a tear spilled from one eye as he gasped, "David. My God. Why—how—is she, is your mother—"

"Still alive. Barely. She asked me to come."

Michael recoiled at the sound of his son's voice. It hurt more than David cared to admit. "She told me about what happened to you over in Afghanistan. I'm so sorry. Are you okay?"

He ignored the question. As far as he was concerned, his father had no right to know anything about David's life. "You know she went to the Justice Project, got the appeal started for you before she got sick?"

Michael nodded. "After Dicky died. I told her it was a lost cause, that I'd made my peace with staying here, but she insisted—"

"Look. I don't give a rat's ass if you rot in here, but she does. She's spent her life, wasted every chance she had, defending you, waiting for some miracle to bring you back to her. It's the only thing she ever wanted in this life and by God, I'm going to give it to her."

"Don't waste your time on me. You should be with her. Comfort her before it's too late."

"Don't you think that's exactly where I want to be? Instead of sitting in this room that stinks of piss and vomit?"

"David, you and your mother, you are everything. All that I have left in the world. I did what I did to protect you."

"Growing up alone, that wasn't protection. Leaving Mom to fend for herself, drive herself crazy with worry, all the stress of following you from one prison to another, all those hours spent waiting and waiting for a chance to see you and have it never happen. Are you trying to tell me it was somehow worth it because you thought you were protecting her?"

David's voice failed to convey the depth of his feeling—a failure so extreme and feelings so tangled up with every lost moment of his life that he slammed the table with his fist. "From what? Answer me that. What was so awful that you thought abandoning your family was some twisted form of protection?"

Michael closed his eyes as if he were trying to imagine David vanished from his world. So goddamned typical. Ignore what you cannot control. Wish away anything you don't want to deal with. Paint over the scabs with a brush labeled denial.

David's breath burned through his chest as if preparing for battle. He waited, the walls closing in. Whatever came next might bury them both. Finally, Michael opened his eyes, his expression turned to anguish. "I was trying to save you from the truth."

"What truth? Stop talking in riddles."

"The truth of what happened that night. Of how I ended up here."

David leaned forward, realizing for the first time that he was taller than his father. "Truth is why I came. Only reason I came. I want it, all of it. And I'll know if you're lying—if you do, I'm out of here."

Michael's face shuttered but his body revealed his agitation as the muscles at his neck corded tight. He nodded slowly. "All right then. The truth. Not that it will do any of us any good."

"Stop stalling. What really happened that night." It wasn't a question; rather a demand.

Michael stood, began pacing, his gaze focused on the cracked gray concrete floor. "I relived that night a hundred million times, trying to figure out how it all went wrong. It was the best night of my life. And the worst. Everything started out so great: Dicky lending me his truck, winning the game, Maria waiting for me after, going to the river..."

Finally his gaze sought out David, his smile gentle. "Everything I ever dreamed. We fell asleep, though, and when we woke, it was late—"

"How late?"

"Clock in the truck said three-oh-two by the time I got Maria back home. She snuck into the house without waking her folks and I thought we'd dodged a bullet. I was so jazzed I almost didn't go home, almost kept on driving just for the sheer joy of being out there under the stars, alone with what I'd just done, with those feelings...everything was possible that night. I was invincible."

"But you didn't?"

Michael's shoulders slumped and he returned to drop into his chair, angling it so he didn't face David. "No. I didn't. I went home first—not even sure why. Had this vague idea that I wanted to talk to Dicky, that I could somehow get him to rehab for good this time. I mean, that night I was a goddamn Superman, so why not? But I was too late. The place was trashed, all the money I'd been saving gone, and so was Dicky."

"You went after him?"

"I wasn't going to let him steal my future, flush it down the toilet like he had his own. I ran back to the truck but—" He stuttered to a stop, his face vacant.

David tapped the tabletop, trying to draw his attention back. "But what?"

"That's when I saw the gun. Well, not the gun. The towel it was wrapped in. In the back of the truck. At first I thought it was something Maria had forgotten, so I grabbed it. The gun fell out, rattling against the truck bed, so loud it could've woken the dead. But there was no one to hear it except me. The moonlight made it look larger than life, a revolver, biggest one I'd ever seen outside the movies, all shiny steel, lethal, powerful."

Silence fell over them. David waited, watching for any signs of deception in the older man. So far he told the truth— would that continue?

"And then," Michael continued, his voice so low David had to strain to hear it. "Then I picked it up. It felt sticky, but the grip was dark wood so I didn't realize there was blood on it, not then. It felt so good in my hand, so right. I knew exactly where Dicky would be—with that no good so-called friend of his, his dealer, Ronnie Powell. I was going to get back my money, save Dicky from himself, save the day. All because of that gun."

Finally, he turned to face David. "Didn't exactly happen that way."

CHAPTER 19

SAYLOR FINALLY TURNED back to Lucy and slowly, as if it took great effort, eased into his chair. Lucy resumed her seat as well, giving him time to gather his thoughts.

"When we first got Alan, we kept him in a special school near Beth's work. Last thing we wanted was him being traumatized by seeing someone from his past. It's hard to know what will set him off—a song on the radio, cartoons, hell, a box of cookies. It's been a long time since he had an episode, but the boy's been through so much—"

The boy was now a thirty-five-year-old man, but Lucy understood what he meant. "Has he ever spoken about what happened that night?"

A look of anguish crossed Saylor's face. "You don't understand. He's never spoken at all. Not a single word—only sound he's made since that night is when he has nightmares and screams like a wild animal caught in a trap. Doctors said while he does have cognitive dysfunction from blood loss and lack of oxygen, that's all in his higher brain centers—like math and reading and the like. They've never found any damage to his speech areas of the brain. Said his lack of speech is from psychological trauma."

"Elective mutism." She'd once worked a sexual assault case involving a young child who'd also stopped speaking. "Therapy didn't help?"

He shook his head. "Made things worse. It's like his silence somehow protects him from the memory of what happened. So we just accept him for who he is: our loving, gentle, special boy."

"If you truly believe the Mannings are responsible, then why are you so protective of Alan now? What's he have to fear?"

"Nothing with them safely behind bars. But I never want to risk them getting out and thinking they need to take care of the only surviving eyewitness."

"Them? With Richard Manning dead, don't you mean *him*? Michael?"

An uncertain look crossed Saylor's face as his gaze slid past Lucy to the window beside them.

"You think they're innocent?" she guessed.

"No," he said, returning his focus to her. "No. Dicky Manning was guilty. No two ways about it."

"Then...you're not sure Michael was involved? You think someone else was in that house with Dicky Manning?"

His lips tightened as if preventing any words from escaping, but his head bobbed in a reflexive nod.

"If Dicky wasn't alone," she continued, "then why hasn't

his unknown accomplice come after Alan?"

"I don't know. And I don't care. I'll do whatever it takes to protect my family until I'm absolutely certain there's no threat."

Twenty-nine years of living with that kind of bunker mentality? She glanced around the well-fortified property. But Saylor had been sheriff for much of those twenty-nine years, would have used whatever means necessary to find any accomplices—

"Ronald Powell, Richard's drug dealer friend. He vanished the day the murders were discovered. Was that your doing?"

"No." Another glance through the window into the house. "Wish it had been, then maybe..."

"Why are you so certain Powell was involved?"

Pure anguish creased his face. He was silent a long moment. "Because I saw him earlier in the night. With a knife. If I'd arrested him then, none of this would have happened."

Lucy said nothing, knowing that once started, he'd want to keep talking. Usually, it was a technique she used when interrogating subjects; this time she felt as if her role was more one of hearing a confession.

"It was at the stadium parking lot before the game. I'd heard rumors that Powell was selling pot, but by the time I spotted him in the crowd, there was no evidence of any drugs. He was sitting on the trunk of his car—he drove a beat-up old Impala—innocent as could be, whittling these little bear figures he used to sell."

"Bears?" Lucy asked, not sure what they had to do with drugs.

"That's our high school team, the Blackwell Bears. Powell

would carve and sell all sorts of unofficial school mascot figures. Kids loved them—adults, too. He might even have made some money at it, if he'd ever tried to sell them for real. I always figured it was a way to cover the cash from his drug deals—not to mention an easy way to hide drugs during an exchange."

"Hollow out a space inside the carving?"

"Right. Guy pays cash for a special bear, Powell delivers, all looks legit to anyone watching. Anyway, that night I saw him, rousted him, even got him to let me search his vehicle, but I found nothing except a few carving knives, wood, and those stupid bears; he must have already sold all his product before I found him."

"Were you ever able to compare his knives to the wounds on the Martin family?"

He nodded, his face shadowed. "State lab did after we got a warrant for Powell's stuff. Said two of the knives were possible matches. He was long gone by then. Never seen again." He glanced over his shoulder toward the door, one hand sliding close to the shotgun leaning against his chair. "But I'm ready if he ever comes back. No one's going to hurt my boy, not again."

Lucy was silent, giving the emotions pouring off him time to dissipate. Finally, she asked the real question that might help her do her job. "Why did you take the tape and transcript? What happened during that hour you were with Michael Manning?"

He looked past her, eyes squinted tight against the morning sun streaming in below the porch roof. Without saying a word, he stood and disappeared inside the house. Since he left the shotgun behind, she assumed he'd be returning—and in a few minutes, he did, bearing a thin stack of papers and an old cassette tape. "See for yourself."

She glanced at the transcript. He didn't wait for her response to the terse words on the page. "I'm not proud of what I did. Broke every rule in the book. But I'd do it again. My job was to protect this community and I couldn't do that without getting Michael Manning to talk."

"You understand by giving this to me, it might get him set free?"

His sigh heaved through his body as if it had been waiting twenty-nine years to be released. "It's not enough, not by itself. But if you find other evidence, if I made a mistake, well, then—" He swallowed, then finally met her eyes. "If I did wrong by that boy, then maybe it's about time someone set things right."

November 14, 1987

SHERIFF ANDREW SAYLOR: This is Blackwell County Sheriff Andrew Saylor interviewing Michael Manning. The date is November 14, 1987, and the time is 8:43 p.m. Mike, did the deputies inform you of your Miranda rights?

MICHAEL MANNING: Yeah, but I don't understand—

SAYLOR: You don't understand your rights?

MANNING: No, those I understand just fine—

SAYLOR: Good. Saw you play on Friday night, Mike. You were amazing.

MANNING: Thanks. When can we leave?

Saylor: We?

MANNING: Me and my brother.

SAYLOR: Your brother isn't going anywhere.

MANNING: He needs a doctor. Rehab. Locking him up isn't going to do him any good.

SAYLOR: You think this is about your brother's drug habit?

MANNING: Isn't it?

SAYLOR: No. It's not even about Dicky sending two of my guys to the ER.

MANNING: They rushed him—and I saw Howard hit him with his shotgun, knock him out. Dicky needs the ER or at least a doctor. They dragged him in here unconscious, probably has a concussion.

SAYLOR: Believe you me, a concussion is the least of Dicky's worries.

MANNING: What'cha mean? I don't understand. And why am I here? Just let us go, it's been hours. You can't just keep us here.

SAYLOR: Sure I can. Especially when your brother just confessed.

MANNING: Confessed to what?

SAYLOR: He said you were there, Mike. That you were just defending him, like always, like the good little brother you are. What happened? Tell me in your own words. He surprised you, didn't he?

MANNING: Who? Dicky?

SAYLOR: Don't play dumb with me. You know who I'm talking about. Peter Martin. He walked in on Dicky and you had to protect your big brother so you shot him.

MANNING: What? No! Mr. Martin? Why—

SAYLOR: To save Dicky. That's what he said. In his confession.

MANNING: He's crazy. You can't listen to him. Lord only knows what he took, and besides, his head is all messed up. He needs a doctor.

SAYLOR: We'll get him one. Just as soon as we get all this cleared up. Let's start with the gun.

MANNING: Oh, yeah. It's not mine. I found it. Was going to bring it to you guys, but I had to get Dicky first when I saw he'd taken our rent money, knew he'd be out trying to score.

SAYLOR: Right. You took the gun with you and went to meet Dicky. How many shots did you fire?

MANNING: What? I never—

SAYLOR: Dicky says you did. Says you're the one pulled the trigger. And before you say anything, let me tell you straight-up that despite everything, I talked the state's attorney into giving up the death penalty.

MANNING: Wait. Death penalty? What the hell you talking about?

SAYLOR: Emotions are running high. I can't guarantee your and Dicky's safety if you leave here. Your only hope is to take the deal I'm offering. It will save both of your lives.

MANNING: I have no fucking clue what the hell you're talking about. I want a lawyer—one for Dicky, too. We're getting the hell out of here.

SAYLOR: Dicky waived his right to counsel.

MANNING: He's in no shape to waive anything. You shouldn't even be talking to him.

SAYLOR: I don't know. He cut a pretty good deal, given the circumstances. But it's contingent on your corroborating everything. If you don't, the deal's off and the death penalty is back on.

MANNING: I don't...I can't—

SAYLOR: Dicky told us everything. All you have to do is agree to it. We know he didn't do it alone—two weapons means two killers. And he made sure we knew it wasn't your idea, said you came looking for him, couldn't stop him, he was out of control. That you were only protecting him when Peter Martin walked in.

MANNING: Walked in on what? What was Dicky doing? Robbing their house or something?

SAYLOR: Don't play dumb, Mike. I'm trying to help you here. Giving you a chance to save you and your brother from the chair.

MANNING: I'm not playing dumb. I don't know what you're talking about.

SAYLOR: I'm talking about Lily Martin. I'm talking about her son, Alan. You'll be happy to hear he survived. Doctors say he'll make it. So that's another factor. He's an eyewitness, will seal the deal at trial if you let it go that far.

MANNING: Survived? Survived what? What the hell do you think we did?

SAYLOR: This. Look at the photos, Mike. Look at that pretty lady and see what your brother did to her. Fifty-three stab wounds. That took some time.

Sounds of retching and coughing.

SAYLOR: No, you don't get off so easy, damn it. Look. Here and here. All that blood, that's all that's left of her face. And here's her little boy—we only got a few shots of him before the medics took him to the hospital. Oh, but here, this is the one sure to buy you the chair. This one makes me want to weep. It's why those folks outside want me to let you go, why they want to take care of you and your brother themselves. Look here, Mike. Look at beautiful baby Glory. Only seven months old. Look how your brother butchered her.

MANNING: Stop! We had nothing to do with this! How could you even think—

SAYLOR: I'm not thinking and neither is that crowd outside.

Now, we know you were there, Mike. Your brother said so in his confession. You don't back him up and he fries for sure, you as well. You want to live? You want him to live? Tell me, tell me now.

MANNING: No, no...I can't...

Sounds of sobbing.

SAYLOR: Sure you can. It's easy. Just tell me you went to the Martins to find Dicky. Tell me how worried you were about him using again. Tell me how you wanted to stop him but you got there too late.

MANNING: No, please...I can't...

SAYLOR: You're not betraying him, Mike. You're protecting him, saving his life. Tell me how Peter Martin walked in with that gun and you took it from him, shot him three times. How it was over so fast you didn't even know it happened, didn't realize you had blood on your hands—literally. We have your bloody fingerprints all over that revolver. You were there, Mike. There's no denying it. Only question you have left to answer is: do you want to spend the rest of your life in prison or do you want you and your brother to die in the electric chair?

Chapter 20

DAVID STARED AT Michael. He was telling the truth—at least David believed him. So far.

Michael continued, "I knew how to shoot—our dad took us hunting when we were kids. But I'd never held a pistol or thought of aiming it at a human before that night. It changes you, thinking like that. Like suddenly the world is divided into tiny man-sized parcels, some worth saving, others less than human, okay to kill."

"What happened?"

"I drove on over to Powell's place. He squatted on land owned by the government, was supposed to be some kind of ag-development project that never went nowhere. A few acres between the river and the Martin farm. Trees enough to hide his marijuana plants, an old barn, fire pit, a few rusted-out trucks and tractors. I don't even remember how I got there—one minute

I was feeling like God, staring up at the stars, and the next, I was holding a pistol in my hand, burning with rage, aiming it at my brother and Powell."

Michael shook his head so hard that the chair legs tapped against the uneven floor. "Idiot. Damn idiot."

"But you didn't kill Powell."

"Of course not. He and Dicky were stoned out of their minds—mixing PCP with peyote and pot. I was damn lucky they didn't kill me, state they were in. Running around naked, screaming, tearing at their hair. Took me hours to get them talked down to the point where I could get Dicky in the truck. Never seen him like that—burning up like his body was trying to eat itself. Eyes so wild—he didn't even recognize me. Lost in his own world.

"That's what I'll never understand. Dicky wasn't like our father, never went to war, never had anything happen bad to him. What was so great about that drug-induced nightmare that he'd leave his only family, steal the food and rent money, and risk his own life to get there again?" He scraped the chair, tugging it closer to the table, scrutinizing David's face. "You've been around the world, seen more than I can ever imagine. You have an answer for that?"

An attempt at deflection? No, David decided, he truly wanted an answer. "I wish I did. I've seen addiction come in all forms: drugs, gambling, women, power, adrenaline..."

Michael squinted at his son. "But never you, right? I read somewhere it might be inherited."

"I'm too much of a control freak—hate feeling vulnerable." It was weird sharing a confidence that intimate with a stranger like his father.

Michael nodded, satisfied. "Good. I mean, not good that you can't let loose, relax—you should talk to someone about that."

A chuckle escaped David. "Like I should take advice from you."

"Learn a lot about living locked up in here. How to stay alert without letting fear eat you alive, how to not get bored, how to learn to find peace within yourself, how to get along with folks." He shrugged. "Not that I'd recommend it, but after all these years, I'm not sure I could live anywhere else. I know how to be a prisoner, know where the lines are drawn, what to expect, how to survive...Outside, I'd be lost."

"Is that why you wanted Mom to drop the appeals when I was a kid? Why you gave up?" Gave up on us, gave up on your family, on me, David wanted to add but it'd be too cruel.

From the anguished look that twisted Michael's face, he'd filled in the blanks on his own. "No. It was Dicky. After they sentenced us and I realized what was really happening, that it wasn't all some horrible mistake, I asked for a new lawyer. But they said if I contradicted his story, our plea deals would go away and we'd both be facing the death penalty. Maybe he was a lousy brother and it was his fault we were in this mess—his and that damn gun—but I couldn't do that to him."

"So last year when he was killed—"

"I told your ma I'd cooperate if she wanted to try again. It'd been so long, I figured there was no hope in hell, but it meant so much to her. She was lonely—you were gone, covering the war—and I figured it'd be good for her. Never dreamed she'd be able to take it this far. She's a strong woman, your mother. Best woman I've ever met. Better than I deserve, that's for sure."

David didn't argue the point. It was the truth. But he still needed the rest of the story of that night twenty-nine years ago. "Keep going. You got your brother in the truck, left Powell."

"Powell took off into the trees, no idea where. By then, the sun was coming up. We were heading down the lane—the one that ran from the river to the Martin farm—when I saw the boy on the bike. Or more importantly, he saw us. The Blackwell kid, Caleb. No idea what he was doing up so early on a Saturday morning. Bad luck for us, I guess, because right after we got home, the cops came. Dicky freaked out, tried to run. It took three of them to get him down, way he fought, the PCP making him go berserk."

David had read the arrest report: one deputy with a broken collarbone, another with bites that had required a trip to the ER, and the third was the one who'd used his shotgun butt against Dicky's head. Despite the fact that Dicky had been knocked out for several minutes, they'd deemed him too great a risk to take to the hospital, had instead hogtied him and hauled him into the county lockup. Back then, police could get away with shit like that.

No one questioned the fact that they'd interrogated a drug user with a concussion while he was intoxicated and then detoxing from a powerful combo of hallucinogens. No one even considered that Dicky might be especially susceptible to suggestion or coercion...not that the deputies were that subtle in their methods. When Dicky finally saw a doctor a few days later he had two skull fractures, a few cracked ribs, and bruises head to toe. Resisting arrest was the official cause of his injuries.

"Dicky was never the same after that," Michael mused. "Not sure if it was the drugs or one too many cracks to the skull or just waking up in prison realizing his life was over. Without me near to watch over him, he'd have been a goner within weeks."

"That was the one thing you asked for when you finally signed your confession two days later."

"That we stay together. Only thing they didn't lie about."

"So the rest of your confession? About how Dicky went crazy, stabbed that woman and her children and you defended him by shooting the father when he tried to stop Dicky?"

"Bullshit. Every word of it." Michael leaned back, lips pressed together, waiting for David's disbelief.

"You had the gun. Your fingerprints in the baby's and the father's blood on it. You seriously want me to believe you just happened to pick up the murder weapon?"

"Not just happened—we were framed. Everyone knew Dicky's truck, knew he was an addict. Easy as pie to throw the gun into the back, set the cops on us. Just happened so fast—because of that boy seeing us driving away that morning. That was a piece of bad luck we could have done without."

"But that means whoever threw the gun in the truck—it had to happen after the Martins were killed but before you found it at three in the morning."

Michael shrugged. "Could have been anytime from when Dicky lent me the truck to go to the game, around sunset—I remember the light in my eyes—to when I got home again. The truck was at the school all during the game, then parked along the road after—Maria and I hiked into the trees down by the river. We couldn't see the road, didn't want no one to see us. Anyone could have driven past, tossed that gun in the back."

"They never traced it to who owned it?"

"Nope. It was old, but no idea who it belonged to.

Leaving me and Dicky playing a game of hot potato and getting burned."

He was telling the truth. David was sure of it. For the first time in his life, he believed his father. His mother was right—had been right all those many years she'd had faith in Michael's innocence. But... "Why? If your brother was under the influence of drugs, his confession would have been thrown out—it was your confession that condemned you both. Without it, you would have been free."

Michael's sigh circled through the empty room, carrying with it the weight of guilt. "You have to understand how it was back then. A crime like that, so terrible, incomprehensible... people needed answers. The sheriff needed a quick arrest, needed to let the people who elected him know they had the right man. More than that, people were frightened, angry, ready to take matters in their own hands. And after the way Dicky beat up those deputies, no way were we going to get any protection from the law."

"You thought they'd kill you?"

"Either the cops would take care of things before we made it to trial or the mob outside would have if we were released." Michael paused. "But it wasn't just us I was worried about. Your mother as well. She kept trying to tell them she'd been with me, that I was innocent. Got death threats, shots fired at her house, her family was run out of the county. It had to stop before someone got killed."

David considered that. It sounded like something out of another era...but it was Blackwell County. He could believe it happening. Even now, years later, remnants of that frontier mentality were alive and kicking out there where the cattle outnumbered the humans four hundred to one.

"More than that," Michael said, his voice low as if in confession. "I thought—they had me convinced—" He twisted his body away from David, head hung.

"You thought your brother was guilty. You thought he killed that family."

Michael nodded. Was silent for a long moment. When he spoke again, he kept his body hunched, facing the rear corner of the concrete-walled room. "He and Powell. They could have done it any time that night. Powell's place wasn't all that far from the Martins' house. Wouldn't have even remembered it after, they were so goddamn high. Might not even have known what they were doing."

"But the gun?"

"I couldn't be sure when or how it got into Dicky's truck. For all I knew, he or Powell came down to the river and tossed it there sometime during the night. Not like Dicky could remember a damned thing—all he knew was what the cops fed him. And Powell, he vanished after that night. I figured the cops were at least half right: there had been two men and one of them was Dicky. And the only way I could save Dicky from the chair was to give them the other half."

He touched his forehead, not quite making the sign of the cross, more like tapping an SOS into his skull. "I was a stupid kid, half out of his mind with worry. The sheriff kept me up two days and nights. By the end, I would have said or signed anything just to get out of there. Then I saw Dicky, saw how bad he was, knew he'd never get any better, would die in prison if he didn't have me watching over him...and the judge banged his gavel and it was too late."

CHAPTER 21

IT WAS AFTER one o'clock by the time TK finished scanning and photographing everything she could from the Martin case. No food or drink was allowed in the records area, so she was now starving and anxious to leave this dungeon hell, to see the light of day.

Prescott took his time searching her bag, even gave her a quick pat down for no good reason as he'd already inventoried all the boxes and returned them to their proper places. But finally, she was up the two flights of stairs and through the doors, breathing fresh air—superheated that it was—and blinking at the midday sun.

That's when she realized she had no vehicle. And since the Sweetbriar was now off limits, her options for lunch were distinctly curtailed. Vending machines at the motel? Try the drug store down the block from the Sweetbriar, see if they had any snacks?

She pulled her phone out, ready to call Lucy, when she realized the battery had died. Of course it had; she hadn't had a chance to charge it since they'd left Pittsburgh. Gazing into the watery heat rising off the blacktop highway she wondered how far it was to the fast-food places outside of town.

The door from the sheriff's department swung open behind her. She glanced over her shoulder—Sheriff Blackwell himself.

He took a deep breath, puffing his chest out, and smiled at her. "Hate being cooped up inside all day, don't you?"

"At least your office has windows," she replied. "That records room made me feel like a mole rat."

"You sure don't look like one." He dangled a set of car keys from his fingers. "I'm headed home for lunch, would you care to join me? I'd love to discuss the Martin case, hear any new insights or findings."

She hesitated—was it collaborating with the enemy? No, Blackwell had been a kid at the time of the killings, and was a witness. Of course he'd be interested, no skin off his back if his predecessor had gotten things wrong. "Sure," she answered. "I'm famished."

"You okay riding with me? Or do you want to follow?"

"Lucy took our ride, so if you don't mind—"

"Of course not, I'd love the company." He escorted her to a silver Escalade with the Blackwell County Sheriff's seal emblazoned across it, held the passenger door open for her, and even offered her a hand up into the high-riding front seat.

His old-fashioned courtesy made her smile. She didn't tell him that she'd spent most of her adult life climbing in and out of

Humvees and Stryker armored vehicles.

As they left Canterville behind and headed into the countryside, TK noted again of how remote this area really was. In a way it reminded her of Afghanistan, long stretches of emptiness peppered with a few homes huddled together. At first glance, it appeared desolate but then glimpses of cattle and green trees growing along the riverbank brought the landscape to life.

"Drought," Blackwell said, following her thoughts. "Spring rains were a fraction of what they should have been and everyone's suffering. We've already had a few wildfires despite the fact it's only May. Hate to think what the summer might bring."

TK assessed the grasslands and parched fields. A fire could devour acres with nothing stopping it until it hit the river. Given the sparse population of Blackwell County, the idea of humans having any control over this land seemed ludicrous. Again, the same feeling she'd had in Afghanistan. Isolation, desolation, the two weren't that far apart.

"What was it like growing up here?" she asked.

He considered the question, steering the large SUV with one hand draped over the wheel, the other propped up against the window. "A lot different than kids have it now," he finally answered. "We roamed free—ran amok, our folks would have said. None of this helicopter parenting from family or the state." He nodded, his gaze fixed on the distant horizon. "Carefree, that's the word. We were masters of our universe."

"Are many of your friends from back then still living here?"

"Unless it's to join up or go to prison, almost no one ever leaves Blackwell County. My mother hates that I stayed. She had her way, I'd be in Austin, a state senator or running for governor or some such thing." He sounded wistful.

"The Martin case, that was why you became a cop?"

He smiled at the horizon. "Probably a large part of it. I don't have a family of my own, other than my mother, but I like feeling like I do. Sheriff of a place like this, it's a lot like being a father. At least I like to think so."

She thought about that. Made sense. Fit his manner as well—not overbearing or controlling, unlike many police officers she'd met, or fellow MPs for that matter. He seemed as if he enjoyed his job, enjoyed the people he served.

"Do you think the Mannings are guilty?" she asked.

"You're the independent reviewer, have seen all the evidence. What do you think?"

"I think if it'd gone to trial and I was on the jury, it might have been a difficult decision to make."

"How long you been doing this, Miss O'Connor?"

"TK, please. Almost a year working with the Beacon Group. I've worked half a dozen cold cases."

"And how many of those had a neat and tidy answer with no questions leftover?"

She thought about that. She was proud of her clearance—so far it was one hundred percent—but each case had left in its wake unanswered questions. Especially for the families. Closure was far easier on paper than it was in real life.

"None," she admitted.

"Me, too." He turned to glance at her. "To answer your question, I think all the evidence pointed to the Manning boys. I'm not sure it could have been closed any other way, not back then, not with the people involved or the emotions running as high as they were. Those boys were lucky they made it out of this county alive—folks were talking lynching for the first time in over fifty years."

"So you think they did it?"

"Not what I said. Not at all what I said."

They turned away from the river and onto a blacktop drive that ran between whitewashed fences. On one side of the drive, cattle grazed in a field, on the other was tall grassland.

"Have to be careful of overgrazing with the drought," he said, glancing at the cattle with an appraising eye. "Welcome to the family spread."

"How large is it?"

"Blackwell Ranch? The original acreage was modest, only five sections—that's thirty-two hundred acres. But my granddad and dad bought out a lot of other family's holdings, now we're over twenty times that size."

TK did the math. That was over sixty-four thousand acres. "So you own pretty much everything I can see?"

He chuckled. "Technically, now that my dad's gone, my mother does, but yeah. It's the Blackwell way. When times get tough, we buy from folks in need. Lease it back to them at an affordable price. They make a living wage working the land for us, keep their homes, everyone's happy."

Sounded like a benevolent dictatorship to TK. They rounded a graceful curve and arrived at a large white house that looked like something you'd see back around the Civil War. It was three stories high with columns running from roof to foundation. The windows were tall and narrow, making it seem even more imposing.

"Home sweet home," Blackwell said as he parked the SUV

on a circular drive at the front of the house. He left the keys in the ignition and hopped out. TK climbed from the vehicle and stood, shielding her eyes against the sun and looking up at the massive structure. "Family lore has it that Hollywood modeled Tara in *Gone with the Wind* on Blackwell Manor."

She nodded mutely. She'd thought Valencia's family home at Beacon Falls was impressive, but this place would have swallowed it whole three times over. At least.

As they climbed the steps to the front door, someone behind them whisked the car away—a butler or valet wearing white gloves. They'd have it detailed and keep the AC running so it wouldn't be hot when Blackwell was ready to leave, she imagined.

"Oh, I should warn you," he said in a low voice. "Don't let my mother bother you any. She spends her days running a multi-million dollar corporation surrounded by men who are afraid of her, so she enjoys any chance she has to agitate. It's her idea of fun." He threw her a wink. "Don't worry. I'll throw you a lifeline if you get in too deep with her."

TK wondered exactly what that meant. It took fourteen steps to cross the front porch, the columns even more massive up close. By the time she reached the towering front door, Blackwell already had swung it open for her, revealing a wide-open foyer with a chandelier, marble floors, and two staircases along the rear wall that met at the second floor.

"Men used one side and women the other," he told her, tossing his duty belt onto a credenza that probably cost more than the house she'd grown up in back home in Weirton, West Virginia. "That way, there was no chance of the men accidentally glimpsing the ladies' ankles."

"Amazing what once passed as scandalous, isn't it?" A dark-haired woman in her sixties approached from an archway on their left. "Caleb, you didn't tell me you were bringing company to lunch."

"Mother, may I present TK O'Connor?" he said in a formal tone. "TK, this is my mother, Carole Lytle Blackwell."

"Nice to meet you, ma'am," TK stuttered, not at all sure what the proper etiquette was. She glanced down at her worn jeans and boots, couldn't help but compare them to Carole's silk designer dress and high heels. "Thank you for having me."

"Any friend of Caleb's is always welcome," Carole said with a smile, although her eyes were fixed on Blackwell, not TK. Her accent was from back East, definitely not Texan. "Come on in." She pirouetted on her heels and led them through a sitting area to a dining room. The table could have seated twenty easily and there was enough china in the cabinet to serve a dozen courses.

Thankfully, Carole kept going past the intimidating formal dining room to a more comfortable and casual room at the rear of the house. It had windows on three sides with a Spanish tile floor and a table topped with a matching tiled mosaic. A vase of fresh flowers sat in the center of the table and there were three places set with bowls of soup waiting for them along with glasses of ice water.

The Blackwell servants were efficient and fast, TK thought, eying the place settings. Pitchers of iced tea and lemonade waited on a sideboard along with platters of ham and roast beef and side dishes.

"We like to keep lunch casual," Carole said as Blackwell pulled her chair out for her and she slid gracefully into it. "So much more intimate than having servants hovering, don't you think?"

TK nodded, startled when Blackwell moved to also hold her chair for her, catching her off balance so she dropped into her seat. Carole pretended not to notice. "I think you'll enjoy the gazpacho. The recipe has been in Juanita's family for generations."

The chilled soup was surprisingly spicy—a perfect combo for such a hot day. "It's delicious."

"So, TK, what brings you to our little corner of heaven?" Carole asked in between sips of soup.

"She's here with the team looking to re-open the Martin case," Blackwell answered for her.

Carole arched her delicately plucked eyebrows. "Really? Well, I hope you all are more considerate than all those conspiracy theorists on the Internet. The things they imply—"

"Like what?" TK asked.

"That Lily Martin was killed by an irate lover," Blackwell said. "Or Peter was killed because of his gambling debts and the rest of the crime scene was just a cover-up."

"A few have even contacted me to ask for confirmation if Roscoe was having an affair with the Martin woman," Carole said. "Really, the man's been dead and buried for over two decades. Can't they show him any respect?"

"Well, now, Dad did have a reputation with the ladies."

TK looked between the two. Seemed like a pretty inappropriate conversation to be having between mother and son, much less in front of a total stranger, but from the indulgent look Carole responded to her son's comment with, it was obvious Blackwell and his mother didn't share a traditional relationship.

Still, she made a note to tell Lucy about it. Even if it was almost thirty-year-old gossip, it might still be worth following up.

"Great men have great appetites," Carole said in a chiding voice. "Besides, wherever your father may have strayed to, he always came home to me."

Blackwell took a sip of soup, head bobbing in a nod that made him appear like a little boy rather than a grown man. He set down his spoon and stood. "Shall I carve?"

Without their answering, he brought the meat platter to the table and began slicing large chunks of beef and ham. TK hurried to finish her soup, only to have a woman in a maid's uniform appear from nowhere and whisk it away, leaving her a clean plate. The same maid moved the side dishes to the table within easy reach before vanishing once more.

"What do you think happened to the Martins?" TK dared ask Carole while Blackwell distributed the meat to their plates.

"Me? Dear heavens, I have no earthly clue. But I can tell you that neither Lily nor Peter were the saints everyone made them out to be. Lily latched on to any man who looked at her twice, desperate to leave Peter. And Peter—" She rolled her eyes. "Whatever happened, it destroyed poor Roscoe. He just never was the same after, was he, Caleb?"

"No, ma'am, he wasn't."

TK frowned. It was Caleb, the son, who'd actually gone inside the scene, seen the bodies. Why would Roscoe, the father, be so devastated? "How so? Did he go inside with you, Caleb?"

The sheriff didn't seem to mind her use of his first name, but it was his mother who answered. "Didn't you know, dear? Roscoe killed himself a year later—on that very same day."

TK stopped chewing and had to force herself to swallow.

That tidbit of information had not been any of the files she'd read. "He did? How awful for you both."

Carole cut a piece of beef into smaller pieces and speared them with her fork. "Can't help but wonder if the two were related. But of course, they couldn't be. After all, Drew Saylor caught the killers, didn't he?"

Her words dangled in the air between them, and TK stared at the mother and son as they ignored her to focus on their food.

Could they really be implicating Roscoe Blackwell in the murders of Lily Martin and her family?

CHAPTER 22

AFTER FINISHING WITH Drew Saylor, Lucy returned to Canterville. She grabbed lunch for her and TK at the fast-food place. TK didn't answer her texts and her phone went straight to voice mail. Lucy debated going to the sheriff's department to check on her, but decided against it. Last thing she wanted was to micromanage. TK was a former Marine, used to fending for herself, and would only resent a hovering supervisor. Instead, Lucy headed back to her motel room. She went in through the side entrance, avoiding the prying eyes of the clerk on duty.

She'd left the AC running in the room and it smelled musty, but the maid had been and gone again so she didn't have to worry about any interruptions. She did take a quick look in the bathroom—no signs of any scorpions. But that was kind of the point, wasn't it? Scorpions wouldn't necessarily leave any signs even if they were there.

Shit. Back home she was the strong one, dealt with spiders or snakes in the garden without worry. Was she really going to let some weasely insect send her into a freakout?

No, she was not. She would deal with this like the fully trained federal agent that she was. Well, used to be.

First, assess the situation. Her luggage was on the rack, above the floor. She was wearing her boots and her only other shoes were a pair of sneakers she hadn't had a chance to unpack yet, so they were safe. What possible avenue of approach could the enemy take?

She glanced at the two beds, neatly made by the housekeeper. Both had bed skirts that dragged on the floor. Scorpions slithered and crawled, but did they climb?

No sense taking chances. She tucked in the skirts under the mattresses of both beds. Then she piled pillows to use as a makeshift laptop desk on the second bed, emptied her notes and files on the bed beside it, and spread out a towel as a placemat for her burger and the chocolate shake she'd indulged herself with.

Satisfied that she'd established a secure perimeter, she plugged in her laptop and phone; took her boots and brace off, leaving them on the bed; and settled in front of her laptop, her legs crossed in front of her. Perfect.

As she ate with one hand, she downloaded the scans TK had sent to their cloud account. This was everything the prosecution had not been obligated to turn over to the defense. Maybe the missing piece of the puzzle lay somewhere in the photos and scanned reports. It was like an itch she couldn't pin down—or that ghost-limb syndrome Nick said amputees felt— this feeling that something was off, didn't fit the picture the evidence painted.

Or that someone had arranged the evidence to paint. That was always a risk—humans were naturally inclined to turn chaos into order, whether it was inventing stories of constellations from random star groups or settling on a "logical" explanation for a murder.

Once the files were downloaded, she separated them into chronological order and placed anything from the actual crime scene, whether photos or coroner's report or lab analysis, in one folder; anything peripheral to it such as witness statements, the transcripts of Michael Manning's interviews and confession, memos from the state's attorney, warrants, etc., in another.

She opened the crime scene folder. She'd already read Saylor's notes and his deputy's report from being first on-scene. Time to fill in the blanks with what they actually encountered.

First, the exterior. Thankfully one of Saylor's people was camera-happy and had snapped a lot of photos—only about ten percent of them had made it to the defense, probably because many were duplicates. Made sense. If you were documenting a homicide, you wouldn't risk something happening to one shot, so you'd snap several as backup.

The exterior appeared just as Saylor had described it: the unoccupied vehicles, one with a door open and bags of groceries spilled near by. Hmmm...groceries. And the open door. Could either help narrow their timeline?

She switched to the second folder, the one with the extra detritus that accumulated during an investigation. Scanned the files until she found what she was looking for. Thank you, Sheriff Saylor. The man had followed the book to the letter. Including tagging the grocery receipt as evidence. Lily Martin had bought her groceries at four-fourteen on Friday, November 13th.

And yes, there were two witness statements, one from the store's cashier and one from a bag boy, to verify that she'd been there Friday afternoon.

Lucy turned a legal pad sideways, drew a horizontal line across it, and then a vertical hash mark labeled: 4:14 PM FRIDAY AT STORE. At the far end she placed a second hash mark labeled with the time of the call to the sheriff's department: 7:09 AM SATURDAY.

Time to drive from the store to her home? She pulled out her map, realized she'd driven almost the same distance when she'd gone to the Saylor house. He was a little more east and Lily would have turned off sooner and gone a bit more north. Guesstimate with a note to drive it and double check: twenty to thirty minutes.

She added a third hash mark labeled: 4:45 APPROX ARRIVAL HOME. Made another note to ask if Lily's car battery was dead Saturday morning. If the interior light was left on because of the open door, that might give them another way to measure when she was interrupted while unloading her groceries.

She stayed with the exterior. Peter's truck. It was parked beside Lily's wagon, but at an unusual angle, pulled wide to the left to avoid the open car door and spilled groceries. He'd arrived home after Lily—did they know when?

Another scan of the second folder gave her the answer. Peter had worked the morning in the fields before leaving for a shift at his part-time job at the feed store. He'd clocked out at five-oh-four. Which would have put him home around five-twenty according to a helpful entry in Saylor's notebook. Thirty-five minutes after Lily came home with the groceries and failed to finish unloading them.

What had happened during that time? Saylor had asked himself the same question, circling it and adding two question marks. It was clear Lily was interrupted—what were the odds that a mother with two kids would have left half her shopping out in the driveway?

Lucy could think of a thousand interruptions that would have pulled her away when Megan was young. A scraped knee, spilled milk or juice, dirty diaper, hungry baby...but why did Lily never return to gather her groceries or close the car door? And what could have been so urgent that she wouldn't have at least reflexively shut the car door?

Only something life-and-death.

Lucy filed away the thought, not wanting to jump to conclusions, and kept moving through the crime-scene photos. No obvious disturbance once you got past the vehicles and went down the front walk until you reached the front door: it was ajar a good four inches.

She flipped to the crime scene sketch that showed the position of Peter Martin's body inside the door. Then she moved back to the photos. He still wore his vest from the feed store and near the body was a silver Thermos. The kind a husband would bring home from work to refill for the next day.

If Peter was killed as soon as he came home, then the killers were already in the house with Lily and the children.

But all this was Friday afternoon and early evening. While Michael Manning was playing football in front of a thousand fans. She leafed through the alibi statements the defense attorney had gathered. Seemed like he'd done a rather half-hearted attempt to mount any kind of defense in case his clients changed their minds about their plea deal. According to his notes, while Michael had been with the team, Michael's brother, Richard, had no alibi, although he claimed to have been with his friend, Ronald Powell. Said they'd left the game around six-thirty in Powell's vehicle.

Six-thirty. Almost an hour after Pete would have gotten home—if he'd driven straight home from the store. Maybe he stopped somewhere? That would totally skew the time line if he had.

Lucy made a note to try to follow up on that idea as well as asking Saylor exactly what time it was that he'd seen Ronnie Powell at the game. She continued through the crime scene photos, pushing her forgotten lunch aside, knowing this part would be difficult.

The first photos weren't too bad because they were taken from the doorway to the baby's room, and you couldn't tell what was in the rocking chair facing away from the door and toward the crib.

The next photos circled around the room. A few were directed up at the ceiling, where thin ribbons of blood could be seen. As if the photographer didn't want to capture the painful reality of what had happened in that room. But finally, they ran out of other details to photograph and focused on Lily and her baby.

The brutality that Lily suffered was immense. Ravaged was the word that came to mind—no, savaged, that was better. It had to have gone on for quite some time, long enough for her restraints, normal household clothesline, to cut into the flesh of her wrists and ankles. There was no sign of a gag. None of the cuts were deep—they all seemed designed to maximize the torture while also prolonging her agony.

Not the frenzied attack she'd first imagined, Lucy realized. Thorough. Methodical. *Personal.*

She blew her breath out and braced herself for the next series of photos: the baby. She clicked through them quickly but then stopped and forced herself to examine them more closely.

After, she sat, eyes closed for a long moment. Then she went back through them one last time.

She'd found her missing link. The thing that changed everything.

Her chest was tight, her breathing shallow as she called Nick—he was the only person she could trust to objectively evaluate her theory. Thankfully, he'd just finished with a patient and had time to talk. She outlined what she'd found and emailed him a few of the photos so he could see what she saw.

"Could it be possible that this entire crime centered on the baby?" she finished. "That she was the true target? The attack on her was so extreme—worse than even the mother's. The mother was tortured, her death prolonged, but the baby, that beautiful, innocent baby..."

She had to blink back tears and catch her breath. "That baby, she was butchered by an animal. It's the only evidence of pure, unadulterated fury and hatred at the entire scene. Tell me I'm wrong, Nick. Tell me I've lost it."

He was silent for a long moment. "No. I think you're right. From the evidence you sent, I think it was the baby who was the killer's focus. He wanted to punish the mother. But the infant? He wanted that baby erased, annihilated."

"Why? What threat could a seven-month-old baby be to anyone?" Then she answered her own question. "Unless that baby wasn't who everyone thought she was. Lily might have been the mother, but what if Peter wasn't the father?"

"But he was targeted as well, so it wasn't a fit of jealousy on his behalf."

"Maybe the real father? Maybe he was a married man, needed to hide the affair?"

"Possible." He drew out the word.

"Or maybe he was a married man and his wife found out about the baby?"

"Are you saying a woman might have done this?" Despite everything the two of them had seen, crimes that shattered the very definition of human depravity, his voice still held a hint of disbelief.

Lucy loved him for that.

For the first time in the months since she'd been sidelined by her injury, she felt as if she was finally back, body and soul reunited, focused, on mission.

At this point, she didn't know or care who had butchered the Martin family. Man, woman, child, it didn't matter. If it was the Manning brothers, she'd make sure Michael Manning never saw the light of day again. If it wasn't, she was going to find them.

Because, civilian or not, that's what Lucy did best.

CHAPTER 23

"DON'T MIND MOTHER," Blackwell told TK after lunch as he led her out to the back patio. The heat was tempered by shade trees and a breeze as they strolled down a flagstone path toward the garage, a building that resembled a small airplane hangar. "She and my father were completely devoted to each other but their marriage was rather unorthodox."

"Was she really implying that your father might have been involved in the Martin killings?" TK asked, wondering why Caleb and his mother seemed to think she needed another suspect to investigate if indeed the Manning brothers were innocent. And didn't Roscoe Blackwell, dead for twenty-eight years and unable to defend himself, make the perfect fall guy?

Buy why?

Caleb shrugged and answered her question. "People always talk about how open-and-shut that case was but, as I said earlier, no case is without its unanswered questions. The Martin case is no exception."

"I know," she said, purposely adding a touch of breathless wonder to her tone.

Caleb beamed in response, obviously enjoying her undivided attention. The more she could get him to talk, the more she might be able to understand. Was he dangling his father as a suspect in order to strengthen the case for Michael Manning's innocence? Did Caleb actually want Manning released from prison? Maybe to make his predecessor look bad? But then why was his mother playing along? Other than the fact that she obviously was still bitter over her husband's affair with Lily Martin.

She matched her gait to Caleb's and brushed his arm. "I have so many questions. Maybe you could help. Like what time did Peter get home? If he was shot because he surprised the killers, then how long were they in the house before he arrived?"

"Mother was right about one thing: Peter was a gambler. My father had all the gaming shut down here in Blackwell County, but I heard people say that Peter would leave work and go spend his paycheck in illegal games over in San Angelo or up in Abilene. Which means he might not have gotten home until late evening, early morning. Who knows?"

"Leaving Lily and the kids unprotected."

"Well..." He slowed his pace, glanced back at the house. "I don't know about that. My father wasn't home most of that night. I remember him and my mother arguing about it after he and I returned from the crime scene the next morning. She accused him of spending the night with Lily Martin."

"The night of the murders?" TK stopped and stared. "You

don't really think—"

He looked away. "Every family has their secrets. My father took his with him to the grave."

TK had no idea what to say to that. Was he trying to point her in a direction that was too painful for him to investigate himself? Maybe Caleb actually was interested in finding the truth. But if he believed the Mannings might be innocent, why had he waited twenty-nine years?

Because that's what you did for family, she thought. You protected them, no matter the cost. Like her own father had.

A rustling came from the bushes around them and a Jack Russell terrier came bounding up to Blackwell. "Here, Lily," he called, squatting and clapping his hands. "C'mon here, girl!"

"Lily?" TK asked. "You named the dog after—"

"Not me, my mother," he said as the dog came bounding into his arms, tail wagging. "All my life, far back as I can remember, any bitch we keep is named Lily." He rubbed the dog's belly and looked up at her. "I'm afraid my mother isn't exactly the forgiving and forgetting type."

His tone was normal—just two folks talking about family pets. But his gaze moved past hers and his smile died.

She turned to glance back at the house. Carole Blackwell stood at the window watching them, an unfathomable sneer twisting her features. A sudden chill forced TK to step back, away from the older woman's dead cold stare.

Maybe Caleb *was* trying to tell her something, something he couldn't admit to himself.

Caleb glanced away, talking to the dog as much as to TK. "Like I said, families are complicated, mine more than most."

"How old were you when it happened?"

"Thirteen—no, wait—twelve. My birthday was the day after." He shrugged, appearing boyish and charming. She had to keep reminding herself that he was in his forties. "Kind of got forgotten in all the chaos, as you can imagine. Poor kid—the son, Alan, I mean. They called me a hero for finding him in time—said he'd have died for sure if I hadn't been there. But it wasn't me who was the real hero. It was Sheriff Saylor. Standing up to my dad and making sure things were done right, that folks felt safe again."

The dog rolled at his feet, tail thumping against the lush lawn as it begged for more loving. A man playing with his dog, what could be more innocent?

As she turned her back on Carole Blackwell's all-seeing gaze, TK's training told her to keep her hands free, prepared to face a threat. But she couldn't stop her instincts that had her wrapping her arms across her chest, rubbing the goose bumps from her flesh. The sun beat down, relentless, but she couldn't get warm.

Maybe it wasn't Caleb's father he was protecting, but his mother.

She'd felt like this before. In another sunbaked land, half the world away. First time she met her squad's new leader, a fresh-scrubbed piece of American pie who still had creases in his lieutenant's uniform. She'd ignored her instincts then, allowed him to charm her, crawl below her defenses.

Not this time.

TK cupped her hand over her eyes and squinted in the direction where the Martin house had stood. "You were their closest neighbors."

"Yes, but you can't see their house from here—could

barely see the fence between our land."

"I don't see a fence."

"Long gone. My dad bought their holdings, merged their land with ours."

Was he giving her yet another motive for his father to annihilate an entire family? Of course, now that Roscoe was dead, it was Carole Blackwell who had gained.

"Do you want to see it? It's still there—pretty much the same as it ever was, except for the graffiti. Kind of a rite of passage for kids around here—sneak into the Martin house, spend the night, make their mark."

Before she could answer, he strode briskly off the path, crossing over the manicured landscaping until it ended abruptly in a meadow of parched wild grass. The land curved down and she made out the single-story frame house partially hidden by trees and scraggly bushes.

"C'mon," he said, turning back to the path toward the garage. "It's on our way."

They continued onto the garage where the Escalade stood waiting, motor running. But that's not what surprised her. Beside the Escalade were three more cars—all Cadillacs—and beyond them sat a Bell Ranger helicopter.

"Nice bird," she said.

"Glad you like it. First thing I bought with the proceeds of the forfeiture auctions. I keep it here since so far I'm our only pilot." His cheeks flushed and he looked twenty years younger in the light streaming through the hangar doors. "If you like, I can take you up some time. You really appreciate the beauty of this land when you see it from the air."

"That'd be nice," she murmured, not sure if she'd just

made a date with a man almost twice her age or if she was just being polite. So many things about Caleb left her uncertain—it was intriguing and exciting and a touch frightening. Which made for a dangerous cocktail of attraction.

She climbed back into the SUV and they headed down the lane to the highway. After a half-mile or so, they swung onto a rutted dirt lane.

"That's the federal land." He pointed to the west. "Powell grew his weed there, squatted, and sold other drugs there as well."

"Did they ever find him? He disappeared that night, right?"

"Never seen again."

"Too bad." They drove another three quarters of a mile and she glimpsed the sun gleaming from the Martin house's tin roof. They parked at the end of the drive. "Any chance you could try to find Powell? It might answer a lot of questions."

He considered. "The man is long gone. Probably Mexico. If he's not dead. It has been twenty-nine years."

"I know. Don't remind me."

"I'll run his name, see if anything pops. But no promises."

"Thanks, Caleb. You want to find out what really happened that night as well, don't you? I mean, it wouldn't just be the Mannings we'd be clearing if someone else is responsible." She hesitated, aware she was crossing a line. "Your mom, she doesn't really think your dad did it, does she?"

He frowned, turned east to look toward his home. The Martin house might have been invisible from his lands above, but there was no mistaking the Blackwell estate. A trick of the topography made it appear as if the Blackwell mansion floated above the trees, gleaming white as the sun blasted it head on.

"No, not really. His suicide hit her hard—I think making up stories like that helps her to not blame herself." He turned back to her, his gaze searching. "Does that make sense?"

"Of course. When someone goes like that, it's hard to fill the void of the questions they leave behind." Especially if you're a crazy old bitch, she thought, wondering if maybe Roscoe had been driven to kill himself—or had some help from his wife.

She felt sorry for Caleb. Bad enough he was the one who found the bodies. At such a young age, it would have scarred him for life. But to also have grown up in that house, raised by that woman, never certain if she might be a killer...She shook herself, reining in her imagination. All she had were innuendoes and vague gossip from twenty-nine years ago.

Caleb continued toward the empty house. The place would have been spooky even without knowing its history. Spray-painted pentagrams and other occult symbols vied with profanities on the once-white siding. Windows were broken, tattered curtains caught in the glass fluttered despite the fact that there was no discernible breeze. It was hotter down here, so humid that TK found herself taking deep breaths as if the air took more effort to move.

Caleb went still, staring at the front door still about ten feet away, his gaze lost in memory.

"You sure about this?" she asked.

"It still gets me, every time." His voice was haunted. A shudder rocked through him and he nodded as if answering a question in his own mind.

"Okay. This is about where I left my bike. Lily's car was there and Pete's truck there." He pointed at the gravel driveway overgrown with weeds. "I ran to the door, was going to ring the bell when I saw it was open."

Together they walked over the cracked sidewalk pavers to the small concrete stoop in front of the door. The door had once been Kelly green, but what little that hadn't been covered in layers of graffiti was faded by the sun and by years.

TK watched as Caleb pushed the door open. It moved slowly, hinges squeaking with disuse. A rush of musty air emerged, carrying the stench of marijuana, urine, and decay.

"Right there," he said, pointing to the narrow foyer. "That's where I found Pete."

"What did you do?"

"I wet my pants." He grimaced at the memory. "Ran back to my bike, but knew I couldn't leave them, not like that. I have no idea how I found the strength to do it, but somehow I went back. I was so scared—even now, I've never been that terrified. I listened, couldn't hear anyone else inside, I knew Pete was dead—that was obvious—but what about Lily and the kids?"

As he spoke, he pulled his Maglite from his duty belt and turned it on, lighting their path as he entered. A rustling came from the rear of the house, a small animal or bird. It stilled again as their footsteps creaked against the rotting carpet and the house went completely silent.

"The kitchen looked okay and the phone was right there, so I called my dad. It was the only the number my fingers remembered how to dial."

"How long did it take him to come for you?" TK could only imagine the anguish of waiting, not knowing if the killer was still nearby.

"I'm not sure. Probably only a few minutes. I hid out in

the bushes on the side of the house until I saw his truck. But that was the side where the baby's room was."

TK's heart about broke at the sadness coloring his voice. "You saw?"

"I couldn't help it." His voice caught. "I looked inside the window. And there was Lily, staring right at me. Except her eyes—they were gone."

CHAPTER 24

LUCY WAS STILL trying to wrap her mind around the idea that an infant was the killer's main target when her computer alerted: Wash inviting her to video conference. "Wanted to fill you in on what I found with the forfeiture stuff."

"I need to update you and Tommy on the Martin case as well. Is he there?"

"Right here." Tommy's image filled the screen behind Wash. He didn't look happy, rather a strange mix of excitement and confusion. "You should see what we found."

Wash shushed him with a hand. "Me first."

"Let me guess," Lucy put in before the two could start squabbling. "The forfeitures are bogus, based on trumped-up charges, and mainly designed to siphon money into the sheriff's coffers."

"Maybe, we're not sure. Still working on the money trail."

"But that's not what we found," Tommy interrupted again. "Tell her."

Wash continued, "It's not easy tracking every item at auction back to their owner, much less proving that any charges were falsified. So I started with the big-ticket items. The cars."

"Okay," Lucy said. "Makes sense. Vehicles are easier to track with registration and VIN information."

"Right. Except..." He trailed off, eyes wide with excitement.

"Except," Tommy picked up the conversational baton, "we found a pattern. Cars reported as abandoned, impounded, tagged for forfeiture—"

"Normal procedure," Lucy put in. "The last registered owners would have been notified, and if they didn't claim the vehicle and pay any fees, the car would be auctioned by the county and re-titled in the new owner's name."

"Only these weren't," Wash said, his wheelchair bouncing as he did a mini-wheelie of triumph. "At first we thought maybe they were junkers, too old, so they were sent straight to scrap. But then I saw that a few were new, high-end models. They would have made good money if they had been sold at auction."

"Maybe the county claimed them to use as unmarked vehicles? The FBI gets vehicles from the DEA for undercover ops all the time."

Both men shook their heads. "Nope. They weren't sent to auction, weren't used by the county," Tommy said. "They were sent to be scrapped."

"We wouldn't have found out who the owners were if the salvage yard the county contracts with didn't have an owner who was particularly careful about keeping his own records, separate from the county's, including VINs."

"So while Wash tracked the vehicles, I tracked the owners."

"And the owners were?" Lucy asked, getting a bit annoyed by their roundabout path to what mattered. "Who were these mysterious vehicles that were mysteriously destroyed registered to?"

Tommy and Wash exchanged glances. Wash nodded to Tommy, giving him permission to answer. "Women. All from other states. And all of them eventually reported missing."

Lucy leaned forward. "You have my attention."

The screen changed from their faces to an array of photos. All women, all in their mid-twenties to early thirties, all blonde. Lucy counted fourteen of them. "How long has this been going on?"

"Best we can tell," Wash answered, "fifteen years or more."

"So not just since Sheriff Blackwell instituted the new forfeiture system?" Didn't mean the forfeitures weren't still some kind of criminal enterprise. But fourteen women missing...

"What do you want us to do?" Tommy asked.

"Wash, keep tracking the forfeitures. And Tommy, you follow the women. Send me everything you have on them—where they were last sighted, their histories, any police reports."

"Sure, we can coordinate with several missing persons' groups. Families who haven't given up, still searching for answers."

"Don't promise them anything," Lucy warned. "It might be nothing—this part of Texas, a vehicle breaking down and being abandoned wouldn't be that unusual."

"But fourteen of them?" Tommy protested.

"Over fifteen years," she reminded him. "But, there's one thing that bothers me."

"What?"

"It's a hell of a lot easier to get rid of a body than it is a car."

"Unless you have access to a scrap yard," Wash finished for her.

"Exactly."

"Which means it could be anyone at the sheriff's department," Wash said.

"Or even the county clerk's office," Tommy added. "All they'd have to do is change the paperwork, sending the cars straight to scrap instead of auction."

Wash nodded. "But it probably has nothing to do with the Martin case. They were killed over a decade before the first victim we've found."

"That's okay. Keep working this." A knock sounded on Lucy's motel room door. "Hang on, guys," she told the others as she edged off the bed to answer.

It was David. He looked drained after his day at the prison but carried a plastic shopping bag.

"Good, you got my text."

He handed her the bag. "Had to improvise a bit. The only store I came across was a small general store."

Lucy dumped out the contents: tape, Magic Markers, and rolls of wrapping paper covered with toothy grinning clowns who resembled serial killers she'd caught. And the last item, the most important: an old-fashioned cassette recorder. "This will do just fine. Help me cover the walls. How did it go with your father?"

"Fine." He sidestepped her question, eying her beds. "What the heck did you do?"

"There was a scorpion in the bathroom and I wasn't sure if they could climb." She ignored his raised eyebrow and skeptical grin; taped one edge of the paper to the wall, turned backwards so she had a white surface to write on; and gestured to him to unspool the roll as she followed with more tape.

"Where's TK?" he asked as they worked. "I thought she'd be here."

"So did I. She's gone radio silent."

"Do you think she's okay?"

Lucy had wondered the same thing. If she'd been working with her team back at the FBI, she wouldn't think twice about an agent following a lead independently as long as they kept her updated. But with civilians like TK, she wasn't sure if she should interpret the younger woman's silence as a commitment to her work or as sullen protest over being assigned to records' duty. "What kind of trouble could she get into from the basement of the sheriff's department?"

He frowned.

"Tommy," she called over her shoulder to the computer, "did you have a chance to go over the blood analysis I asked you about?"

"Yes, and I think you're right." She turned the laptop around and adjusted it so he and Wash faced the paper-covered wall.

"Walk me through it."

"The state crime lab found two blood types on the revolver. One matched the father, Peter Martin. The other matched the baby."

David crouched down so he could face the computer. "We already knew that."

"Right," Lucy said, making notes on the papered wall, "but no one was looking at the blood types the way we are. They just wanted to be able to tie your father's fingerprints in blood to the murder victims. Tell him the rest, Tommy."

"Since they didn't use DNA back in 1987, they used blood types as a crude identification method. The sent it to the lab for confirmation with HLA typing, but it takes much longer. Months back then. Since all the state attorney wanted was to verify that the blood belonged to their victims, they never forwarded the final results to the defense—it wasn't exculpatory, the Mannings had already been sentenced by then, plus it's pretty technical, they may not have even realized what it meant. I'm guessing they probably filed it without even looking at the report."

"But we *are* looking at the report," Lucy said as a knock came on her motel room door. "Thanks to TK and her scavenger hunt."

"Okay," David said, "so?"

"So," Tommy leaned forward into the camera, "Peter Martin was not Glory Martin's father."

———•———

TK AND CALEB drove away from the Martin house in silence. He was visibly shaken by their visit to the crime scene and she felt awful stirring up the old memories. Not to mention the bizarre lunch with his mother. She couldn't imagine living with *that* every day.

"Do you want me to keep looking?" she finally asked.

His Adam's apple bobbed up and down as he swallowed hard and nodded. "Yes. I've been avoiding it for far too long, but now I think it's time. I need to know the truth." He turned to look at her, ignoring the road. "Wherever it leads."

She nodded back, the weight of responsibility settling over her. "I'll need to tell the others about your father."

"I know." He blew out his breath as if relieved by his decision to trust her. "What do you need from me? How can I help?"

The offer stunned her. After all, he was pretty much giving her *carte blanche* to pry into the deepest corners of his family's past. She thought about it, hesitated, then finally asked, "Your father. How did he—"

"Pills. Mixed with his most expensive bottle of bourbon. Mom and I were out, picking up my birthday present."

Right. When Roscoe Blackwell chose the anniversary of Lily Martin's death as the day to kill himself, he'd also chosen the eve of his son's birthday. "Oh, Caleb. I'm so sorry—"

His one-shoulder shrug was more protective defense than acknowledgment of her words. "It was a four-wheeler. Roscoe didn't want me to have it, had forbidden it. Ever since the Martins, he kept me close, didn't like me to go anywhere unsupervised."

"He was trying to protect you."

"Or control me. Or keep me from finding the truth—back then I was obsessed with the case, like everyone in the county. Who knows?" He turned into the motel parking lot. They parked in front of her room, the engine running.

"Anyway, Mother was always of the mind that it was better to ask forgiveness than permission, so she took me to pick out my ATV. To me it meant independence, a chance to escape Roscoe. To her, I think it meant a chance to snap Roscoe out of his funk. They weren't talking, weren't even fighting, and she was frustrated with him—more so than usual."

"You found him?"

He nodded. "I think he planned it that way—no, that's not fair. It could have been either of us walking in on him in his study. I ran in, wearing my new helmet that Mother insisted on, and he was in his big chair, facing away from the door, staring out the windows that overlooked the first land the Blackwells had ever owned."

"At least that's what I thought." His voice dropped low and his hand slipped from the gearshift to rest close to TK's arm. She slid her own hand over his and gave him a comforting squeeze. "I ran around the desk and spun his chair around only to see he was covered in vomit. The stench—to this day I can't stand the smell of bourbon, never touch the stuff. The coroner was kind enough to call it an accidental overdose, but we all knew the truth."

Truth. It impressed her that he was willing to open these old wounds to find the truth. But with it, maybe would come some peace.

"Thank you, TK," he whispered, not looking at her, his gaze unfocused, still caught up in memories. "I've never told anyone that before. Never been able to—"

"You're welcome. I promise, I'll do the best I can."

"I appreciate that—you have no idea how much it means to me." He shook himself and turned to her, his expression lightening. "Are you free for dinner?"

The question startled her. She pulled back from him. "I'm not sure that's a good idea," she stammered.

"No, no. I'm sorry. I didn't mean it that way. I meant going somewhere where we can talk more, about the case, no prying eyes."

"Oh. Of course." David and Lucy could fend for themselves for a night. "That sounds good."

"Great. I'll pick you up at seven. Nothing fancy—there's a steak house over in San Angelo that you'll love."

"All right. See you then." She opened her car door and got out.

"TK?" he called across the seats before she closed the door. "Thanks again."

She smiled. It had been a long time since anyone had placed their faith in her like Caleb had. "You are very welcome."

She closed the SUV door and went to drop her bag in her room. Then she went over to Lucy's room and knocked on the door. Lucy opened it and ushered her in just as she heard Tommy Worth say, "Peter Martin was not Glory Martin's father."

CHAPTER 25

As TK ENTERED the room and waved to Tommy and Wash via the computer, Ruiz paced the space between the two beds while Lucy scribbled lists on paper taped to the wall opposite the window.

"So what if she wasn't Peter Martin's daughter?" Ruiz said. "That means someone else might have wanted Lily dead, but it doesn't clear my father. It's a motive, not evidence."

"Plus, we don't know who the real father is and if they had opportunity," Wash put in.

"I might be able to help with that," TK said. All eyes turned to her.

"Where were you?" Lucy asked. "You weren't answering your phone."

"It died." TK noticed the bag of food sitting near the TV; maybe Lucy hadn't forgotten her after all. "I was having lunch with Caleb Blackwell. And his mother—who is a total narcissist, but that didn't stop her from sharing gossip about the case."

"How is gossip going to help my father?" Ruiz asked. "It's not evidence."

He seemed much more invested in clearing his father's name than he had last night. She wondered what had happened at the prison. "No, but it might open up new lines of inquiry. For example, one tidbit that Carole Blackwell let slip was that her husband, Roscoe, was one of Lily Martin's lovers. He might have been the father of her child."

She relished the moment of silence that followed her pronouncement.

Ruiz wove his way between TK and Lucy, his body vibrating with energy as he searched for room to pace. "If the Blackwells were involved, that would explain everything. They run this county, are untouchable. They own the sheriff and the county commissioners, could cover up Roscoe's involvement, no problem." He made it to the bathroom door then spun back. "They framed my father and uncle, sent them to jail. I know it."

"Be careful," Lucy cautioned. "We're just speculating here. Like you said, none of this is evidence." She turned to the computer. "Do we have any record of Roscoe Blackwell's DNA or blood type?"

"Not in the information I have," Tommy answered.

"TK, do you think you could convince the sheriff to get his father to volunteer a sample?"

"No, because Roscoe Blackwell committed suicide on the first anniversary of the killings."

Ruiz slumped against the bathroom doorframe, his face dropping.

"Which means we'd have to get a warrant and collect DNA some other way," Lucy translated for Tommy and Wash.

"Even so, it's still not evidence that he killed them," Ruiz said, his monotone pronouncement sounding more forlorn than ever. "We'll never be able to prove my father was innocent."

"Don't give up yet. It's the first real motive we have," Lucy answered, now sketching a time line on the wall. TK liked how she didn't waste time on commiserating, but focused on the mission. "Wash," she called over her shoulder, "any luck on narrowing the gaps in our subjects' movements?"

"Not much," he said. "Everything points to Lily getting home around five o'clock on Friday but we weren't able to trace Peter Martin's movements after he left the feed store. I did find some activity on his bank statements that correlate to what the police report alluded to as 'a history of illicit gambling.' Those took place outside of Canterville, in San Angelo as well as in Abilene."

"But none on the night in question?"

"Nope, sorry. He could have gotten home on time right after Lily or he could have been anywhere. Impossible to say."

Lucy put a question mark on her time line under Peter's name and circled it. "Tommy, how about our times of death?"

"Were you able to talk with the original coroner who

was on scene?"

"No. He died years ago. But I did speak with the daughter who took over and she's pretty sharp. Said she learned everything from her dad, so I'm guessing he knew what he was doing."

"His report reads that way. I was hoping to learn more about the different dry times of the various blood evidence," Tommy explained to TK and Ruiz. "Sometimes that can be more accurate than core body temp or vitreous fluid to pinpoint TOD."

"Give it to us, Tommy," Lucy said, her pen poised over her time line. "What kind of window are we looking at?"

"It's different for each victim. Best I can tell, Peter Martin died first, not last. Between twelve and sixteen hours before his body was found."

"Someone do the math for me," Lucy asked.

Ruiz spoke up. "Between three-thirty and seven-thirty Friday night." His voice was flat as always but his face lit up with excitement and his posture straightened as fresh energy shot through him. "Which means my dad couldn't have done it."

"Probably still not enough for an appeal," Tommy cautioned. "Not with the state pathologist's report contradicting it. You'll end up with a battle of dueling expert witnesses."

"Did your father explain what happened?" TK asked. "Why did he confess if he was innocent?"

"He thought it was the only way to save his brother. At the time, he thought Dicky was guilty and would either get the death penalty or maybe even be lynched. The sheriff convinced him that if they both pled guilty, it would save Dicky's life—and neither would get the chair."

TK frowned. "Still, why not fight it?"

"With what? The only evidence pointed to my father. That damn gun. But if the Blackwells were involved, they could have easily planted it."

"If so, I don't think the sheriff was part of any cover-up." Lucy turned and fished out a set of papers and a tape cassette from the cascade of reports scattered across her bed. "The sheriff—the old sheriff, Saylor—truly believed he was saving their lives. From a lynch mob. But your father did ask for a lawyer and never received one. Plus, Saylor pretty much fed your father everything he needed to confess."

"You found the missing hour," TK said.

Lucy nodded. "And one of our missing witnesses. Alan Martin was adopted by Saylor. They live out past the Martin place, near the river."

Ruiz scanned the transcript. "Saylor knew and he kept this hidden? My father could have been free years ago—"

"He knows. That's why I don't think he knew anything about Roscoe Blackwell's possible involvement. Saylor was trying to protect Alan—was afraid if your uncle went free, either he or his buddy, Ronnie Powell, would come after Alan to silence him. I think he's trying to make amends now."

TK was glad she wasn't on the receiving end of Ruiz's glare. "A little too late for that."

"What about Alan?" she asked. "Did he see anything?"

Lucy shrugged. "He's got some pretty severe cognitive

dysfunction. Plus elective mutism."

"What's that?"

"He doesn't speak," Tommy answered. "Often the result of psychological trauma, the child simply shuts down any effort to talk about anything, especially the event that triggered it."

"Is there a treatment?"

"Counseling and time are usually the best ones. If he hasn't spoken in thirty years, he probably won't."

"What about something that doesn't involve talking?" TK asked Tommy. She could get a photo of Caleb's father, show it to Alan. As well as photos of Ruiz's uncle and Ronald Powell. After all, just because Ruiz's father might have falsely confessed, that didn't mean Dicky Manning was also innocent. "Maybe we could try a photo array?"

"Hard to tell. Remember, this kid is severely delayed. I'd have to assess him before I could make a determination."

"Saylor is very protective of Alan," Lucy added. "He's pretty much made sure the kid has had no exposure to anything to do with the case for the past twenty-nine years. I doubt he'll allow it."

"We could try," TK protested. "What's the harm?"

"Let's move back to our timeline," Lucy said, obviously tabling the idea of approaching Alan for now. "We have a window for Peter's death, what about Lily and the baby? We know Lily arrived home before Peter, but if he was killed first, then the killers must have been in the house for quite some time, right?"

"I think your coroner was right, they died after Peter. Probably around two to six hours after." Tommy paused, his voice clouding with sadness. "It took them a long time to die, too. The baby went first. Lily lasted a bit longer—hard to say exactly how long."

Everyone fell silent, no one making eye contact. Finally, Lucy heaved her shoulders and added the data to her time line. She stepped back. "Given what we know now, is everyone ready to eliminate Michael Manning as a suspect?"

She turned around and gazed at each of the team in turn. First, Wash, who simply nodded, then Tommy, who said, "Yes," and finally TK. TK looked at Ruiz, who for the first time since she'd met him, appeared hopeful, invested in his father's innocence. "Yes."

Ruiz met her gaze and nodded. "Yes," he said in his gravelly voice. "My mother was right all along, God help us."

"Okay, then," Lucy said. "Where do we look next?"

Silence ruled the room for several moments. Finally, TK spoke up. "I still think we need to find Ronald Powell. If he was involved, whether it was with Dicky Manning or someone else, or if he can supply an alibi for the Mannings, it could help Michael's appeal."

"Wash, where are you on that?" Lucy asked.

"I traced him to Mexico—he did two years in a prison there for narcotics possession back in the 1990s. But I haven't been able to find where he went after that. There's no further record of him in Mexico."

"Maybe he came home?"

"I'm checking the best I can, but we're talking records dating back a quarter of a century."

"He's no good to us if he's dead," TK said.

"She's right. Start with current databases: vehicle

registration, tax records, social media, death certificates." Lucy stared at the time line, hands on hips. "Don't talk to him yet, though. I want to take that interview myself. Because I'm pretty certain it wasn't Dicky Manning and Ronnie Powell. The wounds, they don't read 'mindless drug-induced frenzy.' To me, they read like deliberate, cold-hearted torture."

"Maybe," Tommy said. "But I can understand why they ignored the coroner's findings after the Mannings confessed. I mean, who the hell would want to torture a mother and her seven-month-old baby?"

Lucy spun to face the computer. "That's the real question, isn't it?"

"Caleb said there was a possibility his father was there that night," TK said.

"Possibility? So he has no firsthand knowledge?" Lucy turned her gaze on TK.

"No, sorry. Remember, he was just a kid at the time. Overhearing bits and pieces of his parents' arguments."

"You spent the day with the Blackwells. Why would they suddenly dangle the suggestion of Roscoe's involvement now? Even if Michael Manning wins his appeal, there's no need to provide us with an alternative theory of the crime. It's not as if anyone would be re-opening the investigation, especially not with Caleb Blackwell as sheriff. What do they stand to gain?"

It was the same question TK had been asking herself all afternoon. "Maybe they're not pointing to Roscoe so much as away from someone else?"

"Like who?" Ruiz demanded.

TK shrugged. "I'm not sure. Maybe his mother?"

Wash chimed in from the computer. "There's no way a woman could have done this, right? I mean everyone was assuming it was at least two men, so how could a single woman—"

"If Carole Blackwell thought her family was threatened by Roscoe's affair with Lily, of course she would take whatever measures she thought necessary to eliminate that threat," Lucy answered.

"But the sheer violence—"

"Profilers call it 'overkill.' And it's actually more reflective of a woman driven to kill than how a man probably would have done it," Lucy explained. "If we're talking simple problem-solving, a man would have just shot whoever needed killing and walk away. Or if he was worried that the crime might point to him, he might try to mask his involvement by making it look like something it wasn't."

"Like a drug-induced frenzied attack," Ruiz said.

"Exactly. But the way the killer took extra time with Lily and the baby—way more time than necessary to fulfill their objective, also increasing their risk of exposure—that means it was deeply personal. They just didn't want them dead, they needed to see them suffer, needed to, in effect, erase them from existence."

CHAPTER 26

LUCY SENT TOMMY and Wash to continue their work while David went to call his mother with an update. Leaving her with only TK to deal with. "Good work with the evidence," she started. "But what else happened with Blackwell?"

"I got to see the crime scene. He gave me a tour of what he saw as a kid."

Now Lucy was intrigued. "Any new insights?"

To her surprise, TK hesitated. "No, not really. It's just hard to understand that kind of experience—the horror, the impact—from reading the reports. It wasn't what I expected."

"The human side of every crime. For me it's the most difficult part to handle. The real face, real lives impacted, whether victim or witness, or in David's father's case, accused."

"I think it was somehow cathartic for Caleb, walking through it. We're going out to dinner tonight."

"Really?" Lucy tried and failed to keep her tone neutral. It hadn't escaped her attention that TK was now calling the sheriff by his first name. "Do you think that's a good idea?"

"Why not? Not like he's a potential suspect, even if his parents are. Since he was a witness, we need to interview him anyway. Nothing says it has to be done in an office. In fact, I might get more out of him in a less formal setting."

Lucy wasn't convinced but also couldn't argue against it. She had no hard evidence that Caleb Blackwell was involved in any wrongdoing, either with the forfeitures or the missing women. "Did he happen to mention his forfeiture program?"

"Said it helped the department buy a helicopter—he's the pilot. Promised me a ride, so I could get a feel for the land."

"A county this size with its own helicopter?" Lucy frowned. "There's no way those forfeitures can all be legit."

"Why not? Maybe Caleb simply is more efficient and thorough about using the forfeiture laws than most rural departments. Big cities like Philly use forfeitures for funding all the time."

"You mean the program that ended with them in federal court? And that is heading to a multi-million dollar class action suit?"

"Bad example. Still doesn't mean Caleb is doing anything wrong."

"There might be more going on." Lucy explained about the missing women.

"But we don't have any evidence that police are involved," TK protested. "Much less Caleb. Could be that someone realized Blackwell County is a good dumping ground for vehicles they want disappeared?"

Lucy doubted that—and from the way TK's eyebrows had knotted, she knew the younger woman did as well. "I'm just saying. Be careful."

"I am. I will." TK paced the space in front of Lucy's makeshift timeline.

"I had a question about one piece of evidence. I couldn't find any report of fingerprints being taken from the bullets. Did you see one?"

"No. The evidence log showed that they sent the revolver to the state lab for analysis, but not the bullets. Probably not in their budget—plus, why bother when they had the other prints in the victims' blood?" She turned to Lucy. "Unless you're wrong about Saylor and he was trying to cover for someone else."

"I'm tired of conspiracy theories and gossip. The lawyers are going to need more than a coerced confession to get Michael Manning out of prison."

"Really? Why wouldn't that be enough?"

"If he had appealed right away, it probably would have been, but now after so long, it's another story. The most the courts would do with what we have so far would be to grant him a new trial. If that."

"Maria doesn't have that long."

"No, she doesn't. We need real evidence."

"We only have one witness, Alan Martin. But at least we have new suspects we can show him."

"Your photo array idea?"

"I used it in Afghanistan with women and children too scared to talk. I know how to do it, make it non-threatening. Hell, I was a Marine in full combat gear carrying weapons uninvited in their homes in the middle of the night, barely able to speak their language, and I still got good intel. At least let me try."

Lucy considered that. "Exactly what did you do in Afghanistan?"

TK shrugged, looked away. "Support. Enablers, the brass called us. The guys would go in, searching for insurgents, enter a village or compound. I'd search the women and children, their quarters, talk with them."

Her words came slowly as if she was redacting her own history. But Lucy could read between the lines. Translating "guys" into "special ops" and "enter" into "raid." She'd been right; TK had seen real action.

"Anyway," TK finished, despite the fact that she'd really told Lucy very little, "I can do it. If you let me try."

"Go, get the photos. I'll take them to Saylor, see what he says."

"But what if he was involved?" TK protested.

"I'm not about to interview a fragile witness like Alan without his guardian present. Take it or leave it."

TK nodded and ran out the door before Lucy could change her mind.

Lucy called Nick to ask for his advice in dealing with Alan, but he was in with a patient. She could wait until he was free, but they really didn't have many other avenues to pursue. Except maybe one. She called Wash. "How difficult would it be for us to run fingerprints? Do we have any access to AFIS?"

He hesitated. "We have run comparison prints—usually to identify John Does whose prints were taken before the modern databases existed. You don't have more bodies out there, do you?"

"No," she assured him. "But those bullets, they bother me."

"Why not ask the sheriff to run them? They'd be easy to do nowadays with local tech. No need to send to the state lab."

Because she didn't want to trust Blackwell or his people with potentially valuable evidence. Especially not if Blackwell's family might be involved.

Wash picked up on her concern without her saying anything. "You think if you bring their attention to them, they might disappear or miraculously get wiped clean? Like those scrapped cars?"

"Then why leave the bullets there for us to find at all? Unless the prints on them point to someone else—"

"Someone they want us to find? Like his father, Roscoe?" He gave a low whistle. "I thought my mind was twisted, but that is...just diabolical."

"Should I ask them to run them or not?"

"Once they're run, they become part of the official record. Took Michael Manning twenty-nine years to fight his way free of that red tape."

"But, I'd love to know—" He was right. Despite her curiosity, she couldn't play into Blackwell's hand. The sheriff was definitely playing a larger game, one she couldn't see.

"We could run them unofficially," he suggested. "One of our guys is a certified latent-print examiner with access to AFIS as part of our partnership with NamUs and NCMEC. Problem is, if there is a match, we'll have some explaining to do about why the prints came from us instead of local law enforcement."

"Which might make them inadmissible and destroy the chain of custody." Satisfying her own curiosity, but not doing

Michael Manning any good. She had to remind herself that, unlike the FBI, her job here was to free a man, not convict one.

"Isn't that against the law? Tampering with evidence?" He sounded more excited than nervous about the prospect.

"Not to mention obstruction of justice. Damn if we do, damn if we don't."

"Sorry, boss. Wish I had an answer. Maybe ask Valencia?"

No way in hell was Lucy going running to the woman who just hired her—talk about amateur hour. It was Lucy's case. She'd make the decision. Every reflex drilled into her by the FBI told her to trust the system and follow procedure, but that idea left a sour taste that burned through her gut.

Before she could decide, a knock came on her door. She looked through the peephole: Augusta, the woman whose life had been turned upside down by the county seizing her possessions and jailing her husband.

Lucy opened the door and stepped outside, blocking Augusta's view of the evidence strewn around her room.

"I'm sorry," the younger woman said in a rush. "I hate to bother you, but you seem so much better at this stuff than I am. My father made it here with the money but he's exhausted. Would you come with me to the sheriff department? I don't want to mess this up. It's all the money we have." Augusta opened the plastic shopping bag she clutched, revealing wads of cash.

"They asked you to bring cash?" Lucy was surprised. She'd paid David and TK's fine this morning with a credit card and the notices said the sheriff's department also took certified checks. Of course that fine had only been two hundred dollars, but she couldn't believe a speeding ticket would require this much cash.

Maybe this was how Blackwell and his men were

profiting from the forfeitures? More than the official funds raised by the auctions, but actual cash in their pockets. But then where did the destroyed vehicles and missing women play into things?

"They said it had to be cash. My father didn't feel comfortable wiring it, and since he had to drive from Florida to take us to Dallas once we get Paul out of jail, he brought it with him."

"And your husband, he's been charged with what exactly?"

"They said he was speeding and resisted arrest. Even though he wasn't, he didn't. But we can't risk him having a record. He'll lose his job, so they said if we paid his fine in full, in cash, they'd set him free. They have to keep the car and all our stuff because it was used in the commission of a crime, but I don't care. I just need Paul back. Will you help me?"

"Of course." Lucy texted David and TK to let them know where she was going. As they walked across the street and around to the entrance to the jail annex, Lucy asked, "Exactly how much cash did they ask you to bring?"

"They said to drop the resisting arrest charge and clear his record, it would be a ten-thousand dollar fine." Augusta was practically in tears. "I would have hired a lawyer and fought it— that's what Paul said we should do—but the lawyers charge hundreds of dollars an hour, and when I called, most said they'd need at least ten thousand dollars up front as a retainer anyway. And that's with no guarantees, Paul could have still gone to prison. So I called my dad instead and asked for the money. Paul's going to be furious. But what else could I do?"

Lucy opened the door, the same one she'd entered through earlier that morning when she came to bail out TK and

David. Same deputy at the counter as well, adding to the sense of *deja vu*. He kept eying her as Augusta set her bag of cash on the counter and explained that she was here to pay the fee to release her husband.

"It's all here," she said, tearfully. "You can count it."

The deputy frowned at the cash and then again at Lucy, who helpfully had her photo ID out—the retired federal agent government-issued photo ID. Technically, it was no better than a driver's license, but it certainly seemed to impress the deputy. "Ma'am, let me check our records," he finally said. "I'll be right back."

Augusta sagged against the counter, palm pressed against her belly as if she was about to be sick. "What if it's not enough? We don't have any more—"

Lucy took her by the arm and steered her to a bench, the bag bundled into her lap. "You hold on to this, Augusta. Don't worry. Everything is going to be just fine."

A few minutes later, the deputy returned, accompanied by a rumpled-appearing man in a sweat-stained polo and jeans. "Paul!" Augusta cried, running to him.

Right behind them was Caleb Blackwell. "I understand we had a clerical error here," he said with a genial smile. "Seems there was a misplaced decimal in the computer. Ma'am, your husband is free to go. With our apologies."

"What about the fine?" Augusta asked, holding up her bag.

"Since it was our mistake, we won't worry about it." He was talking to Augusta but looking at Lucy. "These things happen from time to time."

"Of course they do," Lucy said. "You'd be amazed at the

errors a single misplaced keystroke could lead to—sometimes I think computers are out to get us. Augusta, I'm sure your car and all your possessions will be returned as well. After all, if there was no offense, then there was no reason for a forfeiture to have occurred in the first place. Am I right, Sheriff Blackwell?"

His smile was forced but his smile never wavered. Politician, Lucy reminded herself. No wonder she was worried about trusting him with potentially crucial evidence. "Of course you are, Mrs. Guardino. Hoskins, let's get these fine young people their vehicle and let them be on their way."

Augusta threw her arms around Lucy. "I don't know how you did it, but thank you!"

"You're welcome. Go enjoy your new life in Dallas."

As the deputy hustled Augusta and her husband out the door, Lucy lingered. "Seems like your forfeiture process could use a little fine-tuning."

"The process is just fine," Blackwell said, a warning edging his voice. "But I think you're right, the men are maybe getting a bit overzealous. Perhaps some extra training on the finer points of the law. What do you think?" He made it sound as if they were partners.

Last thing Lucy wanted was to antagonize him, especially when she was getting ready to make a request of his department, so she nodded. "I think that's a good idea."

She waved to Augusta and her husband as the deputy pulled their van up from the impound lot and had them sign the paperwork.

"So, Mrs. Guardino. What brought you back here? I thought your associate finished with the evidence review." His tone was formal, his expression guarded. He must have assumed

TK told her about his family's possible involvement with the killings, but clearly was uncomfortable discussing it here. Not that she blamed him. TK was right. Any interviews with Blackwell would be better done in private and away from the sheriff station.

"Oh, she did, pretty much. There are just a few loose ends," Lucy said breezily. "You know how it is with lawyers looking over your shoulder. Can't leave anything undone. Besides, poor TK spent most of the day shut up in that records area of yours, and it wouldn't be fair to send her back. I thought I'd come finish up for her."

"That's mighty nice of you. Wouldn't expect a former FBI agent to get her hands dirty like that, rummaging through a bunch of dusty files."

Lucy smiled at him. "Oh, Sheriff, you'd be surprised at what I'd do for a case."

CHAPTER 27

DAVID PACED HIS cramped motel room, weaving in and out of the document cartons he'd moved over from the Sweetbriar. To think that after all these years...it was painful even to hope.

Not to mention the guilt at the fact that he'd actually believed his father was guilty, capable of committing such a heinous crime.

He'd tried to call his mother but the nurse said she was having a bad day, had finally fallen asleep. Now he sat on the edge of the bed and buried his face in his hands. He was such an idiot. All that anger was what had driven him through school, given him the strength to face the bloody streets of Baltimore working the crime beat, sent him halfway around the world to more blood and death. As if he needed to see the worst people could do in order to understand his own life.

And it was all a lie.

Maria—he had to tell his mother. Or should he wait until the lawyers got back to him? Last thing she needed was the pain of false hope.

She'd never given up on Michael. David sprang from the bed and grabbed his keys. She deserved to know her faith had not been misplaced. Even if it might take the courts and justice system time to agree.

She deserved to hear from him, in person, that he now believed. Just like she had all those years. He believed in his father.

He opened the door to find TK standing outside, hand raised, poised to knock.

"Good," she said, breezing past him into his room. "You're still here. I need your help."

TK glanced around Ruiz's room crowded with the files he'd moved from the Sweetbriar. She spied his laptop perched on the nightstand between the two beds. "Do you have a printer?"

"Yeah, why?" He closed the door and moved to the TV console. Tucked beside the TV, one corner hanging off the edge, was a small inkjet. "What do you need?"

Energy radiated from her like electricity. "I'm going to crack this. Tonight."

He frowned and shook his head at her. "What are you talking about?"

"This case. Your father's case. We're going to find out who did it."

———◆———

LUCY MADE HER way down to the records area in the basement of the sheriff's department. A tall man in his sixties, his gray hair cropped tight, military style, manned the reception desk. PRESCOTT, his nametag read.

"Why should I waste more of our department's time and resources on your wild-goose chase to free a killer?" Prescott asked after she explained who she was.

"Deputy, someone has given you the wrong impression of exactly why we're here," Lucy answered. "I was an FBI agent for fifteen years. Last thing I want is for a killer to walk free. We're here to review the evidence and prevent that."

He frowned. "I thought you were working for the Justice Project—all those bleeding hearts want is to empty the prisons and blame everything on honest cops."

"We don't work for them. We only want the facts. If we can find evidence that supports the original conviction, we give that to the Justice Project and make sure it's on the record. Hard to argue against the truth, right?"

"Yeah, except those lawyers never seem to realize that. Okay." He gave her a grudging nod. "What do you want from us?"

"It's a little thing, really. Just tidying up loose ends so the lawyers can't use it against us." Lucy chose her pronoun carefully and edged closer to Prescott so their bodies were now aligned, facing the same direction, standing side by side. "In the chaos of the original case, no one ran fingerprints from the bullets found in the murder weapon."

"Why should they? We already had Manning's prints in the victims' blood on the revolver."

"Ah, but if his prints are also on the bullets, then we

could argue premedication."

His eyes lit up. Every law enforcement officer knew the power of premedication when it came to prosecuting a suspect. "Right. Good. Let's see the lawyers try an appeal after that."

"Exactly. How long would it take to run through the local and state databases and AFIS? We can't just compare any prints found only to Manning's, that would appear prejudicial."

"With our new systems, everything's tied together. I can probably have an answer for you by tomorrow. How's that sound?"

She clasped him by the arm. "Deputy Prescott, you're my hero. With your help, we're going to nail the coffin shut on this actor. Can you ask your people to email me a copy of the results?"

"Sure, no problem. You'd get them anyway with that court order." His smile turned to a smirk. "Guess the lawyers are gonna regret getting that—opened the path up to our ending any chance of their appeal."

"Thanks again. I'm so grateful for your assistance on this."

"Least I can do. That was the worst crime we've seen around here in living history. Hope to never see anything like that again."

"You and me both. Take care, now."

———— ♦ ————

TK BOUNCED ON her toes, loving the charge of adrenaline racing through her as she faced Ruiz. God, how she'd missed this feeling. Having a mission, a direct course of action, and knowing she was the one to get the job done. She felt alive again. "I need you to print out some photos."

Ruiz's frown deepened. "TK, what did you find?"

"Nothing. Not yet. But that kid, Alan? Lucy agreed to talk with him. Show him photos taken from the time of the murders." She turned to the case files, rummaging through them. "I need copies of your dad's, your uncle's." She pulled their booking photos from the files. "Also Powell's—we have one of him somewhere, right?"

He moved past her to another carton. "Here." He handed her an old DMV photocopy.

"Good. Now, I just need two more. You should be able to find them online." She thrust his laptop into his hands. He sank onto the bed and balanced it across his knees.

"Let me guess. Roscoe Blackwell."

"Try his obituary or funeral." She plopped down beside him, grabbing the computer before it could bounce free. A quick online search and she found what she wanted: Roscoe Blackwell's obituary photo. She sent it to the printer. Found another story about his funeral that had a good shot of Carole Blackwell clutching Caleb's hand at the graveside ceremony. In for a penny...

Ruiz retrieved the photos from the printer. "I still can't believe a woman could have done it."

"Not me. I suspect everyone. And why not a woman? All she'd need is to threaten one of the kids and Lily would have done anything she said. You don't need physical strength to stab someone or pull a trigger. Once you've made your mind up, all it takes is the mental will to do it."

She sorted through the photos. The three from the case files fit into the palm of her hand, the two from the printer were larger. Would it make a difference to Alan Martin? If he had brain damage, she didn't want to confuse him.

"Does Lucy know you're doing this?" Ruiz interrupted her thoughts. "Last I heard from her, she was at the sheriff's station. Something about helping a woman with the forfeitures."

TK rolled her eyes. She wished Lucy would stay on mission. The forfeitures were a waste of time, had nothing to do with the Martin case. "She knows."

David nodded, still looking a bit stunned that they might actually be able to save his father. As if it had only just hit him that he might, someday soon, have his family back—for the first time in his life.

TK couldn't help herself, she let her excitement overcome her, and kissed him on the cheek before dancing out of the room, clutching the photos.

CHAPTER 28

LUCY WALKED BACK from the sheriff's department wishing she'd brought her cane with her. Funny how she could push through the pain when she was doing her rehab—much more grueling than a simple crossing of a street and a parking lot. Thankfully, there really wasn't anything more she could do today except finish reviewing all the files TK had scanned that morning. Then she'd talk to Nick, come up with a plan to interview Alan without causing him any trauma.

Which meant taking her brace off and putting her feet up. Even the thought made her move faster. Until she reached the motel parking lot and noticed something missing: her rental Tahoe.

Where the hell had TK gone now? Wherever it was, she still wasn't answering her phone.

Lucy knocked on David's door. "Have you seen TK?" she asked, hating how amateurish it made her sound, not knowing where her team was or why they'd left.

"She went to talk to Alan Martin. Wanted to show him photos. Said you knew."

"Alan? Photos?" Anger cut off her questions. She hadn't specifically told TK to wait for her, had assumed she could figure that out for herself.

Usually Lucy would applaud initiative in her team members—Lord knew, she'd followed plenty of leads on her own without asking permission from superiors—but this wasn't the FBI and these weren't trained agents. "Can I borrow your car?"

"I was going to go see my mother," he said.

"It's not that far out of your way. You can drop me off. I'll bring her back in the Tahoe."

He frowned, then nodded and led the way out to an older Ford Escape. She climbed into the passenger seat. "I really appreciate it."

"Sure. Not like there are many taxis around here."

"Which photos did she take?" Lucy asked. No way would they get a second chance at this. She tried TK's cell again. No answer. Fuming, Lucy left a terse message, "Call me. Now."

David sensed her agitation. "She only did it because she wanted to impress you. Don't sell her short. You know how she got that Bronze Star?"

"No, how?"

"Pilot friend who saw it all told me. When she and a wounded SEAL were separated from the rest of the team, she protected him as insurgents attacked their position. Killed several and held their ground until the team made it back to them. She's not stupid and she's not running off half-cocked. She knows what she's doing."

Lucy was silent, staring at the parched fields with their wilted grass and cracked hard packed earth as they drove. "It's not so much that I doubt that. It's just that I—"

"Don't trust her. You should."

"Maybe she needs to trust me."

He shook his head and laughed. It was nice to hear—so different from his usual voice. "I think you two are maybe more alike than either of you will admit."

She started to protest, then realized he had a point.

Her phone rang. Wash, back in Beacon Falls.

"Found Powell," he said.

"Great. When can we interview him?"

"Not so great. He's dead. Killed in a car crash in Colorado eleven years ago."

———◆———

TK WAS DRIVING with one hand while trying to follow a map that was missing most of the roads she was passing when her phone rang. The battery was still dangerously low; she'd only had a short time to charge it while Lucy had been leading the team through their discussion. "O'Connor," she answered, expecting it to be Lucy ready to ream her out for taking the Tahoe.

"It's Caleb. One of my deputies told me your boss asked him to fingerprint the bullets from the murder weapon."

"Makes sense. They're the only remaining pieces of evidence that haven't been fully tested." There was a long pause and she glanced to make sure she still had bars and the call hadn't been dropped. "Is that a problem?"

"No. Just thought you should know. Those prints will come back to my father. It was his revolver."

Now it was her turn to remain silent. "How long have you known?"

"Ever since I became sheriff and saw the case files with photos of the weapon. It's been in the Blackwell family for generations. Well, until now. You might as well tell your boss about Roscoe, earn some brownie points. At least some good could come from this mess." His tone was dour.

TK's phone buzzed with a call waiting. Lucy. Again. She ignored it.

"Just because his weapon was used doesn't make him the killer." TK found herself trying to give him hope. Some hope, though—because her money was on his mother. Plus, how difficult would it have been for Carole Blackwell to dose her husband's bourbon with those sleeping pills?

"It's a pretty damning circumstantial case. And who needs proof with Roscoe dead and buried?"

"Michael Manning," she reminded him. "But I might have the answer to that." She leaned forward and peered through the windshield, trying to make out yet another farm lane's street sign. Ahh...at last something she recognized: the sign for the federal ag research land. The Martin place was down the road from it. "The Martin house is between your land and Drew Saylor's, right?"

"Kind of. Our land circles back down to the river, meets up with Drew's western boundary. Why?"

"I'm headed to his place now to speak with Alan Martin— I mean, Alan Saylor. Did you know Drew had adopted him?"

"Sure, everyone did. Kid's like deaf and dumb, though,

had brain damage. He never came back to school—no one ever even sees him. From what I hear, he needs constant care, is homebound."

Not quite what Lucy described. TK hoped Caleb had gotten it wrong. She spotted the lane leading to the Saylor spread and turned off the county road.

"Drew Saylor is very protective of his boy," Caleb continued. "Best to let me talk with him first, ease into the idea."

"No need, I'm here now." She pulled up to an electronic gate. Seemed like overkill with no one around for miles except for Caleb and his mother. "Are we still on for dinner?"

"Sure. Call me as soon as you're done there."

"Will do." She spotted an intercom mounted to the gate and pressed the button.

No response but she thought she saw movement at one of the windows at the house. It was hard to see, the sun was shining right into her eyes. She tried again and this time a man answered. "Who is it?"

"My name is TK O'Connor. I work with Lucy Guardino and the Beacon Group. We needed to follow up with a few things. It won't take long, I promise."

An even longer silence. Then the gate clicked and swung open as a man appeared on the front porch, a shotgun in his hand. Caleb was right. Drew Saylor did take his privacy very seriously.

"I already told Guardino everything I know," he said as she exited the Tahoe.

"Actually," she said, climbing the steps to the porch and ignoring the weapon he still held. "I was hoping to speak with your son, Alan."

CHAPTER 29

TK KNEW GAINING Drew Saylor's confidence would be tough. As soon as she mentioned Alan, he straightened and stepped back, raising the shotgun ever so slightly. Pure protective reflex.

She countered by plopping down into one of the canvas chairs on the porch. Giving him the high ground while also making it more difficult for him to get rid of her. "Tell me about Alan. I was surprised you brought him back here after you adopted him, but now that I see how beautiful this place is, I guess I understand. It's very serene."

He gave a small grunt, glanced through the screen door into the house, and relaxed his grip on the shotgun. "Wish it was something like that, but it boiled down to money. Took all our savings, me and Beth, to get the adoption finalized, plus all the costs of his special school. We didn't have much choice. I was still sheriff then, and this place has been in my family for generations and is paid off, so we stayed."

"Your wife, is she here? I'd love to meet her."

"One of her nurses is on vacation so she's working three-to-eleven this week. Maybe you could come back tomorrow when she is here." He gestured toward the steps.

TK beamed up at him as he spoke. Not moving an inch. Finally, all the command authority drained from his voice. He slumped into the chair opposite her. "What do you want with Alan?"

"Nothing, if you think it would be too upsetting for him," she reassured him. "But it'd be a huge help to us if he could take a look at a few photos."

"What photos? Why?"

"New evidence has come to light. In addition to the fact that you coerced Michael Manning's confession and denied him his Miranda rights." It was dirty pool, reminding him of his own failures in the case, but what choice did she have?

"What new evidence?" His eyes went flat as did his voice. "Only evidence we had was Michael Manning's prints on the murder weapon in the victims' blood. Nothing you find can argue that away. No matter how that confession came to pass, it was a solid case."

"Would you still think that if I told you Lily Martin was having an affair with Roscoe Blackwell? Or that he was the father of her baby? And the revolver used to kill Peter Martin belonged to him?"

He recoiled, sucking in his breath, his poker face demolished by her words. "You think Roscoe could have—" He shook his head. "No. I mean, he was one coldhearted son of a bitch, but if you'd seen...no, I can't believe it."

"But you can believe a good kid like Michael Manning shooting Peter Martin in cold blood?"

"That's different. He was protecting his brother."

"Right. The brother so incapacitated by the time you arrested him he couldn't even sign his name to the booking form? You really think he was able to restrain Lily Martin and systematically torture her for hours without leaving behind a single piece of evidence?"

His lips twisted in consideration. "Not a night has gone by, twenty-nine years, this case hasn't haunted me. But I always thought the right people were behind bars. Was most afraid that I hadn't been able to hunt down Ronnie Powell, that he might some day return to hurt my son. Now you're telling me it was Roscoe Blackwell? That I screwed up, ruined two men's lives, and let a killer walk free?"

She waited, giving him time to think. A man appeared at the door behind Saylor, his palms spread against the screen as he looked wistfully at TK. Unlike Saylor, he had light-colored hair and eyes. He was thin, in his mid-thirties, and when TK met his gaze, his face lit up as if she was the answer to his prayers.

She slowly rose and approached Alan as if he were a wild animal. But he didn't bolt. Instead, his smile widened and he pushed the door open a crack, the hinges squeaking.

Saylor looked over his shoulder, smiled at his son, and beckoned for him to join them. "It's all right."

Alan bolted through the door and flung his arms around TK, lifting her off her feet in a movement filled with pure joy.

"You look a lot like his favorite counselor at the center in Abilene," Saylor explained, getting to his feet and gently tapping his son on the arm. "He never gets to meet new people—does better with a strict schedule and structure. But he obviously likes you."

Alan finally released TK from the bear hug and stepped back, eyes downcast shyly.

"So nice to meet you, Alan," she said. His gaze snapped up at the sound of his name. "My name is TK."

Saylor slid his phone from his pocket, squinting at the screen. Moments later, the sound of a car approaching caught her attention. Saylor was also on full alert, reaching for his shotgun once again. TK was no stranger to bunker mentality but couldn't imagine living like that for twenty-nine years. If they could prove Roscoe Blackwell was the killer, maybe Saylor and his family could finally enjoy some freedom from fear?

Then she recognized the vehicle. David Ruiz's SUV. It stopped at the gate and the passenger door opened. A very unhappy Lucy Guardino climbed down, glaring at TK as she limped down the drive.

———◆———

AT LEAST DREW SAYLOR hadn't shot TK, Lucy thought as she made her way to the gate. David waved and did a U-turn, heading back out the drive.

Saylor touched his phone and the gate swung open. She'd only managed a few steps, cursing her rebellious left ankle spiking with pain, when Alan came running toward her. He said nothing, not verbally, but his body language spoke volumes as he wrapped her into a joyful hug.

"Nice to see you again, Alan," she said, patting his arm

like she'd noticed his mother doing that morning. He responded by gently releasing her, one palm pressed against her injured side as if supporting her. Pretty observant kid. Made her wonder exactly how impaired he really was.

TK joined her as well. "Thought we agreed I'd be doing this. Without parental supervision."

Implying that Lucy thought TK was too young and inexperienced to handle a tricky interview by herself. Not far from the truth, but how was Lucy supposed to trust her when she'd only known TK for a day and had yet to see how she would handle herself?

"We only have one shot at this," Lucy said. "Figured it was better as a team effort."

They joined Saylor on the porch. He looked nervous, as if unused to having so many strangers at his home. Alan seemed perfectly at ease, plopping down on the porch swing and patting either side of him for TK and Lucy to join him. TK glanced at Lucy and took the lead, sliding in on Alan's left.

"Mr. Saylor," Lucy began to apologize, glad that TK hadn't disturbed the boy but also embarrassed by the younger woman's actions.

He held a hand up. "TK explained it to me. I had no idea, never dreamed I could be so wrong."

"I told him Caleb Blackwell identified the murder weapon as belonging to his father. And about Roscoe Blackwell's affair with Lily Martin." TK kept her voice soft as if these were ordinary facts to discuss rather than ones that provided a man with a motive to annihilate an entire family. Alan's family.

The fact that Sheriff Blackwell had volunteered the information about the revolver was a bit surprising, but it fit with everything else that they were uncovering. Still, Lucy couldn't help but wonder at the man's motivations.

"They're running the bullets for fingerprints," Lucy told Saylor. "Roscoe Blackwell's prints should be in the database, right?"

"They were in our elimination set—privacy issues, those were destroyed once the case was closed. But they should also have them from his suicide. You'll need to ask them to pull those from the old archives—they're paper only, wouldn't have been scanned into any of the newer digital databases."

"We'll ask Prescott to take care of that."

TK made a noise. "You got Prescott to cooperate?"

Lucy ignored her and edged Saylor farther away from Alan. "Did anyone ever talk to Alan about what happened?"

"They tried." Saylor turned so both their backs were to the porch swing. "It was clear he remembered something terrible. He'd go into a full-blown panic attack. But he was never able to communicate anything or answer any questions, not even with a yes-no head nod."

"How does he communicate?"

"Beth taught him a little sign language—he can only manage a few words, but it's enough. He knows his alphabet, can read at a second grade level. Mostly, we just know him well enough that we don't need any words—you've seen how he is. Emotionally, he's as honest and easy to read as the six-year-old he was when it happened."

She sighed. "Some days I wonder if we wouldn't all be better off that way."

"Despite what happened, most days he wakes up and sees the world as filled with joy. As if seeing it for the first time." His expression was a mixed blessing: sorrow and gratitude and love. "Kept me going all these years. Don't know what I'd do without him."

"Has anyone ever tried a cognitive interview? Not direct questions, more of a sensory based re-creation of the events—"

"I know what a cognitive interview is," he interrupted her. "Look, what I did with the Manning brothers, those interrogations, you have to understand, I'd only been elected sheriff a few weeks earlier. Not a clue what I was doing. Hell, back then, no one knew what we know now. Not an excuse, just saying, I learned along the way."

"Twenty-nine years is a long time to be living afraid for your family's safety."

He hung his head. "I really thought…but if I was wrong, if it wasn't the Mannings and Ronnie Powell, then I can't let an innocent man rot in prison."

"Can we talk with Alan? Have him look at some photos? With you right here with him, of course."

Saylor's forehead creased with worry. "Let me see them first."

TK sprang up and reached for her canvas laptop bag sitting near the railing. She fished out a handful of papers and gave them to Saylor. He shuffled through them. "Not this booking photo of Dicky. It's much too scary. The others, I guess they're okay."

Lucy glanced at TK. Alan seemed to have bonded with her. "You sure about this?"

"Yes." The younger woman straightened, a Marine's backbone shining through her posture. "I can do it." She glanced at Saylor and then Alan. "Without upsetting him."

She resumed her seat beside Alan on the swing. "Alan, I hear you're a pretty smart kid when it comes to remembering things. Do you remember the Goldilocks story I was just telling you?"

He nodded eagerly.

"How many bears were in it?"

He held up a hand with three fingers.

"Three. That's right. Good job." She squeezed his arm in encouragement. "Okay, now this one might be tougher. I want you to remember way, way back to when you were little. Something scary happened back then—but it's only a memory, a story, like Goldilocks, so even though it's scary, you don't have to worry because your dad, he's right here and so are Lucy and me."

Alan's smile faded, sunshine banished by storm clouds.

Saylor moved to squat in front of his son. "Hey, champ, if it's too scary, just let me know and we can stop any time. Got it?"

Slowly, his lips tight, eyes creased, Alan nodded.

"Okay," TK began again. "So what I want is for you to think back, way back to before the scary thing. Anything you remember is fine. You and your mom and baby sister went to the store, right? Then you drove home. Was there a song playing on the radio? It was almost dark outside, so maybe the birds were singing or the insects chirping? Do you remember anything from back then?"

Alan squinched his face with effort, then nodded again. He tugged his hand free from TK's and began motioning with it.

"That's his sign for cookie," Saylor interpreted. Then he frowned. "He's signing 'bad cookie boy,' over and over. Is that right, Alan? Bad cookie boy?"

Alan opened his eyes wide and nodded so eagerly his chin

almost hit his chest and the swing rocked. His hands never stopped moving, the same motions over and over, as if he couldn't stop. He opened his mouth as if screaming and moved his legs up and down as if running. And still the same signs.

"Bad cookie boy. Bad cookie boy," Saylor translated.

Alan twisted his head to seek out each adult's gaze, his own imploring, begging for understanding. His face twisted with frustration and more than a hint of fear as he grew more and more agitated. Saylor pulled him into his arms, hugging him tight, stroking his upper arm, until he calmed.

"What does it mean?" TK asked Lucy.

Lucy motioned to TK. They left Saylor and his son and moved to the opposite side of the porch. "The evidence inventory list, there was a box of cookies on there, right?"

"Empty box, found in the trash. Prints on it came back to the elimination set plus two unknown."

"The elimination set included Roscoe Blackwell?"

"Roscoe, Caleb, Alan, his family, and all the first responders on scene." TK frowned. "I saw photos of Roscoe over at Caleb's house. The guy was huge, built like a big, burly bear. No one would ever call him a boy."

"He would have seemed even bigger to a scared six-year-old." Lucy stepped toward the swing where Saylor had coaxed a smile out of Alan once more. Resilient kid. She hated asking any more of him. "Does Alan have a separate sign for man?"

"Sure. Show her, champ."

Alan beamed at Lucy and moved his right hand from a salute-like motion at his forehead down to his chest. Very different from the duck-quacking motion at his forehead that he'd performed earlier.

"Okay, no mistaking those two." She turned back to TK. "Do you have the scan of the grocery receipt from that day?"

"Yeah, here you go." She held her phone out to Lucy. The red low battery light was blinking furiously.

Lucy scrolled down the list of groceries bought and never eaten twenty-nine years ago. "One box of cookies." She used her own phone to search the other evidence, including the crime scene photos, comparing it to the grocery list. "No other cookies found in the house."

Saylor approached, keeping his voice low. "We assumed she'd given them to Alan to keep him busy while she unloaded the car and that the unknown prints came from store clerks or other shoppers." He glanced over his shoulder at Alan who was now swinging happily. "Do you really think the killer stopped to eat cookies? In the middle of all that carnage? And Alan saw him?"

"Or knew who he was, somehow connected him to cookies. We should run those prints from the box through the current databases." Lucy hesitated. "Besides Alan, there's only one other boy who's involved in this case."

He nodded grimly. "I know. Caleb Blackwell. But he was only twelve—I just can't see it. Maybe Alan meant something else. TK asked him to focus on the time before the killings. Maybe it was him getting into the cookies and Lily told him he was a bad boy?"

"No way of knowing. How long was Caleb a deputy under you before he was elected sheriff?"

"A little more than ten years, why?"

"So he started with the department about fifteen years ago?"

TK frowned. "Lucy," her tone held a warning, "we should focus on the Martin case."

Lucy ignored her. "No concerns during that time?"

Saylor shook his head, obviously puzzled yet also considering the idea that one of his deputies could have been a killer. "No. Nothing. A bit of a brown-noser, played the politics better than most, but I used that to my advantage, set him to more administrative duties."

"So he wouldn't have been involved in anything like impounding abandoned vehicles?"

"Well, sure, he still patrolled. We all did back then, even me. What's this all about?"

"It's about fourteen missing girls and their cars all being turned into scrap metal by order of the sheriff's department. All in the past fifteen years, all right here in Blackwell County."

CHAPTER 30

"NO," SAYLOR SAID. "I don't believe it." Lucy couldn't blame him. She was basically implying he'd had a serial killer under his command.

"Neither do I," TK put in. "Those vehicles could have been diverted by anyone."

"I may have put two innocent men behind bars," Saylor continued. "Let's not condemn another without concrete proof."

Lucy raised her hands in surrender. "You're right. TK, could you call Prescott, ask him to run those prints on the cookie box? Tell him it's for the same reason as running the bullets. He won't argue."

"Sure, but my phone is about dead. Can I put it on your charger?"

"Table by the door," Saylor told her. TK went inside.

While they waited, Lucy told him about what Wash and

Tommy had discovered while researching the forfeitures.

Saylor stalked to the corner of the porch farthest from where Alan swung. Lucy joined him.

"What if it was Caleb?" he asked in a low voice. "The Blackwells control everything in this county. No one can touch them."

"The FBI can. I still have contacts there."

He hung his head. "Could I really have been such a fool? Not seen it? I mentored that boy, treated him like a son—he lost his own father so young."

"I've been wrong before," Lucy said. But the more she fit the pieces together, the more certain she was. Although her theory was worthless without evidence.

TK rejoined them a moment later. "No idea what you did to the man, but Prescott was happy to oblige."

"Good. We're going to try the photos, see if Alan responds to any of them."

Saylor's expression was grim as he moved across the porch and squatted in front of his son while TK resumed her seat beside Alan.

"Hey, champ," he started. "I need you to stop swinging for a moment and look at some pictures. Kind of like the flash cards Miss Reynolds uses at the center. Just point to anyone you know, okay? And if you don't know them, no problem, you just don't point and shake your head. Sound good?"

Alan nodded eagerly, holding his hand out.

"No, I'll hold them. You just look," Saylor told him. He turned over Michael Manning's booking photo.

Alan squinted intently, then balled his hand up and shook his head.

"Okay. Good job. Let's try another." This time it was Ronnie Powell's DMV photo. Again Alan shook his head. Saylor sank back on his heels, obviously reluctant to proceed. "Good, good. You okay to do a few more?" Alan nodded eagerly. "How about this man?"

This time Alan pointed and nodded his head. He tapped Roscoe Blackwell's photo and smiled at Saylor as if expecting a reward for his efforts.

Saylor glanced at Lucy and TK. He seemed relieved. "Guess you're wrong. It was Roscoe, not Caleb."

Lucy approached Alan. He revealed no trace of fear or anxiety. "Alan, you're doing real good." She nodded to Saylor. "Your dad has just one more to show you, okay?"

Before Saylor could show Alan the final photo, his phone chimed. He slid it from his pocket and glanced at the screen. "Someone just turned into the lane." He stood. "It's Caleb Blackwell." He turned to Lucy and TK. "How much does he know?"

"Nothing about our new research," Lucy assured him.

"He told me he might stop by to see how Alan did with the interview," TK put in.

Alan tugged on his father's arm, craning his neck to look at the last two photos still gripped in Saylor's hand. Suddenly, he bolted from the swing, leaving it careening, hitting TK in the back. A wild, keening noise filled the air as he pushed past Lucy, knocking over two of the canvas chairs, and ran into the house, hands covering his head.

"Alan!" Saylor called. "Stop!"

Lucy caught sight of the photos he'd showed Alan, scattered on the porch floor. One was Dicky Manning's booking photo, the one Saylor had deemed too scary and had folded inside out to hide the image.

The one Alan had reacted to was pinned face up beneath the leg of one of the overturned canvas chairs. It was the first time Lucy had gotten a good look at it. The almost thirty-year-old image was of Carole Blackwell with her son, Caleb, beside her. Whose face had frightened Alan so much? The mother's or the son's?

Alan disappeared inside, the door banging in his wake. Saylor shook his head and started after him. The roar of Caleb Blackwell's SUV stopped him. The truck was coming around the bend and soon would be at the gate.

"We'll take care of Blackwell," Lucy suggested. Whether Blackwell was here to protect his mother or himself, she wanted to keep him away from Alan.

Saylor hesitated, his gaze on the door his son had vanished through. He shook his head in frustration. "No. When he's like this Alan won't respond to me, only his mother. He'll be in his closet, his safe place."

"Like before," TK whispered.

"Like before," Saylor said, his voice haunted. "I found him the first time. You'd think he'd let me—" He shook his head once more, then straightened. "Could you keep an eye on him? Let me handle Caleb."

"Just send him away," Lucy said. "Then we'll figure out what to do about all this. In the meantime, we'll be right inside."

TK frowned at her, but Lucy gestured for her to follow as Blackwell's SUV pulled up at the gate. They entered the house, shutting the door behind them. Through the window, Lucy watched as Saylor kept his shotgun at the ready and slowly climbed down the porch steps and headed across the dry grass to meet the sheriff at the gate.

"Check the back," she told TK. "Find another way out of here."

TK's frown turned puzzled. "Why? You can't seriously think Caleb is guilty? If it wasn't Roscoe, then it must have been Carole Blackwell Alan was reacting to. Maybe Caleb has been covering up her crimes all along."

"Either way, doesn't matter." Lucy grabbed her cell phone. They had no proof Blackwell had come for anything except information. Did he know they suspected him? How?

She'd had three bars out on the porch but now, nothing. No service at all. She glanced toward the front windows. He'd come prepared.

"Must be using the jammer," she muttered. Which meant Blackwell was ready for anything. Damn, damn, damn. Lucy scanned the room. She had her Beretta and a spare magazine, but surely Saylor had more weapons. Ahh...beside the china cabinet was a standing gun safe. She strode over to it. Locked. Digital keypad. Of course, with someone like Alan living here, they wouldn't take chances. "Are you armed?"

"No. Lucy—"

She spun to TK. "I have one job and only one job for you right now."

"What?" TK was watching out the window, her body tense.

"You take that boy and you get him to safety. Here, take my weapon." She unclipped her holster and held out the Beretta. TK took it, eyes narrowed as her fingers closed on the pistol's grip.

TK released the Beretta's magazine, checking the chamber and rounds, then reloaded, all in the fluid motions of an expert. Between the former sheriff running interference out front and the former Marine taking point on Alan's escape, they just might be able to save the boy. Lucy hoped.

CHAPTER 31

DAVID DROVE AWAY from Drew Saylor's house intending to head straight to Abilene and his mother. But he couldn't stop thinking about Caleb Blackwell's mother, Carole. Could she have killed an entire family? Or covered her husband's own crimes?

Growing up, the Blackwells had always seemed like distant, benevolent royalty. The mansion on the hill overlooking the river was their palace. When spotted in public they waved politely, but never seemed real—certainly never concerned with the hard-scrapped lives of people like David and his mother.

All his life, people like the Blackwells had looked down on David and his mother for their relationship with a pair of convicted killers. What if the real killer was closer to home?

He couldn't resist. When he saw the turn for the Blackwell estate, he took it. He needed to meet Carole, the woman who might hold the key to his father's freedom.

He'd been surprised Caleb had run for sheriff. Surely he had enough to keep him busy with all the various Blackwell enterprises? But Carole Blackwell was only in her early sixties, she probably still controlled the business. David remembered her as a woman always smiling with her mouth while always frowning with her eyes—and she didn't miss a thing, had once caught him filching a brownie from a Founder's Day bake sale and hauled him over to his mother, berating him right in the middle of practically the whole county.

Maybe being the top lawman in the county was Caleb's way of finally standing up for himself, David wondered as he drove the winding road up to the manor, noticing that even the Blackwell's manicured lawn suffered from the drought.

The house was bigger than he'd remembered, seeing it from the distance as a kid. What would it have been like, growing up here? Caleb had also lost his father not long after David's dad was sent to prison, so, like David, it was just him and his mother.

Along with a bevvy of servants, he amended the thought as he rang the doorbell and a uniformed maid answered.

"The sheriff is out," she said before he could introduce himself.

Caleb would have been only a boy at the time of the killings. Carole Blackwell would have more valuable insights about her husband's possible involvement. Or, maybe even her own.

If she lied, he'd be able to see the truth in her body language. All he had to do was get her talking. "That's all right. I'd like to speak with Mrs. Blackwell. Tell her it's David Ruiz."

He'd remembered to grab his electrolarynx and use it.

The maid frowned at his strange voice and hesitated. A voice from behind her called out, "It's okay, Maggie. Let him in."

The maid gave a small curtsy and stepped back from the door. David crossed the threshold into the marble-floored foyer that was larger than the apartment he'd grown up in. A tall woman with salt-and-pepper hair wearing slacks and a blouse much too elegant to be called business attire approached, dismissing the maid with a wave of her hand.

"David Ruiz. Of course. I've followed your investigative reporting, although I have some doubts about your current crusade for justice for your father. But I am curious. What can I do for you?" As she spoke, she entwined her arm with his and led him through a formal living room the size of a basketball court to a more intimate sitting room.

He chose his words carefully. "I'd like to talk to you about the Martin case. Some new evidence has come to light that I hoped you could help with."

"Of course, anything. Please, sit down." She didn't seem perturbed by his voice at all.

He took a seat on the couch. All the furniture was an elegant shade of blue with subtle patterns woven into the fabric. The main color in the room came from wallpaper that appeared to have been hand painted with watercolor washes. The setting sun beamed pink-tinged light in through the tall windows, bathing the room in a rosy glow.

"Let me get us some refreshments," she said, leaving the room before he could protest.

While she was gone, he turned on the recording app on his phone and slipped it into his shirt pocket where it would catch every word. He wasn't concerned with forgetting anything she told him, but rather was interested in what Lucy and TK would think since they'd be able to hear the emotional context in her speech he was deaf to.

It was amazing how many people lied during the course of a day—or how often. Made him wonder about many of the subjects he'd interviewed when he was a journalist. So far Carole Blackwell's body language had been totally genuine. A baseline. It would be interesting to see how she reacted when they discussed the killings in more detail.

Carole returned, surprising him by carrying a covered tray and setting it on the coffee table in front of him. Behind her came a maid carrying another tray, this one with two glasses, a pitcher of martinis and a decanter of whiskey.

"Just set that on the sideboard. We'll help ourselves," Carole directed the maid. "Thank you. That will be all. You and the others can leave for the day." She waited until the maid had vanished through a door leading into the rear of the house. "You look like a whiskey man," she said in a hearty tone, pouring him a generous portion from the decanter.

David didn't have the heart to tell her that he rarely drank anything stronger than beer—all the meds he'd been on after his injuries had weaned him free of any desire to allow himself to cede control. A little fuzzy around the edges like last night at the Sweetbriar with TK was the closest he came. He accepted the glass, rolled it between his palms as if getting it to just the right temperature. A sniff told him it was the good stuff—sure to be mellow, warming from the inside.

She poured herself a martini, garnished it, and perched on a dainty chair opposite him, legs crossed at the ankles and tucked below the chair, ladylike. "Now, tell me about this new evidence you've uncovered."

"Well, ma'am, I'd love to first hear what you remember about that time. If you don't mind."

"Of course." She leaned back, sipping her drink, her gaze distant. "You know Roscoe was never the same after? That he—died the following year?"

"Yes, ma'am. I heard. Sorry for your loss."

Her eyes narrowed at him. "That gadget you're using to talk with, you don't really need it, do you? What exactly happened?"

He lowered the electrolarynx and continued without any artifice. "Humvee I was in got hit by an IED. Lost the part of my brain that controls emotions when I talk. Funny thing is, if I laugh or sing, it comes out normal—but seeing as I never did have much of a singing voice, I figured it was easiest and less scary for folks to use this gadget. Put them at ease a bit."

"Of course. I understand. I sometimes feel when I watch people who aren't, shall we say, sincere, that there's a disconnect between what they believe and what they say. Is that what you're talking about?"

"Something like that, yes, ma'am. I hope it doesn't bother you too much."

"No, not at all. It's rather refreshing in a way."

"Anyway, you were telling me about the night of the killings."

She leaned back, appraising him. "I loved my husband very much, but Roscoe was a man of enormous energy and appetites. He was never satisfied, always wanted more. Including, I'm afraid, the affections of younger women. Like Lily Martin."

He nodded. "They had an affair?"

"Yes. One of Roscoe's many." Even her shrug was elegant and refined. "I learned to accept it—none of his women held any threat for me. Roscoe knew I controlled the wealth and property—it was the reason why our parents had arranged our marriage, to save the Blackwell fortune, bind it to the Lytle one. And he also knew I was devoted to him and our family, would never let anything come between us."

"Did Lily Martin threaten to do that? Come between you?"

"We argued about her—not the affair, but the fact that she refused to let go of Roscoe. Even claimed her baby was his. Never proven, of course, but she threatened to go public if he didn't run away with her."

David leaned forward—she was giving herself almost as much of a motive as she was her husband. Although Roscoe Blackwell couldn't defend himself from beyond the grave. "Do you know what happened? That night?"

A strange, wistful smile twisted her face, then was gone so fast he wasn't sure if he imagined it or not.

"No. I don't know the details. But this might be helpful." With a flourish, she raised the lid from the covered tray that sat between them on the coffee table.

Instead of the *hors d'oeuvre* he'd expected, a wicked-edged filleting knife with a bone handle lay there. Dark stains covered it.

"It's the knife that killed Lily and her baby."

CHAPTER 32

TK STOOD WATCH, peeking through the curtains in Alan's room at the scene unfolding in the front yard. Saylor remained a good ten feet inside the gate, talking to Caleb Blackwell. Saylor held his shotgun, his posture alert, ready to use it. Caleb leaned casually against his SUV, clearly certain he held the upper hand.

In many ways he did. If Saylor took action, he'd have to kill Caleb immediately—there were consequences to drawing a weapon on a lawman—and he'd probably spend the rest of his life in prison answering for it. No. All Saylor could do was react to Caleb, which gave the sheriff the advantage.

The only thing they had going for them was the time Saylor bought them while he talked with Caleb, stalling him.

She glanced over her shoulder at the closet. Alan was curled up on the floor; still making that weird noise that raised the hairs on the back of her neck.

How the hell could she have been so wrong about Caleb?

She'd noticed the weird vibe between him and his mother at lunch. The way they'd both been so quick to throw Roscoe out as a suspect when they realized the case against the Mannings was unraveling.

Lucy crouched down and somehow folded herself into the closet alongside Alan's quivering body. She pulled him into a tight embrace and slowly, he went silent.

"It's going to be all right," she crooned to the boy-man, rocking him gently. "TK is going to take you out of here while I help your dad."

TK moved away from her position at the window and extended a hand, touching Alan's shoulder. He finally looked up, met her gaze. She gave him what she hoped was a reassuring smile. "I need you to help me, Alan. Can you do that? Can you show me how to get down to the river?"

His nod was tentative but he let her take his hand. Lucy released him and TK pulled him to his feet.

"I figure you build a house on a river, there's probably a boat or two out back," TK told Lucy. Alan nodded eagerly, his fearful expression easing into one of anticipation.

Lucy climbed out of the closet, wobbling on her bad leg, and turned to Alan. He was taller than Lucy but she somehow managed to reach his forehead and plant a kiss there just like TK's mom used to do when she was a child.

"You can do it, Alan," Lucy told him. "Your mom and dad will be very proud. Take good care of TK and do what she says, okay?"

An uncertain frown creased his face but then he relaxed and nodded. "Get going," Lucy told TK as they moved through the kitchen to the rear of the house.

Lucy paused to raise the handset on an old rotary-dial phone on the kitchen wall then hung up, shaking her head. "It's dead."

They reached the door. Past the small backyard was a dock. The water was too low to see from their position, but on the porch outside the kitchen door stood three fishing poles. Beside them several life jackets hung on pegs.

Lucy held the door open for TK and Alan. "You can't trust the sheriff's department. You'll need to go to the Texas Rangers or FBI. Probably Abilene."

"That's over an hour away. I can't leave you and Saylor that long."

Lucy grabbed TK's arm. "We aren't your mission. Alan is. You get him safe and then worry about the rest. Do you understand me, Marine?"

Reflex jerked TK to attention. "Yes, ma'am."

"Go. Now."

"What are you going to do?"

"Find more weapons and back up Saylor. Hopefully it won't come to that and I'm overreacting, but better safe than—"

"Dead," TK finished for her. Alan clutched at her arm with both hands. "Alan, time to go. Must be nice, living on the river. How about if you show me your boat?"

———◆———

Leaving Alan in TK's capable hands—far better the younger former Marine protect him than a woman with a gimpy leg and no military training—Lucy returned to the gun safe. She didn't have time to waste but it was worth giving it at least a try. Numbers—no idea what Saylor might choose. But letters? There were two obvious four-letter combos: his wife or his son.

She closed her eyes, visualizing a phone keypad—the alphabet began on the two key, right?—and typed in 2526: ALAN. The lock clicked open and she was rewarded with the sight of two hunting rifles, two semi-automatic pistols, and a second pump-action shotgun. She shoved two magazines of ammunition into her back pockets, grabbed the pistols and shotgun, and checked that they were loaded and ready to go as she moved through the living room back to the screen door where she could assess Saylor's situation with Caleb Blackwell.

Both men were standing on opposite sides of the gate, now only a few feet apart. Blackwell was clearly losing his patience.

"I know TK is here—that's her vehicle. What happened when she showed Alan the photos, Drew?"

How in hell did Blackwell know about the photo array?

"I told you, Alan is gone," Saylor answered. "With his mother. After that former FBI agent came around, upsetting things, we thought it best to send him away."

Blackwell scratched his scalp, tilting his hat up, squinting as he scrutinized the house. The setting sun was directly in his eyes, Lucy realized. A small advantage, but one she'd gladly take. There was no proof the sheriff's intentions were anything other than fact-finding, but no way was she taking any chances. Her job now was to buy TK and Alan as much time as possible while learning Blackwell's true intentions.

She set the shotgun just inside the door where she could reach it in two steps, concealed one pistol at the small of her back, her shirttail covering it, and tucked the other in her boot where the Velcro from her brace kept it securely in place. Finally, the damn thing was good for something. As she stood back up, she saw TK's phone still on the charger. Which meant no chance for any cavalry coming to the rescue.

She wondered again at Blackwell's convenient timing. How could he have known they were close to getting the truth? Obviously, he wasn't afraid of anything Alan could communicate, not after twenty-nine years.

But there was no way he could know about the photo array or that she wanted to check the cookie box fingerprints against the current database—one that had his prints on file. Unless...She glanced through the window. Both men still talking, no weapons drawn. As if they were both stalling.

TK's phone. It had been at the jail all night, plenty of time for Blackwell to install spyware if he wanted an easy way to keep on top of the investigation.

Lucy tapped through to the system admin screens. Unfortunately, after having her very own serial killer stalker, she had plenty of experience with spyware and how to find it buried in the recesses of a phone's inner workings. Bingo.

Which meant Blackwell was not here to see what they knew. He was here to tie up loose ends. Why hadn't he opened fire? Three well-armed, well-trained adults against one. Odds were against him, so his stalling meant he had a plan, intended to get out of this alive. Actually gave them an advantage over someone intent on suicide.

Okay, then was he stalling to give backup time to arrive? No. She couldn't see him trusting anyone else with the secrets he'd kept safe for twenty-nine years.

What the hell was his plan? He couldn't let them live—or leave, since as soon as they got past the range of the cell jammer, they'd call for help from the FBI or the Texas Rangers.

Only one way to find out. She pushed through the front door, brushing her hands on her jeans as if she'd just come from the restroom.

"Hi again, Sheriff," she called. It was hard not to wince when she used his title. There were so many new names she wanted to call him instead: killer, psychopath, slaughterer, evil sonofabitch...

"Evening, Lucy," Blackwell called back, using her first name for the first time. Was that good or bad? "Where's TK and the boy?"

Lucy leaned against the porch railing, angling herself so Saylor was out of her line of fire. Was she really considering drawing on a sworn officer of the law? Blackwell's hands were at his belt, posing no immediate threat. Yet.

Even if he was guilty of a heinous crime twenty-nine years ago and maybe more since then, she still had no proof, just a theory. She couldn't simply kill him based on a theory. Neither could Saylor. Not unless they wanted to spend the rest of their lives in prison.

With Blackwell being the highest-ranking lawman in the county, Saylor couldn't even use the castle statute as a defense. No. As much as she wanted to put Blackwell down like the animal she believed him to be, she had to wait, let him make the first move.

"You just missed TK. I sent her with David Ruiz to finish our interviews. Didn't you pass them on your way in?"

He considered that. "Blue Ford Escape?"

"That's right. I'd call her, but there's something wrong with the cell service." The last was for Saylor's benefit, to let him know there was no help coming. "I'm sure she'll be back at the motel in plenty of time for your dinner date."

He nodded, contemplating his next move, sidling to one side, placing Saylor in her crossfire. How long could they keep this game up?

Long enough for TK to get Alan to safety, she hoped.

"Okay, then," he said, turning to open the door of his Escalade. "Guess I'll catch her later. Thanks."

Neither Lucy nor Saylor relaxed their postures until he was inside the SUV and backing down the lane.

Saylor turned to rejoin her. A screech of wheels against gravel sounded. Lucy spun around.

Blackwell's SUV rammed the gate and plowed into Saylor before he could jump out of the way or even get off a shot. His body flew up against the hood, the shotgun flying from his hands, and then he was flung backward onto the ground.

She drew her weapon while retreating back inside the house where she'd have cover. She exchanged her pistol for the shotgun she had waiting and took aim.

Blackwell parked the SUV over Saylor's prone body and hopped out, brandishing his own weapon, a M4 submachine gun, using the engine compartment of the SUV as cover. "Come out and drop your weapon, Lucy. Or Saylor's dead."

Right. Like he wasn't going to kill them both anyway. She checked her phone. Still nothing. That damn jammer he was so proud of getting from the damn forfeiture money.

Blackwell was smart enough that he didn't give her a clear shot. At least not from this direction. If she could get out one of the windows on the western side of the house, she could use the trees as concealment and outflank him.

A few big ifs there. But no time for any other plan.

"What do you want, Blackwell?" she called through the door, to get his attention as she immediately sidled back out of sight and headed into the master bedroom facing the forest.

"Bring me the boy and I'll let you go," Blackwell called back. Did she look like she'd just fallen off a turnip truck? No. He was smarter than that—still stalling, but why?

She entered the bedroom. Even better than a window, there were French doors leading onto a small terrace not visible from the front of the house. She ran outside just in time to hear Saylor engage Blackwell. Not dead and not out of the game. Good.

"I don't understand," Saylor said, his voice reflecting his anguish. "Why leave Alan alive only to come after him again all these years later?"

Lucy climbed down and hid behind the shrubs around the deck. They were something dry and scratchy, with leaves that were withering and begging for water. Somewhere nearby, she smelled smoke as if someone was burning trash.

When she craned her head, she could barely make out Saylor dragging his body out from under the SUV, his face contorted in pain. If he could just keep Blackwell talking a few minutes more.

Blackwell fired a three-round burst that threw up a wave of dirt clods just past Saylor's head. Saylor froze, his hands extended in the universal sign of surrender.

"Alan was supposed to be dead. I even went back the next morning to make sure everyone was dead—and to get my father there. I wanted to see the look on his face when he realized his precious Lily and her darling baby were gone forever. But he showed up too soon and I never got to check on Alan. After that, it was too late—but he also wasn't any threat. He never saw my face and he wasn't talking anyway."

"He's still no threat to you. Walk away, no one needs to know."

As they talked, Lucy skirted the shadows and crossed the dead grass to the tree line. Now she could see the men but still had no clear shot.

Blackwell had the SUV door open, and not just for concealment. He was grabbing something from inside. "Too late now. Tell me where he is."

"Never," Saylor said.

"Thought you might say that." Blackwell threw something into the air. A gas can, its spout open. It spewed gas in a graceful arc, then landed a few feet beyond Saylor, more gasoline streaming into the parched grass surrounding him. "You listening, Lucy?"

Blackwell grabbed one more item from the SUV and held it aloft. A roadside flare. "If I have to, I'll burn this place to the ground, all of you along with it."

He turned to shout into the blue-tinted dusk surrounding the cabin. "Bring me the boy, Lucy, and I'll let you live. Without him, you have no case, so I have no reason not to let you go. Do it now or Saylor burns."

CHAPTER 33

TK JOGGED DOWN the back porch steps and headed toward the dock but Alan didn't follow. "C'mon," she called back in a hushed voice, gesturing. He shook his head solemnly and reached for a life vest, pulling it over his head.

Thanks to her experiences working with scared women and children in Iraq and Afghanistan as their villages were searched and men secured, TK understood how to calm someone's fear and panic without speaking their language. But what to do with a man who functioned with the mentality of a child and didn't speak?

The answer hit her as she sprinted back to grab a vest for herself: whatever he wants. Fastest way to get the job done. Alan proved her theory by now smiling and following after her at an easy lope.

Together they ran down the well-worn path to the dock.

The canyon was a good seventy feet wide but the river was so low from the drought that its channel had dwindled to half of that. There were steps leading down from the dock to where a metal canoe was beached in the mud.

The water was a green-brown and barely any current seemed to move it. TK wondered if it was even worth trying to use the canoe, but as soon as she stepped into the silty mud, she realized even a slow-moving canoe would be better than trying to slog along the riverbank. Fewer tracks, too.

Without her saying a word, Alan flipped the canoe right side up, grabbed both paddles, and stood waiting. TK took her cue and pushed the canoe into the water—at least it was still deep enough for the boat, although it was clear from the flood lines etched into the sides of the canyon that it usually ran four to five times as high.

She held the canoe steady and Alan climbed in, settling himself in the front and holding his paddle at the ready. She jumped in after and pushed off, the current guiding them into the center of the water and pulling them downstream faster than she'd thought it would.

One thing gone right, she thought. Then the sound of semi-automatic fire pulled her attention back to the house. Three shots. No return fire. Hell.

Guess Lucy was right about Caleb. As much as she wanted to return and help, TK had to focus on her mission: Alan's safety.

———◆———

DAVID JERKED BACK from the bloodstained knife. "You've had this? All along? And you didn't tell anyone?" he demanded. "You let my father rot in prison to protect your husband?"

Carole's smile was unnerving. "Why are you so certain it was Roscoe who killed them? Surely, you aren't underestimating me, Mr. Ruiz?"

He frowned, unable to parse the meaning behind her words. She was totally relaxed, no trace of anxiety...Yet, was she confessing to murder?

Then she laughed, a soft sound, almost musical. "If your FBI friend takes this knife to be tested, she'll find my husband's fingerprints all over it along with Lily Martin's blood. And the children's. That should put everyone's fears to rest and allow your father to regain his freedom."

She was so...blasé. As if twenty-nine years of a man's life were meaningless—not to mention his uncle, who'd died in prison. David staggered to his feet, his fury palpable, hammering through him like mortar rounds.

"How long? Why didn't you—" he stammered.

"I had to protect my son," she said, resuming her seat, her posture regal. "If people knew the truth, it would have destroyed him." She nodded to the couch. "Please, sit down. My son will be here soon, but in the meantime, I'll tell you anything you want to know."

His vision swimming, David sank back onto the soft cushions. "Would you have ever come forward? Would you have let my father die in prison?"

Her lips tightened and she shrugged. "Is that what you really want to know? Surely an investigative reporter such as yourself has other questions? After all, this story is bigger than us all."

"Right. Of course." He swallowed, pulled out his notebook, his hands shaking. All those years, wasted on doubt and anger. But now he was finally going to learn the truth. "Walk me through it. Everything you know."

She smiled at him once more, considering her options. Had she killed the Martins? Or had her husband? Maybe both, together, some warped test of their love? His mind spun with possibilities.

Finally, Carole nodded. Then she smoothed her palms against her thighs, straightening her posture as she pulled a small but lethal looking nickel-plated semi-automatic pistol from her pocket and aimed it at him.

"You deserve the truth," she said amicably. "But I'm afraid all I know is what my son told me."

NOVEMBER 13, 1987

HE COULDN'T BELIEVE how easy it had all been. Caleb bent over the handlebars of his bike, pedaling furiously in the November moonlight. It'd taken more time than he'd thought, but it didn't really matter—no one at home would be missing him; he'd told his mom he was going to the football game with friends.

Hah. As if. Carole had smiled and given him a hug, proud that her son was no longer a loser. If she only knew.

But who needed friends when you knew how to get away with murder?

It was the perfect plan. He'd gotten the idea last month from the news—some kid up north, Chicago, Detroit, one of those cities with a lot of blacks, he'd shot up a party, killed a few people, but was only going to juvie for a few years instead of prison because he was twelve. The grownups had gone on and on, arguing about how old was old enough to be tried as an adult and a bunch of other legal shit.

Bottom line: Kid got away with murder because he was twelve. Caleb was twelve—until November 15th. That had given him five weeks to plan.

He already knew exactly who he'd kill: that stupid baby that was causing all the trouble between his parents, making his mom worry that Dad was going to run off with Mrs. Martin, leaving her and Caleb behind. She'd cried and yelled and even threw a vase at Roscoe during one of their many fights.

Roscoe had shouted back, raised a fist, and Caleb had run, wrapped his arms around Mom, protecting her. She'd hugged him back. Roscoe just laughed and slept in the guest room that night.

The next day it was as if nothing had happened. But Caleb began listening carefully when his dad took him over to the Martins' every Saturday morning. He heard Mrs. Martin beg Roscoe to take her away from Blackwell County, to give them a fresh start.

No way. It would kill his mom if Roscoe left. Caleb was not going to let that happen.

Only one answer to save his family: kill Lily Martin and her brat of a baby.

He'd hid in the house, waiting for Lily and the kids to come home that Friday afternoon. He wore a pair of his dad's old work gloves—all the TV shows said to wear gloves if you didn't want to get caught—and his Halloween mask. Richard Nixon. He didn't care about the man being a president; he just thought Nixon's face was twisted and ugly. When he had the mask and gloves on, he felt like he wasn't himself anymore, he was someone else, someone powerful and awful and capable of anything.

Once Lily arrived, everything had fallen into place, like someone else was scripting the events. She'd sent Alan to his room—right where Caleb hid. It'd been so easy to surprise the kid, tie him up, and then sneak back out the bedroom window. While Lily had been in the laundry room and put the groceries away in the kitchen, he'd taken the sleeping baby—only thing the kid seemed to do was sleep and shit—and hid in the baby's room until Lily went back out to the car.

He'd chosen the knife because it was one of his dad's favorites—been passed down for a hundred years. The handle had been carved from an antler and the blade was narrow with a slight curve that ended in a sharp notch. It looked wicked and deadly.

Lily must have agreed because she did exactly as he told her after she saw the knife.

The hardest part was waiting to start the fun until the father came home. He was the most dangerous, but Caleb had a plan to handle him as well. It was so simple. Peter Martin never even saw it coming. Caleb hid behind the front door, holding his father's revolver, and as soon as Peter stepped inside and closed the door, Caleb shot him in the face and twice in the chest.

The sound made his ears ring and he didn't like the smell, but it got the baby crying and Lily screaming, and his real fun could begin.

Alan surprised him, actually tried to get away, but Caleb was twice his size. He sort of liked Alan, so he didn't spend as much time with him—and he let him keep his face. Figured it was the least he could do since the rest of the family would have to have closed caskets. Caleb imagined the scene: two large wooden caskets, one tiny one, and Alan's in the middle, the only one mourners could actually go up and say good-bye to. He'd cry, maybe put one of his old toys inside, turn to his mom for comfort and she'd treat him extra special nice.

He had it all planned out. Now, as he left the scene of his crime, all he needed was to take care of a few last details. First, he stopped at the pullover beside the river where all the older kids parked and made out. An assortment of vehicles waiting for him to frame someone for murder...ah, that was the one, the Manning brothers' truck. He'd hoped it would be here.

He had nothing against Dicky Manning except he was a druggie and drunk, and half the time he talked to people no one else saw. But his younger brother, Mike? Caleb hated him.

Mike Manning had everything Caleb wanted. He was a star football player, was getting out of this place thanks to a college scholarship, everyone at school adored him—even old Mrs. Garrety in the principal's office, and she hated everyone—and, worst of all, he'd stolen Caleb's girl. True, Caleb was only a seventh grader and Maria Ruiz was a junior, but she was nice and beautiful and she always smiled at Caleb when she saw him and he just knew they were meant to be together.

As soon as he got rid of Mike Manning.

Caleb took the gun, wrapped in one of the baby's cloth diapers, and tucked it into the back of Mike's brother's beat-up truck. He kept his father's knife, figured it might come in handy some day, plus it would be easy to hide, along with Roscoe's gloves. The mask he burned in the garbage pit on the edge of their property.

Then he rode to his house, took a long bath, and went to bed, excited about the scene he'd scripted for the morning. After tomorrow, no one would be calling Caleb names any more. Oh no. After tomorrow, he'd be a hero.

Most importantly, he'd saved his family. Roscoe would stay, Mom would be happy, and they'd both finally be proud of Caleb.

CHAPTER 34

AS TEMPTING AS it was to surrender and save Saylor from Blackwell, Lucy knew it would be a pointless gesture—Blackwell would simply kill them both and continue his hunt.

The smell of smoke was stronger here in the trees, choking her. Forcing herself to take slow, shallow breaths, she edged farther along the tree line, searching for a line of sight that would give her a shot at Blackwell. The geometry simply wasn't in her favor. Instead of aiming for a kill shot, she would have to settle for providing Saylor with cover fire and hoping he wasn't too injured to escape while she pinned down Blackwell.

The SUV was between twenty and thirty yards from her vantage point. Close enough for either slugs or buckshot, depending on what Saylor had his Remington 870 loaded with— many law-enforcement officers alternated loads. She sighted with the shotgun, her new position placing her almost directly in front of the Escalade, hoping to drive Blackwell inside the vehicle, seeking cover. Anything to get him and the flare away from Saylor.

The buckshot spread out, pinging against the metal and shattering the driver's side window. Blackwell responded by whirling to face the new threat, firing with his M4, spraying the trees in bursts. Lucy threw herself to the ground as bullets flew overhead, returning fire despite the fact that Blackwell never broke cover.

Silence fell. Blackwell was out of ammunition, reloading. As a trained professional, it should only take seconds—not long enough for Lucy to cross the exposed area between them. She raised her head to check on Saylor. He'd managed to belly-crawl halfway to the house, but it did him little good—he was now totally vulnerable. One of his legs was twisted at an unnatural angle and he left a trail of blood on the brown grass behind him.

She kept her weapon trained on the SUV, hoping Blackwell would show himself. It shouldn't take him this long to reload. Cautiously, she raised up to one knee and saw his head bobbing below the dashboard's center console. Was she talking to someone on the radio? Calling for reinforcements?

She fired at the windshield. The safety glass was no match to the shotgun slug, which tore through it and then out one of the rear windows. If Blackwell had raised his head, it would have blown his skull out.

No such luck. Blackwell used the demolished windshield to his advantage, propping his M4 on the dash and firing back at Lucy. Only a few bursts this time, but enough to flatten her back to the earth.

"You sent Ruiz after my mother?" Blackwell screamed in

fury as he turned his aim on Saylor, emptying his magazine once again in a spray of bullets. The man had no discipline—he might have all the tools of a law-enforcement officer, but he obviously lacked experience in using them. "Hell with all of you. I don't have time for this."

Lucy tilted her face up just far enough to see what he was doing. The SUV reversed back over the smashed gate. Blackwell's arm appeared briefly out of the driver's window, throwing something toward the patch of gasoline spreading over the dead grass. The roadside flare.

It spun through the air, blazing orange against the gathering dusk, and before it even hit the ground, the gas fumes erupted in flames.

A wall of fire burst along the ground, flames dancing like a whirling dervish, devouring everything in sight. The wind gathered them and gave them direction: straight toward Saylor.

———◆———

TK AND ALAN hadn't gone more than a mile downstream when the current slowed and the river dwindled until it was nothing more than a shallow pool blocked by a sandbar. Alan didn't seem to mind, he steered them to shore and hopped out, waiting for TK.

On the other side of the sandbar were a set of pilings and the remnants of a dock with a ladder along one side leading out of the gulley. Numbers were stenciled on the pilings as if they'd had some kind of official designation. The old agriculture research center. Another hundred feet past the abandoned dock she glimpsed a ribbon of brown—the river resuming its course.

TK glanced back the way they'd come. No signs of pursuit and the sun was almost down. Should she haul their canoe over the sandbar and try the next length of river?

Alan made the decision for them, gleefully running through the mud and silt to the ladder and throwing himself at it.

"Wait," she called, worried it wasn't safe, but he'd already scrambled halfway up. At least she wouldn't have to worry about it holding her weight.

As soon as he was at the top, she climbed the rungs. Up top there was a platform anchored into the solid ground, about ten feet square. On either side were trees and brushes, but heading in land was a well-worn path. She jogged down it, catching up with Alan.

"You need to let me go first," she scolded him. His expression turned from smiling to crushed in an instant. "Stay with me—that's what your dad wanted. I'm supposed to look after you, so you need to listen to me. Okay?"

He didn't make eye contact, shifting his weight as he nodded his head earnestly.

"Okay," she said. She took his hand and placed it on her left shoulder. "Keep your hand there. That way even when it gets dark, we won't lose each other."

He squeezed her shoulder and smiled at her. Amazing how quickly he shrugged off any negativity. She sure as hell could use a little of his positive attitude in her own life.

Moving slowly through the deepening shadows, they walked down the path. About twenty yards later, the trees ended and a wide expanse of cleared land opened up before them. In the dim light, TK made out rows of abandoned farm equipment. She recognized a thresher, a disc plow, two portable irrigation sprayers, and a hay baler—the kind that could make six-foot-high round bales.

In addition to the farm equipment were an assortment of junked-out cars, several small tin-roofed sheds, a silo, and a larger metal barn. She shook her head at the waste. Bad news for the taxpayers but good news as far as finding a defensible position. The place reminded her of the abandoned buildings where she ran parkour, a maze of obstacles ready to trip up the unwary.

It was clear from Alan's confident stride that he knew the area well. She turned to him. "Ever play hide-and-seek here?"

He nodded eagerly. As overprotective as his father was, she doubted Saylor let him play near any of the more dangerous machinery—but that baler, there was plenty of room to hide inside its maw, and the thick steel was as good as bulletproof. She led him over to it. Everything looked stable—last thing she wanted to risk was those heavy steel jaws slamming shut on one of them, but they were locked into place.

"How about here?" she asked. "Is this a good place to hide?"

He nodded and climbed in, avoiding the rollers, squeezing his body into the recess where the hay bale would fit and grinning at her.

"Okay. You wait there and don't you come out until I tell you to. Deal?"

Another eager nod and he crossed his heart, sealing their bargain. TK left him and walked a spiral path out from the baler, searching for high ground with cover and a good view of the road. If danger was coming, it would be from there.

She climbed to the top of one of the silos and took stock. One semi-automatic pistol, thirty-one rounds of ammo divided in two magazines, and cover of darkness. It would have to do. Then she looked up river, back the way they came. The sky was indigo above and a brilliant crimson streak below. Only instead of dipping below the tree line and disappearing, the red and gold was growing, filling the horizon.

And moving. That wasn't sunset. That was a wild fire. Raging out of control.

---·---

DAVID STOPPED TAKING notes halfway through Carole's recitation, simply unable to focus on the words on the page. It was unbelievable; she was so damn proud of her son, the monster who'd butchered an entire family in cold blood.

"Why are you telling me all this?"

"Why not?" she countered. "None of it is admissible, much less believable. There's not a single shred of proof. You can't even tell anyone. After all, Caleb saved Blackwell County and the people here. Who'd believe you if you tried to tell them he was a cold-hearted killer? No one. Not with your," she sniffed, "pedigree. Not to mention how obviously self-serving it would appear. If you ever tried to tell anyone, it would hurt your father's cause more than help it."

"You kept this knife all these years—"

"To implicate Roscoe. He's so much more helpful dead and buried than he ever was alive. The knife was a bit of an insurance plan. In case someone like you and your mother started digging."

He shook his head, his mind swimming with the implications and ramifications of everything she'd told him. "I don't understand. What do you want me to do?"

"That's for my son to decide. Unlike his father, Caleb is a big-picture thinker. I'm sure he has a plan for you." She tilted her chin toward the window. "That's him now." There was the sound of the front door opening and a man's footsteps. "Caleb, dear," she called out. "We're in the front parlor. Come say hello to Mr. Ruiz. I was just telling him all about your childhood exploits."

CHAPTER 35

AS SOON AS Blackwell was out of sight, Lucy ran across the lawn to Saylor, dodging flames. Saylor lay, not moving, blood oozing in a puddle near where his hands covered his head.

He looked dead. Lucy raced to him, squatting down in the ground, the flames consuming the gasoline spill and drawing dangerously close. Sweat dripped from her face as she examined him for injuries.

"Saylor. You're hit." Damn, was it a head shot? His pulse was good. She pulled his arms away from his head and saw the left one was where the blood was coming from. A through-and-through at the fleshy part of the forearm.

Saylor groaned and raised his face out of the dirt. "Ain't dead yet."

The wind gusted sparks across to his jeans. Lucy smacked the flames out with her hands. His right leg was twisted mid-thigh—where the Escalade's bumper hit him when Blackwell ran him down. "Hold tight. This is going to hurt."

She pulled his arms over his head and dragged him toward the Tahoe TK had left behind. As she moved him, she finally saw why Blackwell had been stalling. The fire here in Saylor's yard was the least of their problems—the trees and grassland surrounding the property were alight with flames.

He must have started the fire to cut them off and then came here to make sure they didn't escape before it reached them. Too bad he hadn't thought of the river. Or maybe he had. Maybe that's why he ran over Saylor, leaving him too injured to travel by boat.

A dead man could be left behind. A wounded one took time and energy. Time they didn't have the way the trees were crackling as the drought-parched forest was consumed.

With the fire surrounding them on three sides and coming closer with each second, she had no time to check Saylor for spinal injuries; had to hope for the best. A howl of pain escaped him—she took that as a good sign. If he was feeling pain, his spine was intact.

Blackwell's final salvo of gunfire had shot out the Tahoe's windows but she saw no sign that his bullets had hit anything vital. She opened the SUV's back door, coughing as smoke filled the air. Her vision clouded with tears and she couldn't see the house or the gate through the haze.

"I can't lift you by myself. Can you put any weight on your other leg?"

He shook his head, his face ashen, eyes clamped shut with the effort of clutching her arms to keep from falling back into the gravel.

"C'mon, Sheriff," she coaxed. "Your boy needs you."

That did the trick. He sucked in his breath, opened his eyes wide, and reached for a handhold. Together they half-dragged, half-pushed his body up and into the SUV. Lucy slammed the door shut, ignoring his groan as the vehicle rocked. No time to make him comfortable, not until they were clear of the flames.

She tossed her weapons into the passenger seat and hopped in, turning the ignition on and fastening her seatbelt with one motion. "Brace yourself. It's going to be a bumpy ride."

Smoke swirled through the broken windows as she turned the SUV around. An immense wall of flames greeted her—the fence was on fire as well as the high prairie grass beyond it. Behind her a roar filled the air as the fire reached the house, rampaging across the porch and up the side to the roof.

"I can't believe how fast it's moving." She aimed the SUV at a slight dip in the flames where she hoped the road and gate lay.

"The drought," Saylor answered her, although she'd expected none. "Plus the wind picks up when the sun goes down."

"We can't stick around here. Hang on." She gunned the engine and plowed through the flames, bumping over something—the gate? Smoke and heat blinded her as sparks flew through the air, carrying with them cinders and ash. It was difficult to take even a single deep breath.

They passed the fence, but the prairie beyond it was an ocean of flame. Thankfully the trees lining the lane revealed their escape route.

"What was that call Blackwell got before he left?" Between the wind rushing through the blown-out windows and the sound of the fire, she had to shout.

"Dispatch was relaying a message from his mom," Saylor replied. His words were coming with short gasps between them, but his voice was strong. "He told them he'd thought he'd seen a small fire near here and was getting the helicopter up to check it out."

She squinted into the smoke. They should be near the road. "Does his helo have FLIR?" The forward-looking infrared imaging was how police helicopters tracked fleeing suspects.

"Yep. It'll be easy to find TK and Alan—they'll be the only human heat signatures out this way."

The fire behind them reflected off a stop sign. They'd reached the main road. "You need a hospital."

"I need my son safe," he insisted. "Leave me here and I'll take my chances."

She patted her pockets. Two magazines for the pistols in her back pockets, but somewhere along the way she'd lost her phone. "Do you have your cell?"

His breath came in ragged gasps as he stretched an arm around to his back pocket. She reached back between the seats and grabbed it. The screen was hopelessly smashed and had gone black. She tried the power button. Nothing. It was damaged beyond repair.

She scanned both directions on the highway. No signs of traffic from either direction. Flames crested a small rise behind them, heading along the river. She remembered her landmarks from her earlier drive. The fire would hit the ag research center next, from there the river curved and would lead it to the Martin house and eventually Blackwell's place. Idiot might have condemned his own home by starting the blaze.

But if it saved him from a murder charge, Blackwell obviously thought it was worth a chance. No. *Thinking* wasn't how he was functioning—his abrupt actions back at Saylor's showed that. Blackwell was reacting. Letting his emotions and immediate desires guide his actions.

Which might be the only reason why she and Saylor were still alive.

"Where would TK and Alan go?" she asked Saylor.

"The river's too low, they wouldn't make it far downstream. The ag station. There are a few old barns there, farm equipment, abandoned vehicles. It'd make a good place to hide. Plus, Alan knows it. He likes to explore all the machinery."

She turned onto the highway, heading away from the route that would take them toward Abilene and the nearest hospital—and toward the one that paralleled the river and headed downstream.

———•———

DAVID GLANCED AWAY from Carole as Caleb Blackwell marched into the room.

"Mother, are you all right?" Caleb planted a solicitous kiss on Carole's head before turning to glare at David. "What right do you have coming here?"

Carole patted Caleb's hand as it rested on her shoulder. "It's perfectly all right, dear. After all, if anyone would be interested in the truth, it would be Mr. Ruiz, don't you think?"

"Exactly which version of the truth did she tell you?" Caleb asked, moving away from his mother. "The one where

Roscoe dealt with a simpering, clingy mistress with blackmail on her mind? Or maybe the one where the Blackwell matron defended her husband's family honor by taking care of things herself?"

"The one where her psychopathic twelve-year-old son tortured a mother and baby," David blurted out before he could stop himself. To his surprise, Caleb responded with a chuckle.

"Right. Of course. Mother, your imagination never ceases to amaze me. Especially as we all know the only evidence points to Roscoe." He raised an eyebrow at David, emphasizing his point. "But Mr. Ruiz and I have more urgent business at hand. You and TK O'Connor seemed rather close when I arrested you last night. What would she do to save your life?"

David startled. "Excuse me?"

"Stand up. Keep your hands where I can see them," Caleb ordered, his posture one of command. He drew his weapon and aimed it at David as he settled into a shooting stance. David slowly complied, adrenaline colliding with fear as the blood rushed away from his head, making the room spin.

"Turn around, hands on the back of your head." Within seconds, Caleb had David's wrists handcuffed behind him.

"Am I under arrest? What for?"

"Caleb, what are you doing?" Carole asked. Her body language was more curious than concerned. Her son wasn't the only psychopath in the family, David decided.

Caleb pushed David toward the front entrance. "You were right, Mother. I should have taken care of that boy a long, long time ago. Seems like TK found a way to get him to tell her who really was at the Martin house and now they've made a run for it. But don't worry. I'm going to use the helicopter to hunt them down."

"Just be careful, dear," she said, taking a sip of her martini. "You don't want to leave things half done. Again."

"I've already taken care of Drew Saylor and that FBI agent, Guardino. Mr. Ruiz here is going to help me wrap up any other loose ends."

"Exactly how am I going to do that?" David asked.

"You're going to help me find where TK has taken Alan. Then we'll trade your life for his."

Right. "Why would I do that?"

Caleb's shrug needed no interpretation. "You get to tell the world how my father was the real killer. You get to save your father—isn't that why you started this to begin with?"

"And TK? How's she fit into all this?"

"Let's find them first, then we'll see about that." He shoved David forward. "Mother, there's a wildfire at the Saylor place. It would be best if you evacuated into town. I'll meet you at the sheriff station."

"Nonsense. This is my home. I'm not leaving it."

"Mother—"

"Caleb Blackwell." David felt Caleb jerk to attention behind him. "I said no. I am not leaving my home. You will simply have to stop the fire before it reaches here."

"But—"

"No buts about it. I need you to handle this, Caleb. Can I trust you to do that?"

"Yes, Mother."

David glanced back over his shoulder in time to see Carole Blackwell beaming proudly at her son, the coldblooded killer.

CHAPTER 36

THE NIGHT AIR rushed in through the Tahoe's shattered windows, bringing with it smoke and ashes. Lucy hoped TK had gotten the insurance on the vehicle. The incongruous thought made her want to laugh—adrenaline did that to her sometimes. She pushed the accelerator as far as she dared on the unfamiliar road, each curve eliciting a moan of pain from Saylor in the back.

"Is Abilene the nearest hospital?" she asked. She was pretty sure that was right, but if he had internal bleeding, then this detour to find TK and Alan might be condemning him to death.

"Yep. Once we have Alan safe, we can call for a medevac." His voice was weaker and he was gasping between every word. "Always wanted to ride in a helicopter."

The headlights caught the reflective flash of the large agriculture research center sign. Lucy hit the brakes and they spun onto the lane—the same lane that led to the Martin house and that ended at the rear boundary of Blackwell's property.

The road was rutted out, tossing Saylor around mercilessly. His groans dwindled to mere whimpers. As a clearing with scattered equipment and a barn came into sight, they died out all together. "Saylor, you still with me?"

Silence. Lucy braked the car, leaving the lights on—if TK had brought Alan here, Lucy didn't want to risk any friendly-fire incidents. Slowly, keeping her hands raised, she climbed out of the Tahoe and eased into the swath of light at the front bumper. "TK? It's Lucy and Saylor."

"Is it clear?" TK's voice called through the darkness.

"For now. Saylor's injured."

A few moments later, a form separated itself from the shadows and approached Lucy. "Are you and Alan okay?"

"Yes. I stashed him in the baler." She pointed in the direction of the machinery, but Lucy had no idea which piece she was referring to. "What happened? I heard gunfire."

"Blackwell ran Saylor down with his Escalade, shot out the Tahoe, and shot at both of us. And when he learned David was at his house with his mom, he started the fire and took off."

"I saw the fire. It's spreading fast. Does Caleb think you're dead?"

"As good as. But Saylor's hurt bad. I don't think he'll make it if we don't get him to the hospital in Abilene. Fast."

TK nodded. "I'll get Alan and we'll hit the road."

Lucy grabbed her arm. "It's not that easy. Blackwell said he was going to get a helicopter to look for you and Alan."

"The Bell—no way we can outrun it in the Tahoe." She craned her neck, turning to stare in the direction of Blackwell's property. A single bright light stabbed through the slice of the sky that was still black, untainted by the fire's glow. The helicopter, heading their way. "That's him now. What are we going to do? We can't hide here forever and we can't run."

Lucy glanced around. In the dark, the farm equipment and abandoned vehicles took on an otherworldly aspect, only the faint lines of their silhouettes visible.

"We don't have to outrun the helo," she mused. "In fact, we don't want to."

TK's expression was filled with the same skepticism she'd greeted Lucy with when they first met.

"Blackwell will be using FLIR—which can't penetrate metal. If we leave Saylor and Alan hidden, and if Blackwell is searching for two thermal sources on the move, then we give him two thermal sources on the move."

"You and me," TK filled in the blanks. "Wait. Are you suggesting we hijack Caleb's helo?"

"Fastest way to get Saylor to the hospital and regain control of the situation. What do you say? Up for some night maneuvers?"

"Roger that."

———◆———

CALEB HERDED DAVID around to the back of the house where a small hangar stood. A shiny blue and white helicopter waited for them. Caleb opened the front passenger door and shoved David up onto the seat, his hands still cuffed at the small of his back, then moved around to the pilot's side and took his seat. He strapped in with an intricate set of restraints.

"Don't I get a seatbelt?" David asked as Caleb began to flick switches and the engines came to life. He watched closely—this helicopter was different than the trainer he'd flown while researching his story on Navy pilots, but the controls seemed basically the same.

Caleb didn't even spare him a glance. "You might not be riding long enough to need one."

David shut up, trying to figure out how he could move enough in the cramped quarters to stop Caleb without the use of his hands. Then they were airborne and he had to also factor in the need to not crash.

As they rose past the house, an ocean of orange filled the horizon.

"I still don't understand what you want from me."

"Simple." Caleb pointed to a screen below the flight instruments. "That's the Forward Looking Infrared camera. It sees heat in shades of gray. You're looking for two human-sized targets. Check for movement, that's usually the easiest—although other than the fire and a few head of cattle, there won't be many heat signatures."

David stared at the screen. It was fairly monotone until they crossed over the county highway, which was still radiating heat from the blacktop and he saw the difference in color.

"You haven't told me yet what you're planning to do to TK and Alan."

"And you're stalling. No matter, look there." Caleb pointed to two human-shaped blobs on the screen. One was moving rapidly, the other trailing behind. "They're at the ag station. Perfect. There's a good place to land not far. Wait."

David squinted at the screen. There was another fainter blob, this one stationary. "What's that?"

"Not moving. Probably a car engine. TK must have gotten one of those old wrecks started. We'll just have to slow them down, won't we?" He sent a sly grin David's way and banked the helicopter, heading it back toward the fire.

"What are you going to do?"

"Ever see what a gust of wind does to a campfire?"

"Sends sparks everywhere."

"Wait until you see what the rotor wash from this baby can do. I'm going to herd the wildfire right at them, block their path to the highway. They'll be trapped. Right where I want them."

"Won't we be trapped as well?"

"Not as long as we don't dawdle. We're in, we're out, take care of business and back home in time for dinner with Mother."

"What do you mean, take care of business?" David knew, but he also still had his cell phone with its recording app running. Even if Caleb killed him, there was a chance that some day, someone might learn the truth. "The same way you killed Lily Martin and her family?"

"You don't think it could have been Roscoe or my mother?"

"I think you were a spoiled kid jealous of the time his father spent with a woman not your mother and worried that he'd go start a real family with Lily and her baby. I think you had fun torturing them and Alan. And I think you killed your dad, I'm guessing, because he was going to turn you in."

"You're almost right. It was me. It was a helluva lot of fun. But I didn't kill Roscoe. Mother took care of that. He wanted to lock me up in some mental hospital in Germany. No way was she ever going to let him take her son from her."

David was glad he couldn't hear the emotions coloring Caleb's voice—the body language was sickening enough.

"And those missing women?"

"You know about those?" Caleb's expression was a mix of surprise and pride.

"Lucy figured it out."

"Hang on," Caleb called as winds from the fire began to buffet them. "Oh, sorry, forgot, you can't hang on." He laughed and banked the helicopter again, hovering just above the flames, pushing them with the rotor wash.

The blaze responded with gusto, jumping across the road then racing down both sides toward the ag station. Satisfied that he'd cut off any escape for TK and Alan, Caleb increased their altitude and they sped in front of the wall of flames, heading to where a single heat signature still moved.

David frowned. He'd been hoping TK would somehow manage to get away, vanish into the night before the helicopter could make it back. No such luck.

Caleb hovered over a flat area near the ag station's barn. "I only see one now, the other must be sitting in the car. No matter. The one moving will be TK. I'll take care of her first. Then the boy."

CHAPTER 37

WHEN LUCY HEARD the helicopter returning, she scrambled into position. She shimmied beneath one of the larger pieces of machinery, its heavy-duty steel concealing her from Blackwell's FLIR. Now all she needed was to wait for TK to lead Blackwell to her.

She adjusted the shotgun, making sure its sights were clear then set her pistol within easy reach. They'd only get one shot at this. TK would have preferred to play the role of marksman, but with Lucy's limited mobility that was not an option.

The wind shifted, bringing with it the foul stench of burnt asphalt. She craned her neck out of her sniper hole just enough to see that the fire had shifted. So that's where Blackwell had gone after the helo initially spotted them. Bastard had forced the fire toward their position, ensuring that any escape would be cut off.

Which meant whatever happened, they needed Blackwell alive and able to fly them all out of here. She exchanged the shotgun for her Beretta, which she'd retrieved from TK, swapping it for one of Saylor's semi-automatics.

The sky around her roared and loose debris began to whip through the air as the helicopter circled overhead and then descended to a cleared patch on the other side of the barn. TK raced by, dancing over the elevated route she'd created. She waved to Lucy, her grin visible even in the darkness. She was having fun, outsmarting Blackwell who, with his 2D representation of their positions, would not be looking for TK to come at him from above.

Lucy raised her weapon. TK's acrobatic stunts as she raced over the myriad of equipment were amazing—she hoped to see the younger woman perform them again someday in daylight. TK moved with the precision of a laser-guided missile, fully focused on her mission.

Mission. That's what drove TK. She was a different woman compared to the one Lucy had to bail out of jail that morning. Reminded her a lot of herself—Lucy finally had a taste of what her supervisors at the FBI had faced, trying to wrangle her passion to pursue a case no matter where it led.

"TK!" Blackwell's voice cut through the night. "I know you're here. Come out."

"Come and get me," TK called back, drawing Blackwell into their trap. They'd done a good job of predicting where he'd land. They didn't need him to move very far, just another dozen yards or so.

Lucy strained to see in the darkness, wishing for a pair of night-vision goggles. But this entire operation was low-tech—no fault of her team, simply circumstances beyond their control.

Blackwell stepped past the rusted-out pickup truck that sat at the outer boundary of their designated perimeter. Lucy froze. He held David Ruiz in front of him, a human shield.

How the hell was she supposed to wound Blackwell without killing him, leaving him able to fly, and not also put a bullet through David? She sighted the Beretta, hoping Blackwell would come close enough that she would have clear aim at one of his feet.

Not the ideal solution; helicopter pilots used both their feet at the controls, but it might be all she had. Except both David and Blackwell wore dark pants and dark shoes, and they blended into the shadows too well for her to distinguish them with any clarity.

Damn. She was going to have to come up with a Plan B on the fly—and without being able to communicate the change to TK. Time to see exactly how good the former Marine was.

Blackwell stopped in the center of the small clearing. "I'm losing my patience," he shouted into the hulking shadows surrounding him. "Show yourself. Now!"

His back was to Lucy, giving her the chance to carefully sidle out from her concealment and move into a better position. TK distracted Blackwell by swinging up and over the top bar of one of the irrigation sprayers to land with a loud thump on the roof of an old pickup that had no wheels and was half-sunken into the ground.

"I'm right here," she said, spreading her hands wide to show she was unarmed. Except for the handgun concealed in her boot, but the objective was to keep Blackwell from ever getting close enough to find it.

Blackwell shifted his posture, fully engaged. He held a pistol to David's temple the way a movie gangster would. Again, he reminded Lucy of a boy with all the toys but no clue how to use them like a man, letting emotion overwhelm his training.

Which put him in the class of amateur, but also made him highly unpredictable. The worst kind of subject to deal with. At least career criminals knew how to cut their losses, making them often eager to negotiate. Not Blackwell. He was playing out some kind of psychodrama scripted solely inside his own twisted mind and subject to improvisation without notice.

"Where's the boy?" he demanded, knocking the pistol against David's skull to emphasize that he held the upper hand.

Lucy studied him as she crept closer. She couldn't shoot him, not with the fire moving in and the helo their only way out of here. He was taller, larger than her, so a regulation takedown was out—and would probably get David killed.

"What will you give me for him?" TK said, stalling for time.

TK's gaze brushed past the spot Lucy had abandoned, confusion flitting across her face until she spotted Lucy once more. Lucy spun her hand in the universal "keep talking" gesture. She was asking a lot of TK—basically to play a human target.

TK embraced her role, adding a hint of girlish whine to her voice. "Please, Caleb. I don't have any part of this. I'm no cop. Let me go and I'll tell you where the kid is."

The ground was hard-packed, muffling Lucy's movements but she had to keep looking down to make sure she wasn't about to trip over the scattered debris with her dragging bad foot. She just needed to get a little closer, and she needed David's help—hopefully the reporter had good survival instincts.

"Don't do it, TK," David yelled. "He's just going to kill us all."

Blackwell laughed. "Idiots. You keep chatting like a bunch of girls and the fire will do that anyway." He gestured with his gun to the flames that filled the sky behind the barn.

And with that motion, Lucy saw her chance.

"Down!" she shouted.

David dropped to the ground as she pushed off with her good leg, grabbing Blackwell's gun hand. She forced it away from David with one hand while jamming Blackwell's chin up with her other.

While Blackwell strained to regain control of his weapon, Lucy concentrated on controlling his head. She stepped between his legs, using her momentum to leverage his chin back, flipping him backward and to the ground.

Because as anyone who understood gravity knew, the body followed where the head led. Gravity always won.

Lucy shifted position, ignoring the lightning strike of pain coming from her bad leg as she torqued it. She wrapped her fingers around Blackwell's wrist and twisted viciously. He yelped in pain, dropping the gun. She finished the compliance technique, bringing his wrist up behind his shoulder blade, now in complete control of his movements.

TK shoved past David, who was crab-crawling backward because of his handcuffed hands, and stepped on Blackwell's other hand. She pinned it to the ground while she held her pistol to his head. "Now who's the idiot?"

CHAPTER 38

TK HELD HER weapon on Caleb while Lucy efficiently searched him for weapons and retrieved his handcuff keys. Lucy went to release Ruiz from his restraints. TK was practically bouncing out of her boots, she felt so jazzed. She hadn't felt this way in a long, long time. Not just triumphant, alive.

"Thought the plan was you were going to shoot him?" she quipped as Lucy worked. Caleb was proned out on the dirt, his body sagging with defeat.

"I was going to try for his feet but David was in the way and I realized that helicopter pilots—"

"Use their feet. Right. Good call."

Lucy tossed the handcuffs she'd taken off Ruiz over to TK. TK grabbed them mid-air, that's how focused she was, as if every molecule around her was electrified. She knelt to restrain Caleb while Lucy took over standing guard.

"Could have shot him in the balls," she continued as she ratcheted the handcuff shut on one wrist and reached for the other. "Doesn't need those to fly."

"Hey," Ruiz protested. "What if she'd hit me? I would like to keep that particular piece of my anatomy intact, if you don't mind."

TK grinned over her shoulder at him. "Right. Women around the world would have wept and mourned if anything happened to your precious family jewels."

"You'd better believe it."

"Move it," Lucy put in. "That fire's closing in."

She was right. Not only was the place heating up, but the air was getting choked with smoke. Nice thing, though, was the fire gave off enough light that there was no way Caleb could make a move unseen.

"What was that takedown?" TK asked, securing the second bracelet on Caleb's wrist. "Krav Maga?"

"Brazilian jujitsu," Lucy answered. "My daughter is a black belt in Kempo and is studying for her purple belt in jujitsu."

"You have a daughter? How old?"

"Fourteen."

TK exchanged a grimace with Ruiz. "Wow, you really are old."

In answer, Lucy simply jerked her head toward the Tahoe. "You and David move Saylor to the helo, then get Alan on board. I'll follow with Blackwell."

"Is there room for all of us?" TK asked Ruiz as they ran to the SUV.

"There are two single seats in the back and a bench seat, so yes."

They reached the Tahoe. TK opened the rear door. Saylor was unconscious, his color paler than moonlight, blood smeared over his shirt.

"Damn," Ruiz breathed.

"He's in shock. We've got to get him to a hospital." Together they hauled Saylor out of the SUV and onto the Bell. He barely fluttered his eyes and didn't make any sound. "Ruiz, look around for any first-aid supplies while I get Alan."

TK jogged through the maze of farm equipment to the baler where she'd left Alan. It was on the side of the property closest to the fire and she had to pull her shirt collar up over her mouth and nose to breathe. Sweat dripped from her forehead and her eyes watered with smoke. She ducked her head into the baler's compartment. "Alan, you okay?"

He was huddled exactly where she'd left him, crying silent tears, his body shaking with fear.

"Hey there, told you I'd be back. Sorry it took so long," she said, coaxing him out. "It's kind of scary out here. There's a fire and your dad is sick, but we're going to help him. Ever see a helicopter?"

He stumbled and coughed in the smoke, but she wrapped her arm around his waist and he let her lead him to the Bell.

Poor kid about bolted when he saw his dad lying there so still and pale, but then he seemed to gather himself, climbing on board without TK's help and kneeling beside his father, patting Saylor's forehead and hair.

Lucy followed with Caleb, helping him to climb up into the pilot's seat before she removed the restraints.

"You try anything and we all die," she reminded him. "TK, do you have tactical medical training or do you need me in back to take care of Saylor?"

Of course Lucy had medic training. Was there anything the FBI agent couldn't do? TK thought with a roll of her eyes. But she had to admit, that despite Lucy's age and physical disability, she'd come through when it counted. "No, I'm good."

"David, in back, take care of Alan," Lucy ordered. She moved to take the copilot seat, her pistol trained on Caleb.

The flames were so close they reflected through the windshields, coloring the cockpit red and orange. Caleb sat staring, not reaching for the controls.

TK watched from her position beside Saylor. Ruiz had found oxygen and a trauma kit, so she was setting up an IV. "Come on," she called to Lucy. "We need to get going."

"You heard her," Lucy told Caleb. "Let's go."

He leaned back, crossing his arms over his chest like a petulant child. "What's in it for me?"

"You want to live?" TK shouted, her patience with the man exhausted.

"Not in prison," he replied. "I get you guys to the hospital and you let me go. Deal?"

"No way," Ruiz protested. "You two have no idea—"

"Deal," Lucy said firmly, twisting in her seat to glare at Ruiz. TK met her gaze and nodded. Ruiz opened his mouth, anger and confusion battling on his face, but then looked hard at Lucy and clamped it shut. So much for Mr. Human Lie Detector.

An explosion rocked the helo, sparks and flames shooting through the air. The fire had hit something combustible and there would be more to come, given the farm equipment littered around the yard.

"You have my word," Lucy shouted, panic in her voice.

"Let's go!"

She was a better actor than TK expected. Caleb grinned, thinking he held the upper hand, and hit the controls.

TK shook her head and turned back to Saylor. Poor Caleb, he was so going down. Hard.

They took off, the winds from the fire trying to push them one way and the other, but then they were finally above the fire. TK craned her head out the window and gave a low whistle. "Caleb, you started this fire?"

He was wrestling with the controls, his gaze fixated on the dials and forward view, answering only with a grunt and a nod.

TK didn't have the heart to say anything, but watched in silence as Blackwell Manor burst into flames. She couldn't help but wonder if Carole Blackwell had escaped or if she stayed behind, ensconced in the house she'd killed for.

———◆———

LUCY KEPT CLOSE watch on Blackwell's movements after she removed his handcuffs so he could pilot the helicopter. She didn't trust the man not to try to kill them all. Unfortunately, the fire was giving him plenty of chances to do that without even trying very hard.

The helicopter finally rose high enough above the flames that the fire-generated updrafts and winds calmed a bit. Blackwell glanced around, fingers gripping the controls, orienting himself. His jaw tightened and brow creased, wrinkles appearing below his eyes, which were wide.

Lucy had seen that look before. Usually right before people died.

She followed Blackwell's gaze: a large house perched on a hill overlooking the river, fire blazing from every window. They were headed right for it.

"No," TK yelled from the rear compartment. "That's his home. He's going to crash us!"

"Don't try it," Lucy told Blackwell. He ignored her and moved the controls, hurtling them back toward the ground.

"I have to save her," he muttered, despite the pistol she dug in his side. "My mother's in there."

"She's gone, Caleb." TK tried to reason with him. "She'd want you to save yourself."

"No," he screamed. The noise shattered Alan's calm, and he began to shriek, a wailing that battled with the roar of the fire and the helo's engines.

Lucy pinned Blackwell back in his seat, her pistol jammed up under his ribcage, the pain distracting him momentarily. Good, if he could be distracted, he could also be persuaded.

"Want a chance to save her?" she yelled into his ear. The helo bounced so violently she had to clutch at his restraints with her free hand to keep her position. "Put us down and I'll let you go. You're her only chance, Caleb. You kill yourself, take us all down, and she dies. And it will all be your fault."

They were low enough that the flames from the house reflected in his eyes. Suddenly, his posture relaxed and he nodded—not at Lucy but rather at the house they were racing toward. His hands and feet worked the controls and the helo's engines protested but obeyed.

They slowed but the ground was still coming up much

too quickly. "Hang on," Lucy called to the people behind her.

An updraft caught them, slowing them enough that when they hit the ground, it was with a hard thud, ashes and sparks spraying up all around them. Lucy was jerked away from Blackwell, thrown backward then sideways as the helo lurched and skidded, threatening to topple to one side.

Then finally, they were stopped. The rotors were still spinning, holding the flames at bay. The house was about a hundred feet in front of them, fully engulfed.

To her horror, a figure appeared where the front door would have been. But instead of running free, escaping the flames, it stopped and made a beckoning motion. Then vanished back inside.

She blinked, sweat running from her forehead as the air heated. Surely she'd imagined it?

Before she could stop him, Blackwell undid his restraints and bolted. "Mother!"

"You guys okay?" Lucy looked over her shoulder, torn between wanting to go after Blackwell and needing to take care of her team. Not that anything she did would be able to save them—piloting a helicopter was one thing the FBI had never trained her to do.

The rear door slid open, a rush of superheated air flooding the helo. To her surprise, it wasn't TK who sprinted from the helo to chase after Blackwell, but Alan. David followed but was no match for Alan's speed.

TK was sprawled on the floor against the other side of the compartment, one hand pressed against a gash on her forehead. "I'm fine," she said as Lucy freed herself from her restraints and crawled into the rear. "Check Saylor."

Lucy handed TK a gauze pack from the med kit. She'd done a good job with Saylor: two IVs running wide open and a makeshift splint on his leg. His pulse beat fast but steady. "He's still with us."

She grabbed the shotgun David had left behind, and crawled out the open door, her bad leg protesting. Blackwell was almost to the house, racing down a narrow corridor where the fire had already burned a path, devouring all the fuel available before moving on. Alan caught up with him, tackling him to the ground.

Not even the wildfire could drown out the boy's screams of fury as he punched Blackwell, hitting him over and over, arms flailing blindly. David reached him, pulling him off Blackwell.

Blackwell rolled over, struggling to his feet. The heat was so intense that Lucy found herself holding her breath. Not good. She pulled her shirt up over her nose and mouth, forced herself to take slow, steady breaths. The air was filled with ashes and she stumbled over the uneven, burnt ground.

David released Alan and went after Blackwell, hauling him back as the second-story windows shattered and burst, flames shooting up, filling the sky. Blackwell struggled, intent on getting into the house.

Lucy came up behind him, nodded to David who tightened his grip. Then she hit Blackwell in the kidney with the butt of her shotgun. He dropped to his knees, stunned. She twisted his arms around to his back and replaced the handcuffs once more.

"Get him back to the helo," she shouted at David, her voice shredded by the wind and the heat. She reached for Alan, who stood sobbing, hands still fisted, and wrapped her arm around him. He didn't protest as she led him back to the helicopter.

Behind them the house roared, a noise almost like laughter, booming through the night as the roof raised up, torn free from its anchors, and then crashed back down to earth.

David had taken the pilot seat while TK held a gun on Blackwell, now handcuffed and restrained in one of the rear seats.

"Do you know what you're doing?" Lucy shouted above the gusting flames. She climbed into the front passenger seat.

He nodded grimly. "Kind of. Did a few hours on a trainer for a story. I can get us up—" His voice trailed off in a definitely non-reassuring manner.

"Do it." Lucy found two radio headsets and placed one on David's head and took the other for herself. "I'll call for help."

"Keep an eye on the instruments," David said, no stress revealed in his tone but beads of sweat dripped down the side of his neck. "Especially that one, the horizon indicator."

He worked both hands and feet and they lurched up a few feet, then winds from the fire buffeted them, driving them toward the flames. David hunched over the controls, his face a study of furious concentration.

The world glowed orange in every direction, flames reflected from the instruments, as the firestorm tossed them about like a child's toy.

CHAPTER 39

TK KNEW SHE was going to be fired. Why else would Lucy have sent her back to Beacon Falls alone the day after they caught Caleb Blackwell while Lucy remained in Canterville, finishing up their case?

Lucy could have at least given her time to say goodbye to David Ruiz. She still couldn't believe how calmly he'd taken charge, piloting the helo, saving them all.

TK almost didn't bother coming to her appointment with Valencia. After all, if she was out of a job, with the gym closing for renovations, she needed to find a place for her bike and get on the shelter and emergency-housing lists. People who'd never experienced homelessness had no clue how much work it took. You didn't just show up and expect a good Samaritan to let you crash for the nigh; there were rules and regulations and paperwork and curfews and priorities and quotas...

She rapped her knuckles against Valencia's office door at the very top of the Queen Anne's round turret. The location fit her—Valencia and this job here at Beacon Falls always seemed too good to be true, something out of a fairy tale, just like this house perched on this bluff overlooking so many endless possibilities.

If it was one thing TK was sure of, she didn't belong in any fairy tale. TK's life was made of the stuff of reality: blood and grit and dirt and pain. No happily-ever-afters guaranteed. It was a miracle she'd lasted as long as she had.

But still...it had been nice while it lasted. As she stood waiting, she could almost understand Carole Blackwell's temptation to create her own fairy-tale ending—even if the woman had ended up burned alive inside her own dream-come-true palace. She wondered if Carole knew about the other women Caleb had killed over the years? Had the mother ever in her wildest dreams imagined she'd created such a monster?

Valencia opened the door herself. "TK, thanks for coming." As if TK actually had a choice.

TK stepped inside. The room was octagonal with a tall ceiling that mirrored the conical shaped roof above it. There were windows filling six of the walls, the views stunning. Magical. A realm not suited for a grunt like TK.

She scuffed her boots before stepping on the thick Persian carpet and waited, at parade rest, expecting Valencia to take her seat behind the elegantly curved desk that fit the room perfectly.

Valencia surprised her, moving instead to one of the two overstuffed chairs in front of the windows. There a table between them with a teapot and china cups waiting.

"Please." She gestured to the other chair.

"No thanks," TK said. "I prefer to stand. No sense drawing things out. I know I screwed up. If you're going to fire me, just tell me where to sign the paperwork and I'll be gone."

Valencia frowned, then looked away as she busied herself pouring tea. The delicious aromas of cinnamon and cardamom filled the air, reminding TK of the homes she'd visited in Afghanistan. Those women knew how to make a cup of tea. "Tell me what you did wrong."

TK came to full attention. Appropriate for an after-action account when you were the one responsible for almost getting your team and civilians killed. "I should have listened to Lucy and waited before going to confront Alan Saylor with the photos. She has more experience interviewing witnesses, she'd already met the subject, and she had a plan. I should have trusted her, never gone there alone or approached Alan Saylor the way I did. I endangered my team, his family, and the mission."

To her surprise, Valencia smiled at that. "What would you do differently next time?"

Not that there was ever going to be a next time, but TK humored her. "I would have trusted my team, not gone off on my own."

It was a humbling admission, but somehow saying the words out loud made her feel better. Not because they were what Valencia expected to hear, but because it had been so long since TK could trust anyone. But Lucy and Ruiz? They'd risked their lives for her, despite her blundering stupidity.

So typical. She finally found a team as good as the one she used to have with the Marines, and she went and lost it. Again. What the hell was wrong with her? Wilson had warned her when they ran parkour that she needed to learn she couldn't do it all alone. Had she learned the lesson too late?

"You're not here for me to fire you," Valencia said, interrupting TK's mental flagellation. "You're here because I want to offer you a position on Lucy's new team. On a probationary basis, but you'd be moving from per diem to fulltime. Is that something you'd be interested in pursuing?"

"Ma'am, yes, ma'am," TK said automatically.

Valencia laughed. It sounded human, gruff and throaty, not at all like a fairy-tale princess, and TK relaxed.

"Sit down, please." Valencia gestured again to the chair beside her. TK obeyed. "There's one more thing I'd like to discuss with you. It's a personal request, so feel free to say no." She poured a cup of tea for TK.

"What do you need?"

"I've lived here all my life." She waved in the direction of the rear wing of the house where her personal quarters were, "and I quite enjoy my independence and solitude. But with this new investigatory initiative, Beacon Group will be drawing more attention, and Xander insists that we have on-site security present." Xander Chen was Valencia's assistant—an older man, totally devoted to Valencia and her work. "I understand you have some experience in that arena? Perhaps could assist us in designing a protocol, finding a reputable service?"

"Of course, no problem."

"And while I accept the necessity of having strangers monitoring the grounds, I despise the idea of having strangers prowling around inside my home."

TK startled, jostling her cup, but managing to catch it before it spilled. "Wait. You want me to move in? Here?"

"Is it too much of an imposition? I can assure you, you certainly would have no duties other than overseeing security. And, of course, Xander is also here if you require time off or are gone with the team on an investigation. What do you think?"

TK tried and failed to hide her smile. She raised her teacup, the delicate bone china would not have lasted five minutes inside Sal's gym. What Valencia was offering—a home, a real home—was something TK hadn't had since she was a girl. Something she couldn't even admit yearning for all these years.

Maybe fairy tales did come true.

She touched her teacup to Valencia's. "I guess it's worth trying. On a probationary basis, of course."

———◆———

LUCY HAD JUST stepped out of the shower when her cell phone rang. She grabbed a towel, wrinkling her nose against the smell of smoke that still permeated her hair, and answered. It was Valencia. "She said yes."

"To the job or the place to live?"

"To both. Good call on the living situation, by the way. Oh and she apologized. Said she should have trusted you and that it won't happen again."

Lucy was doubtful about that. But... "She's got a lot of potential. I think it's worthwhile, giving her a second chance."

"So do I. What do you think about David Ruiz?"

"Ruiz? On our team?" She'd assumed the reporter would return to some form of journalism.

"Just a thought. Once his family situation is resolved."

Lucy paced through the room, her wet feet cold against the tile floor. "Let's not rush things. I'm flying back tonight."

She'd sent TK home yesterday while she'd spent the day in Abilene, being interviewed by the state investigators, taking care of paperwork, dealing with the car rental people, and, since her clothes had been ruined, shopping for a cell phone, two new pairs of boots—neither quite as colorful as Megan's, but just as comfortable—and a fun dress to wear while she traveled home.

The dress was totally impractical as she couldn't wear her gun with it, but it made her smile—and she couldn't wait to see the expression on Nick's face when he saw her in it. Might be enough to keep him from asking too many questions about her trip.

"I'll be heading out as soon as I'm sure the FBI forensic accountant doesn't need anything."

"The final nail in Caleb Blackwell's coffin." Valencia's tone held an unexpected trace of venom. As if she took Blackwell's crimes personally.

"Something like that. Although I hear he's already working a deal. Full confession, including the names and locations of his victims to avoid the death penalty."

"What does David think about that?"

"The irony wasn't lost on him. But he's been busy. Thanks for your help, arranging the compassionate furlough for his father."

"Least the state could do since it might take weeks for the official pardon to come through. Not to mention the reparation money."

"He and his father spent the day with Maria. I don't think they're quite at the point where they're thinking about the future."

Movement at her feet caught her eye. She froze. It was the damn scorpion. She'd been poised to step right on it. The ugly creature had its tail raised, ready to pounce.

"I think I have your next case for you. A missing person. Local, this time."

Lucy barely heard her as she held her breath and stared at the scorpion. She was naked except for a towel, her only weapon a cell phone, and…she scanned the space within arm's reach. Her cane was propped against the wall immediately behind her. Beside it was the TV stand where she'd left her Beretta and remnants of her breakfast.

The scorpion must have sensed something. It skittered closer to her foot, its tail quivering, preparing to sting.

Lucy extended her arm, chose her weapon, and with one lightning strike, hit her target.

"Email me the info and I'll review it on the plane," Lucy said, returning her focus to the phone. "I'll have the team ready to go first thing in the morning."

She hung up. The upside-down coffee mug on the floor at her feet rocked as the scorpion protested its confinement. Lucy grabbed the Bible from the nightstand drawer, used it to weigh down the mug, then scribbled a note for the maid: BEWARE OF SCORPION.

She'd finished dressing, loaded her bags into the Mazda she'd rented, and was ready to head back to Abilene and from there to the airport, when there was a knock on the door. She opened it to find a tall man in a conservative navy suit, grinning down at her, his face hidden by a pair of sunglasses.

"Jake Carver," she greeted him, opening the door wide.

"My favorite forensic accountant. Wow, you clean up nice." Last time she'd seen Jake, she'd been helping him to prep for a deep-undercover assignment with the Reapers, an outlaw motorcycle gang.

"You called for an accountant, figured I'd best dress the part." He took off his glasses. "How are you, Lucy? Heard you've moved on to greener pastures."

She nodded through the door to the sheriff's department across the street, bustling with activity despite the early hour. "And yet still causing trouble and making work for the Bureau."

"Yeah, sounds like that sheriff of yours is pretty much done for. Seriously, only you could come to solve a cold case and find a serial killer. Why'd you need me?"

She explained about Blackwell's forfeiture scheme. "Who knows how many victims there are. And besides, if Blackwell somehow skates on any of the state charges, or ever comes up for parole—"

"I'll be there ready and waiting with federal time. No parole. RICO, public corruption, maybe a little misappropriation of funds." His grin widened and he nodded. "Sounds like my kind of fun. But I do have a favor to ask."

"What do you need?"

"Your room, if you're leaving. The clerk said they were full up between the reporters and the hotshot crews fighting the fire. But she said you were booked through the end of the week."

"No problem, it's all yours. I'll change the reservation before I head to Abilene."

"Thanks." He grabbed a duffel that reminded her of TK's rucksack. She gestured for him to bring it inside. "What's with the bed covers?" he asked, tossing his bag into the far corner.

"Be careful," she cautioned.

He froze, bent over, and rose, holding her note in his hand. "What the—"

"Welcome to Texas. Have fun." She started out the door but he called her back, holding her cane in his hand.

"Hey, I think you forgot this."

"Nope. You can trash it. Doesn't go with my new style." She swooshed her skirt with one hand and he laughed.

She could live with the pain, live with the fact that she'd always have to watch where she was going so her bad foot didn't trip her up, but she couldn't live with everyone labeling her as less than who she was.

Her first stop in Abilene was the medical center. Drew Saylor was out of ICU but still pale, although he was awake and chatting with his wife and Alan. Lucy stopped at the doorway, debating leaving instead of interrupting, but Alan spotted her, jumping to his feet and racing to give her a hug. He looked past her anxiously, then frowned a question.

"Hi, Alan. I'm sorry. TK couldn't come to say good-bye—she's already back home. But she told me to give you this." She embraced him in a tight bear hug. "And this is from both of us."

He clutched the bright yellow copy of *Curious George* with glee, spinning to show it to his parents.

"Hope it's okay," she said to Beth and Drew. "I saw a bunch of copies in his room."

"It's his favorite," Beth reassured her, moving to sit beside Alan and read the book.

"Thank you," Drew said. "For everything."

Lucy grimaced. "Not sure you owe me any thanks. If I hadn't involved you, you'd still have a home and none of this," she gestured to the hospital bed and equipment surrounding him, "would have happened."

"Maybe, but I've come to realize that we were, in our own way, prisoners in that house. Now that it's gone, well, we can go anywhere, do anything."

She thought about that. "Glad it worked out. If you ever find yourself near Pittsburgh, give me a call." She glanced at Alan, laughing over the well-worn story. "All of you, you're welcome any time."

She left them and headed down to the third floor. David sat in a chair, arms draped over the railing of Maria's empty bed, a bright orange and green afghan clutched between his hands. He didn't look up at the sound of her footsteps.

"Happened right at sunrise," he said as she placed a hand on his shoulder. His body shook with grief, but his voice was the same flat tone of a computer reading stock quotes. "Her favorite time of day."

"Your father?"

"Was here. Held her in his arms—she didn't even feel any pain, she was so happy." He swiped at his eyes. "Thank you for that. He's gone back, but the lawyers said they should soon have him out for good."

"I bet she was so proud of you. Without you, none of this would have happened."

A sigh heaved through him. "Yeah, but what do I do now? In a few weeks my father will be free, but we're strangers to each other. And my life isn't here—neither is his."

"Sounds like the perfect time to start over. Get to know each other. Find a new home. You could consider coming to work for the Beacon Group."

"I don't know if I'd do you any good finding answers. Maybe the only thing I'm good at is asking questions. At least I thought so. Before I met the Blackwells. I was such a fool."

"Maybe you're not a perfect human lie detector. Doesn't make you any less of an investigator. You got Carole Blackwell talking when no one else did. Got the truth out of both her and Caleb and on the record. Maneuvered him right where we needed him at the ag station. Without that, Drew Saylor would probably be dead, the rest of us as well."

He frowned. "When I was working the crime beat and then when the TV network hired me, I was so damn certain I had all the answers. Now I'm not even sure of the questions."

She glanced out the window at the horizon, so much more distant than back home in Pennsylvania. Yet, somehow the view reminded her of the morning she'd met Valencia at Beacon Falls and they'd stared over the river gorge. She'd couldn't even dare admit it to herself, but at that moment, she'd felt utterly lost.

As if she'd left who she thought she was behind, locked away in an office at the FBI.

Now she understood. This was her chance to ask the questions important to her instead of to some nameless, faceless bureaucracy.

This was her chance to do more than solve crimes; this was her chance to bring justice to the forgotten victims.

And to do it her way.

Lucy turned and smiled down at David as he hugged Maria's colorful afghan to his chest. For some reason, she felt not Maria's presence, but her own mother's.

As if this moment, this realization, had nothing to do with careers but everything to do with family and legacy and something no parent could teach, but that every parent, even misguided, narcissistic Carole Blackwell, wanted for their children.

"Not knowing the answers or even the questions to ask sounds like the perfect place to start," she told David. "I think maybe it's how we begin to live our own lives instead of someone else's, don't you?"

LUCY'S ADVENTURES

at Beacon Falls will continue in

DEVIL SMOKE

Winter, 2016

ABOUT CJ:

New York Times and *USA Today* bestselling author of twenty-nine novels, former pediatric ER doctor CJ Lyons has lived the life she writes about in her cutting-edge Thrillers with Heart.

Two-time winner of the International Thriller Writers' coveted Thriller Award, CJ has been called a "master within the genre" (Pittsburgh Magazine) and her work has been praised as "breathtakingly fast-paced" and "riveting" (Publishers Weekly) with "characters with beating hearts and three dimensions" (Newsday).

Learn more about CJ's Thrillers with Heart at www.CJLyons.net

EDGY READS

www.EdgyReads.com